Roxy Steel lives in the UK and is passionate about what makes us who we are? Why we do the things we do? And how we choose to think, feel and behave differently to impact the world around us in the most positive way? Through self-observation, talking with many friends and family about their and her own inner thoughts and behaviour Roxy came to understand that the biggest impact of who we are all stems from our childhood and the society we are born into. She believes that humans are evolving and each and every one of us is part of that evolution.

The animal kingdom and all activists of past, present and future.

Roxy Steel

BILLY STONE'S TWO WORLDS

AUSTIN MACAULEY PUBLISHERS™

LONDON * CAMBRIDGE * NEW YORK * SHARJAH

A CIP catalogue record for this title is available from the British Library.

ISBN 9781398411340 (Paperback)
ISBN 9781398414198 (ePub e-book)

www.austinmacauley.com

First Published 2023
Austin Macauley Publishers Ltd®
1 Canada Square
Canary Wharf
London
E14 5AA

All the friends and family who believed in me and encouraged me to keep writing, you know who you are.

Synopsis

Twelve-year-old Billy is awoken one morning by a being from another dimension called Max who shone light from his very being. Billy was totally freaked out, as the being spoke without moving his lips; he was using telepathy to communicate with Billy telling him that they have work to do together to save humanity. Knowing that Billy did not believe his eyes, Max teleports him all around the world and takes him to his home Planet Unity, to prove to Billy that this wasn't all a dream.

Humans are on a course of destruction and many things are not working. Radical and fast change is required to change the course of the future; The deforestation of the Amazon and poisons being pumped into the earth's atmosphere and oceans. The monetary, social and education systems. Homeless, starving, thirsty and dying people. The exploitation of humans and animals. The poisoning of the food supply with antibiotics, fertilisers and pesticides. Health systems that treat disease rather than prevent disease. Plastics killing sea life. The separateness of humanity.

Max asks Billy to choose which subject they should work with first. Billy had no idea what a 12-year-old could do to save humans from the destruction and was still not convinced that this wasn't an epic dream, his imagination gone crazy or even that perhaps that he was dead or in a coma! As Max had already taken him on adventures around the planet and beyond, Billy decides to go with the flow to see where this adventure takes him.

Chapter 1

"Billy… wake up… Billy… wake up!" Miss Taylor said sternly.

Miss Taylor was the English teacher at the Wovery School in Wiltshire, England. Billy Stone was a daydreamer, the wonder of the world around him sent his imagination off on adventures of fun, freedom and courage. Billy found school very boring; actually, Billy found life quite boring as his imagination was far more exciting than any school lesson or TV show. Consequently, Billy was always in trouble for not paying attention and being in his own world; a world of vastness, of many stories and adventures.

Billy dreamt of many things, from saving animals to flying high in the Earth's stratosphere. Billy didn't really like the world around him, he found the reality of the adults around him tedious and it scared him that he might end up just like all the adults in his life. Due to his 'oddness', he didn't have any friends and being an only child at 12 years old he was either with adults or on his own. Adults seemed to either be stressed about something or rushing around trying to fit in everything they had to do into their day.

Billy really didn't want to grow up and have things he had to do every single day.

"Billy, it's your turn to read out loud from today's book."

Oh, dear… Billy had been away on an adventure taking him all the way to Australia's great barrier reef, swimming with a 6-foot hump head maori wrasse, manta rays, spaghetti worms and white humpback whales. He was lucky enough to have a laptop and spent a lot of his time researching the internet mainly about planet earth. He loved nature from the myriad of different types and sizes of ants to bats, birds, worms, small and large mammals, sea life, trees, plants and flowers.

Unlike most boys of 12, Billy didn't like to remove legs from spiders or wings from daddy long legs or to hold a magnifying glass with the sun beating down on ants just to see what would happen. Instead, Billy loved to just watch them, in awe at the beauty and magnificence of everything around him. The amazing strength of ants, how they can carry leaves many times their own weight or how organised they are.

He came to the conclusion that ants are far more intelligent than humans, as they all seem to get along just fine working together for the good of them all. He had noticed that animals lived in the now and came to realise that humans are either like him daydreaming or they were worried about the future, feeling bad about the past or just distracted by things to do, lists to write, future plans to make or gossiping. Animals on the other hand were just 'being'.

Doing their thing; eating, sleeping, mating, going about their day, minding their own business and just getting on with life. Billy wanted to be something other than human. As well as nature, Billy liked to study the maps of the world, of individual nations, mountain ranges and the different cultures around the world. He was fascinated with the different clothes that people wore to the slightly different look of people; the hairstyles, colour of skins, their big smiles and general appearances.

He wanted to explore the planet, meet and talk to the people, see the different landscapes, the ancient wonders of the world, he wanted to be standing at the pyramids, close his eyes and be there in a flash with the ancients, see their clothing, hairstyles and faces. In addition to the amazing world we live in, the other topic he was interested in was how we could live in such a beautiful world and have such awful hatred, war, hunger, unnecessary death and a totally unbalanced way of life. Those that have and those that don't, it seemed to him odd that we couldn't all just get along fine and share with each other, our stories, our wealth and our happiness.

Billy was thought of at school by his teachers and peers as not that intelligent, having no concentration, no desire to learn and not socially adept. How wrong could the world around him be? Billy was highly knowledgeable as long as the subject was of interest. He wanted not only to explore the world but also to change it so that everyone was happy and smiling. Although he didn't have any friends, he did not mind, he did not blame anyone and did not feel bad about it. He just accepted that's what his life was like.

Billy's parents were a 'normal' hard working couple. His mum worked at the local hospital, working shifts. She was slim with long brown hair, which for work she tied into a bun. His dad was an accountant who was very tall with glasses and greying hair. They lived an ordinary life going to work, watching TV, doing DIY and gardening.

It was a lovely sunny afternoon after school and Billy went into his room to explore the internet. He felt something different as he entered his room, the air seemed odd and he couldn't quite put his finger on what was different. It was as if someone had been in the room. Nothing had been moved, but there was something different. What Billy did not know was that his world was about to change.

"Billy, wake up… Billy, wake up!"

Billy stretched, yawning from a deep sleep. "Miss Taylor, can I go next please?" Billy said sleepily.

"Billy, wake up, it's not Miss Taylor, you are asleep…you are not at school, Billy… wake up!"

Billy sat bolt upright, eyes wide. He almost jumped out of his skin when he saw a figure standing at the end of his bed. A tall man, in a bright silver and gold robe, shining so brightly it made Billy squint.

"Hello, Billy." Billy heard the words, but he did not see the man move his lips. Billy rubbed his eyes, thinking he was seeing things. "Billy, don't be scared, I mean you no harm." Again the man's lips did not move, but he could hear as clear as the school bell ringing, the words inside his head.

"Errrr, hello…" said Billy. Billy was a bit scared, but at the same time, he was excited because this man did not look like an ordinary man. He had a glow about him, almost like he was exuding light from his very being. A kind face, smiling, he had bright blue eyes, brighter than any blue he had ever seen. His hair was white, not like an old age pensioner, it glowed just like his robes. He just stood smiling at Billy, waiting for Billy to react. "Who are you?"

"My name is Max." Again his lips did not move.

"How do you do that?" Billy Gasped.

"How do I do what?"

"Say something without moving your lips."

"I just think the words I want you to hear, and you 'hear' them in your mind."

Billy thought for a few seconds and said, "It's a trick, you are not real—I am still dreaming!"

"OK, if that's what you want to believe Billy. If so, why don't you wake up now, if you are dreaming, you can wake up." Billy pulled the covers over his head. "That won't help you, Billy; I am still here."

A minute later Billy came out from under the covers. The shining man was still standing there smiling at Billy. Billy jumped out of bed and walked over to the man; he put his hand on the man's arm and nearly fell over as his hands went straight through him.

"Arrhhggg!" Billy yelled. "Who are you? What are you? Are you a ghost? OMG, I am seeing things or are you here to take me to heaven? Have I died? OMG, what is going on?"

"Billy, please calm down, please do not worry you are very much alive. I am from Unity; a world very much like yours, in another dimension. I have come here to help humanity and save your planet, we have work to do!"

"We… have work to do… we… who?"

"You and I Billy, we have much work to do."

Max put his hand on Billy's shoulder and within a split second, Billy and Max were on top of a mountain. The view was incredible, 360° snow-capped mountains. Max did it again and bang, in a split second they were in a savanna with elephants and zebras all around, it was such a beautiful scene, nature, at its best right in front of Billy's eyes. The next scene was a beautiful deserted beach covered in turtles. Billy couldn't believe his eyes and was convinced he was in a strange dream being transported all over the world, his imagination having a wonderful time.

They were back in Billy's room. Max explained that he came from a place where the beings were more evolved than humans on Earth, they communicated via telepathy. When they wanted to be somewhere, they just thought about the place, and they were 'teleported' with their thoughts to the location.

By touching Billy's shoulder, Max connected with Billy energetically so that he could take Billy with him wherever his thoughts wanted to go. They had been to the Himalayas, Africa and Florida all within seconds of each other. Billy was mesmerised by what was happening. He really wasn't sure if he was dreaming, dead or just his imagination had gone crazy. Surely this couldn't really be happening?

"So, what 'work' do we have to do then?" asked Billy.

"We have to save the world, Billy."

"And how are we going to do that then? Just you and me?"

"In lots of way's Billy, there is so much that is not working on Earth, so much that mankind is doing that needs to change; The way the animal kingdom and the earth are totally abused and exploited, the separateness of your world and

195 nations not working together. And that's just for starters, the list is pretty long. This planet is a living breathing organism, it is all one. Mankind is part of that living breathing beautiful organism from the blue whale to the microscopic Mycoplasma including mankind.

Mankind is killing the only home you all have and something has got to change, a shift in global thinking is required. It is love and kindness that will change your planet, not wars or politics or religion. As I said, what is needed is a shift in global thinking, oneness with mother earth, oneness with nature, oneness with animals and oneness with each other, no matter what religion or nation. But first Billy, I need to show you more."

The next moment Billy was travelling down a tunnel at such speed it was like warp speed on star trek. Colours were streaming past them; it was like being inside a rainbow. It was silent, not as you would expect travelling at such speed. Billy felt weightless, like a snowflake floating down from the sky.

He couldn't really think about anything, the experience was just mesmerising, like being in a dream. Floating, yet moving at unimaginable speed. Actually, Billy still wasn't sure if this was in fact a dream. The tunnel twisted and turned left to right, up and down, it really was like the fastest and biggest roller coaster ever invented. Billy was having a lot of fun.

They arrived in the most beautiful place Billy had ever seen. The sky was the bluest and brightest, far beyond what he could ever imagine. The greens in nature were gleaming they were so bright. The flowers were indescribable; the colours were truly magnificent, shades he had never seen before.

A stream was babbling and meandering through the woods, the gentle whisper of the water as it went on its journey, it was singing, Billy could actually hear that it was a melody. There was bird song and animals all around lazing in the sun or eating the grass. "Wow," Billy said with a look of disbelief. "Wowee… where are we?"

"This is my home Billy, we are on Unity. Come, I have more to show you before we go back to your place."

They were then surrounded by a similar show of colour and beauty, on a grassed area there were children playing. They were playing with young animals; puppies, kittens, baby rats, lambs, rabbits, calves, piglets, chicks and other animals that Billy had never seen before. They were running and jumping, the children were laughing. Some were lying down and having a nap, huddled up, the small children and very young animals, sleeping together, keeping each other comforted as they slept.

Max continued. "This is one of the play areas for the very young. All species can come here to meet and play together. This is part of the schooling here on Unity, we integrate with the animals at a very early age. We understand that we are all as precious as each other."

In the distance was a much bigger area where some adult animals were resting and eating, there was not a fence as you would see on Earth, they were all together just hanging out, doing their thing.

Once again they were back in Billy's room. Billy had so many questions racing through his mind... Where was Unity, how come Max wasn't solid and how exactly did he transmit his thoughts into Billy's mind and transport them to the places in a blink of an eye. What exactly needed changing on earth, how were they going to change it all? And... why Billy... why was Max wanting to 'work' with Billy.

I mean, come on...I'm just a 12-year-old boy with an overactive imagination, not academic, not very good at anything. Why me? Billy thought. His mind was racing when Max interrupted his thoughts. "You don't have to be academic to change the hearts of the people, Billy."

"OH... MY... GOD!" said Billy slowly. "You heard me talking to myself... inside my head?"

"Of course, Billy, I can hear your thoughts, that's one reason why I choose you, Billy, because I know how pure your thoughts are, how much love you have inside you. It's love, compassion and kindness that will change your world, not how many exam papers you have. Exam papers really just show how much stuff you can remember or how well the teacher has taught you something.

If school was about love and kindness to everything in this world, you, my friend, would be top of the class! You have an amazing imagination, you are very open to anything new and are amazed by what you see around you in nature. These are the reasons I choose you, Billy. I have been with you a long time, watching you, listening to your thoughts. You are a shining example, Billy."

Billy always felt like someone had been watching him, his whole life he had that feeling but ignored it. Billy just sat on his bed in a daze, still not sure if he was dreaming or if Max was real, and they indeed needed to change the 'global thinking'. How on earth would they do that, seven billion people? Then there was school, Billy wondered how he was going to spend time travelling with Max when he needed to be at school.

He knew that some kids were home-schooled, but that would cost a lot of money, money his parents didn't have. He couldn't skip school, as his parents would surely find out, then he would be in serious trouble! Billy's mum really wanted him to improve on his school work. The last thing Billy wanted to do was upset his mum, he loved her so much and wanted to please her.

If this was really happening, Billy had to find a way. Billy looked at the clock and realised he had to go to school, Max hearing his thoughts, said he would catch up with him later, they could chat some more about Billy's questions.

That morning at school, Billy couldn't think about anything else except Max and all the things he had seen and heard about. School was now even more boring; he had to find a way to stop having to go to school. At lunchtime, he went into the school's computer room, to search the internet. Billy searched and searched about stories of kids not going to school and the reasons why, but he couldn't find any reason that he felt would be agreeable to his mum and then there was the tuition, how would that happen?

In the afternoon, as usual, Billy was daydreaming, the morning's events going around and around his mind when suddenly it came to him; the solution about school. He was so excited he squealed. The whole class turned to see what was going on. Billy immediately turned red with embarrassment. All he could do was smile at everyone, in fact, he couldn't get the silly grin off his face, as much as he tried his muscles wouldn't move, the grin just kept grinning.

Eventually, they all turned away and carried on with class. One of the benefits of being known as a bit weird is that when you do something weird no one takes any notice. Leaving school, Billy couldn't get home quick enough, he ran all the way, still with a silly grin all over his face. He busted through the door hoping his mum was in, he couldn't remember what shift she was on today. She was not in, so he went up to his room hoping that he would see Max. Max was waiting for Billy.

"Hi," Billy said quite casually as he saw Max.

"Hello, Billy, good day at school?"

"You tell me, Max, you can read my thoughts." Billy smiled a cheesy big smile at Max. "Well, you certainly have a big smile on your face, Billy."

"Yes, Max. I am excited as I have decided to tell mum that I want to teach myself. School doesn't suit me, I don't have any friends, so I don't socialise and

I am not interested in the subjects, although I do agree I need to continue to learn math, English and science. However, what I really want to do is to explore the planet, the insects, the animals, the fauna, the oceans, I cannot do that with the exams from school. I need to learn so much, which can be learned from the internet. I can still take my exams in math, English and science then go on to college. So I am going to talk to mum when she gets in."

"Sounds like you have a plan; of course I will share with you as much as possible whilst we are working together, Billy."

Max and Billy continue to chat about the amazing things on planet Earth, Max didn't stay long and said he would catch up properly with Billy the next day. That evening Billy spoke to his mum about schooling, she was not convinced but said she would sleep on it. That night Billy had so many exciting dreams, no school, lots of adventure with Max and having lots of fun.

The next morning Billy woke up very early full of energy and wide awake. He dashed downstairs to see his mum to ask what she thought about him schooling himself. His mum was in the kitchen getting breakfast and packed lunches ready for him and his dad. "Good morning, Mum." Billy said breezily and excited.

"Good morning my lovely boy, you are up early and sounding excited," his mum said with her beautiful soft voice.

She had so much compassion and love for her boy. "Come here and give your mum a hug."

Billy and his mum embraced, Billy held on tightly to his mum, squeezing her as if he was going to fall. "Hey, Bills what's up with you? You are holding on tight son!"

"Just wanna show you I love you mum, really… I love you so much."

"Arrrr, I love you more, Bills."

Billy sat down at the kitchen table to wait for breakfast. "So mum, you have slept on it, what are you thinking about me schooling myself from home?"

"Oh Bills, I haven't had a chance to think about it."

"But you said you would sleep on it."

"That's just an expression Bills, it means I will think about it."

"Oh, OK, no problem, take your time mum, there is no rush." Billy thought to himself, 'there is only humanity to save mum' no worries! He laughed to himself, thinking of everything that had happened with Max.

Later that day after school, Billy rushed upstairs to see if Max was waiting for him which he was. They both said, "Hey!" at the same time. "So Billy, you have questions?"

"Yes, Max, I do. Where is Unity and how come you are not solid?"

"It's not easy to explain in your human words Billy, words are so limiting, but I will try my best to help you understand. Unity is in a parallel universe, both Earth and Unity are existing at the same time, in the same space, but we are undetectable to each other. I am not solid because I choose not to be. If I wanted to, I could slow down my vibration further than I already have to become part of the physical world you exist in, but it is much more comfortable for me to lower my vibration to this level so that you can see me without me needing to be physical."

"OK, so how can I, being a physical being be teleported to another place 1,000 s of miles away?"

"Because when I connect with you energetically, I raise your vibration to match mine, which is why you felt as light as a snowflake when we went to Unity."

"OK, how do you do that and how do you transmit your thoughts into my head? How do you 'think' your way to a place?"

"Billy, human words just can't explain how it is done, for now, I just need you to trust me. Perhaps in time, I will teach you how to do these things, but we need to focus on why I am here, that is,"

Billy interrupted Max. "I know, you are here to change the 'global thinking', and you want me to help you."

"Yes! That's great Billy, I knew you were the right person for the job! OK, your other question was what exactly needed changing on earth and how are we going to change it all.

"Like I said Billy it is a very long list; the deforestation of the planet and the mining of the planets underground resources. The poisons that are being pumped into the earth's atmosphere. The poisons and animal waste that are being dumped into the water tables, rivers and seas.

"This is poisoning the air that you breathe and polluting nature including the sea life. Plastics that are killing sea life. The 'dead zones' in the seas where life does not exist, no life at all.

"The monetary, social and education systems. The homeless and starving or thirsty people, and the dying children. The corrupt government systems. The

Earth's nations not working together, if they were they wouldn't have armies to defend themselves.

"The mass farming of animals that is full of cruelty and suffering and it is one of the biggest causes of the planets environmental calamities. The cruel use of animals in chemical product testing.

"The poisoning of your food supply with antibiotics, fertilisers and pesticides that is causing disease. The mass production of junk food that is causing disease. The health systems that treat disease rather than prevent disease; treating diseases is very profitable business! What shall we start with Billy? You choose."

Billy didn't know what to say he was stunned. He was wondering again, how a 12-year-old could have an impact on any of what Max was talking about. He was just one human out of seven billion…AND he was just a boy!

"Seems like an impossible task, eh Billy? Well, let me tell you. Man has created this situation, so man can also change this situation. What most people do not realise is that you are all creating your realities. Your individual and collective realities with your thoughts. Everything starts with a thought. Think about it Billy when you get up in the morning, what is the first thing that happens?

"It is thought; you think about what is going to happen today. If everyone thinks that they can't do anything to change the world, they need to think again. If everyone starts thinking they can change, they can change their own behaviour, which will have an impact on the people in their lives, those people will see the change, and will be inspired to change themselves.

"You see, you are all connected; change one part and that has a ripple effect, like a stone being thrown into water it affects the whole of the water, not just the part where it entered. If you take a cup of water out of the ocean, is it still the ocean? Humans are a collective consciousness Billy, the more people that think the same thing, the more likely it is to happen, we need to change the thinking into oneness and love for everything. You might wonder where did this all start, Billy?

"Well, it goes back a very long time in your history, but that's a very long story. In more recent times, it's all about profit, consumerism, globalisation, satisfying the human desires for more money, more stuff, bigger houses, faster cars, expensive holidays. So, where did the human desires come from Billy? When did it all change from people being contented with farming their land and feeding their families? Keeping up with 'The Jones', Billy.

"Comparing yourself to others and seeing what they had and wanting what they had. Also, the conditioning from your societies, your religions, your families, your neighbours. It has all come from within you all Billy, so you can, if you observe yourselves, observe others, you can choose to be different. Consumerism will die, Billy, just like communism doesn't work for everyone, neither does consumerism. The bubble will burst, but if you can start the change happening from within the people, from their thoughts, this will have a much more positive effect. As I have said before Billy, it is love and kindness that will change the world. Love and kindness to fellow human beings.

"Love and kindness to animals. Love and kindness to the natural world. Love and kindness to mother earth. Most people Billy, are kind, good people, but you are all blinded and conditioned to think that this is the way life is, but it doesn't have to be like this Billy, life could be different; if the haves would just share with the have-nots and if you all lived from your hearts; love and compassion for everything, everyone, every creature and all of nature. The people need to change the way things are, the way things work around here.

"Come up with new systems, new ideas to become a peaceful society. Humans have been in existence the equivalent of a blink of an eye. What you do next in your evolution won't actually make any difference in the universe. The universe will keep expanding. The universe will keep creating itself. Who knows, maybe we don't need to save the earth, maybe it is just humans that are in danger of wiping themselves and all other living creatures off the face of the planet. Mother Nature will continue to evolve, change and heal. Humanity will be gone. Humanity needs to wake up Billy. Humanity needs to take the next step in evolution. The evolution revolution—Oneness—just like on Unity.

"Some people are already making changes, new environmentally friendly and sustainable products, such as replacements for plastic products, eco-friendly disposable plates that will decompose in 28 days and 'Pineapple' leather shoes. There are people taking it upon themselves to clean up beaches and plastic in the sea. France has made it mandatory for supermarkets to give away unsold food, rather than throw it away. This is great, but this really shouldn't need governments' legislation, if people where living from their hearts supermarkets bosses would want to do this. Who actually wants to throw food in the bin that can still be consumed by someone who is hungry?

"A very small number of dairy farmers are choosing to make milk from nuts and plants which is less impact on the Earth. Charities and individuals are shouting about all the things in the world that need changing, but sadly the masses think that they cannot make a difference. The list of new ideas goes on and will continue to grow. What you and I will be doing together is adding to what is already going on. The evolution revolution, Billy; it is happening!"

Chapter 2

"OK," said Billy. "Let's start with the animal kingdom."

"I am glad you suggested that, I was thinking the same thing Billy but before we start, I just want to say, most people are completely unaware of the atrocities that are going on. You are so conditioned from an early age that things around you are normalised. Some people are aware of how cruel animal farming for example has become, some are doing something about it, others do not want to know the detail and so they bury their heads in the sand and remain ignorant to the facts.

"If you are told a lie enough times it becomes a part of your reality. If enough people are taught the lie it becomes part of the culture, if the culture passes that miss information onto the next generation it becomes part of the tradition. What you have to remember is that just because you have a tradition doesn't mean it is morally acceptable. Tradition and morality are not always the same thing. As you evolve as a culture so do your traditions.

"Billy, young people like you deserve to know the truth, this isn't going to be a pleasant journey Billy but sometimes in life, things are not pleasant and evolution is not always an easy ride! I will promise you one thing; I will only ever tell you the truth. I am not here to dress it up so that it is easier for you. Watering down the truth would be an injustice to the animals and an insult to you, Billy. A small percentage of people are fully aware and choose not to be complicit."

"What does complicit mean?"

"To be involved with others in an activity that is unlawful or morally wrong. You can really only choose something in life when you know the truth; otherwise, you are just following the conditioning that has been happening to you for your whole life."

"You keep mentioning conditioning, what is conditioning?" asked Billy.

"Another great question, conditioning is what happens to humans from a very young age. Let's think of it like a computer program or natural brainwashing and it is what massively contributes to the human personality/ego. When you are born, you do have some nature that is already programmed within you. I am sure you know of examples when someone said, Ooh, he is just like his grandfather, even though the grandfather had died before having a chance to meet the boy.

"Then you have conditioning that is from outside yourselves. It is an influence from the world around us that shapes us, shapes our views, our habits, our behaviour, our values and our morals Billy. Examples: If you grow up in the UK, you are generally conditioned/programmed to eat 3 meals a day. In Nepal and many other countries, for example, you are generally conditioned/programmed to eat 2 meals a day. Both are perfectly fine, it's just what you are used to from when you were young.

"If your parents were very critical, you will probably be the same, you will find yourself criticising others because you have followed your parent's example. If as a child you were not shown love and affection, you will probably grow up finding it difficult to show love and affection because you didn't receive it. If you are born into a religious family, you will believe your religion unless you start asking questions, start critically thinking, or until someone else has an influence on you causing you to change your mind about a thing.

"If you are born in a family that has racist views, chances are you might grow up being a little bit or totally racist, until you start thinking for yourself and basing your opinions on your own experiences rather than external factors, such as families, neighbours etc. If your parents lack respect for others, you will probably follow their behaviour, have their views and values.

"If a friend of yours says; they don't like another student, do you stick with your friend and say you do not like that person too? Or, do you form your own opinion, based on your experience with that person?

"If you are teased at school, about your looks, maybe you are someone with ginger hair and freckles or someone with a big nose or ears or teased about the colour of your skin or lack of family finances, you will feel not worthy Billy and will feel not good enough.

"The world around you shapes you; families, neighbours, school friends, teachers, social systems, religions, governments, into believing you are not enough or believing in a thing. This happens from a very early age, humans are not aware of the programming until much later in life when some of you realise what has been happening all your life. If I told you that a banana is blue, you would say I was crazy, right?"

Billy laughed and said, "Yes, of course, bananas are yellow, well ripe ones are."

"So, you know the banana to be yellow because you have been told what yellow is, it is the same with everything else. You have been told that your family religion is the 'right religion', you have been teased about bodily appearances, so you become self-conscious of them when you are actually perfect the way you are.

"All these things play a huge part in what humans think about themselves, how you treat others and what direction in life you take. So, you have all been conditioned/programmed over millennia and now is the time for people to start seeing the programming for what it is and making the decision to change, to evolve to the next phase in the human evolution, Billy."

"So Max, we can't get away from being programmed, it's going to happen no matter what our parents do?"

"Yes, Billy, however, if your generation learn about this and change the way you program the next generation, then life on Earth will take a new direction. You all have a choice Billy, with every moment; you get to choose if you want to 'reprogram' yourself. The conditioning/programming is also the good stuff about humans.

"If you have been brought up to always be honest and truthful to say please and thank you, not to drop litter, to eat with your mouths closed, pick up your feet when you are walking, accept all people as equals and respect them, then these qualities generally stay with us. One thing that most humans have been conditioned/programmed to do is eat animals and their secretions (milk and milk products like cheese, yoghurt, cream and butter. Honey and birds eggs) and exploit animals in many other ways. Like I just said, this is not a happy story; it is brutal, unkind and unthinkable.

"The facts about how humans treat animals all over the world, farmed animals, wild animals, domesticated animals, whether for food, entertainment or clothing it's all about profit and lack of empathy/compassion, lack of equality of all living beings Billy. Most suffering is due to profit, if you follow the money, that's where it all starts. However, humans are numb to this. It is normalised from when you were growing up because it is part of your traditions and cultures.

"OK, so here we go Billy, let's start with the area that causes the most suffering, due to the sheer numbers; animals for food. Remember Billy, you need to know the truth to make an informed choice about whether you want to be complicit in animal abuse. What I am about to share with you will enable you to consider if you are comfortable with continuing to be complicit."

"What does complicit mean again, Max?"

"To be involved with others in an activity that is unlawful or morally wrong. So, in the example of eating meat, by eating the meat, you are just as involved with the killing of the animal as the person who does the killing. Humans just need to decide if they think it is morally wrong or not to enable them to make a decision."

Food

"Mass-produced meat is focused on maximising production output while minimising production costs, which means that the welfare of the animal is very often at the bottom of the priority list. In the UK, over 1 billion land animals are killed every year for meat, dairy and eggs. The UK has around 66 million people; 1 billion is a massive number of animals killed every year for the pleasure of your taste buds."

"Max, just how much is a billion?"

"It's a thousand million, Billy."

"We kill a thousand million every year, Max?"

"Yes, Billy and that's just in the UK, which as you know is a small place in the world."

"I can't actually imagine what that number really looks like."

"Well, Billy, 1 million seconds is around 11 days and a billion is around 31 years, does that help you feel how massive a billion really is?"

"Wow, a billion really is so much bigger than a million; thanks, Max, that helps."

In a blink of an eye, Billy and Max were in the rafters of a big barn housing pigs.

Pigs and Their Piglets

"So Billy, as you can see below, it's not a very nice place."

"Woow, that stinks, Max, and look at those poor mums down there, they are in small cages."

"As you can see the pigs don't have much room."

At one end of the barn were hundreds of pigs in pens, crammed in together, the other end where lots of mums in cages with her babies suckling her milk.

"Pigs are officially entitled to less than one square meter of space each and the majority of sows (female breeding pigs) are kept in farrowing crates, as you can see Billy, she can't move around, she is either lying down or standing up."

As Max was speaking Billy was just taking it all in, the words, the scene and the stench. "Farrowing crates were made illegal in several countries across Europe, but are still used as the standard farming practice here in the UK. The mummy pigs are kept in these crates every time they are pregnant for up to 5 weeks at a time. The majority of sows in the UK are artificially inseminated in order to ensure they are kept continuously pregnant to maximise profit.

"The cycle of forced impregnation and confinement is repeated over and over again for about 4–5 years or until the sow is too exhausted to carry on. At this point, she is then slaughtered for low-grade meat such as pies and sausage meat. Wild piglets remain with their mothers for around 12–14 weeks, but in UK farms piglets are taken from their mothers after only 3–4 weeks and given antibiotic drugs even though they are perfectly healthy. Around half of all antibiotics sold in the UK are used on farmed animals with 60% of these being used on pigs which you humans then ingest."

They were teleported to another barn, where there were lots of baby pigs in a pen. A man picked up a piglet and with what looked like his mums gardening tool for cutting the roses, he chopped off the piglets' tails. Billy gasped. The piglet squealed and squealed. He was tiny, screaming his little head off. Billy was shocked and speechless as he watched the scene below. "In 2007, it became illegal to cut off dogs-tails in the UK as it was considered cruel and unacceptable; however, it is standard practice in pig farming." Next, the man picked up what looked like his dad's wire cutters and started clipping the teeth, again the piglet squealed.

Whispering, Billy asked, "Why Max, why are they doing that, Max?"

"Farmers inflict mutilations on piglets soon after birth, by amputating their tails and clipping their teeth, all of which is done without anaesthetic or painkillers. This is done because they are so overcrowded in pens and not stimulated by natural soundings, which means they do not behave naturally; they have a tendency to eat each other's tails, or even try and chew on each other's legs."

"I am totally dumbfounded Max, why don't they just give them a better life, more space and natural surroundings, rather than torturing them by mutilating their bodies?"

"Follow the money Billy; to give them more space and a natural environment would be too expensive."

"What about free-range pigs, Max?"

"There is no legal definition or formal standards for free-range pigs; this means retailers can label pork products as free-range without having to adhere to any standards or guidelines. It gets worse Billy, if piglets are not growing fast enough or are sick and injured, they are seen as unprofitable to the industry so are killed, in a very brutal way," Billy's jaw dropped open with pure bewilderment.

"Other possible forms of mutilations are: castration, ear docking or tagging or notching and tattooing none of which are for the benefit of the piglet. When the piglets reach slaughter age at around 6 months, they are transported in cramped and overcrowded trucks with no water or food, regardless of the weather. They are often driven many miles to the slaughterhouse, the final part of their life journey, a scary place to end such an innocent life.

"Electric prods are used to control the pigs, to keep them moving in the direction of the path of death. One of the methods of slaughter for pigs in the UK is the gas chamber, where groups of pigs are herded into metal cages which are then lowered into a chamber that is filled with carbon dioxide. Once inside the chamber, the pigs scream and thrash, fighting for their lives for up to 30 seconds.

"One-third of pigs in the UK are killed in gas chambers. The other certified 'humane' method of pig slaughter in the UK is electrical stunning with the aim to render the animals unconscious before they have their throat slit. A pair of large electrical 'tongs' are placed on either side of the pigs head; however, stunning is often poorly executed, it's very difficult when a pig is moving its head to get an accurate placement of the 'tongs' also, the workers are rushed, as they have a lot of pigs to get through in a day.

"This results in an estimated 1.8 million pigs in the UK regaining consciousness on the production line each year and being fully conscious as their throat is slit and then die from blood loss or become awake as they are submerged in a boiling hot water bath, which is used to remove the hairs from the skin; at this point, they will probably drown. There are around 11,000 pig farms in the UK. Around 1,400 of these farms house more than 1,000 pigs and hold around 85% of the total pig population in the UK, very much like this farm, Billy."

"What about the pigs we see in fields, Max?"

"Only 3% of UK pigs spend their entire lives outdoors Billy. Not all pigs are reared in conditions like this Billy; however, the vast majority of the pork products sold in the UK come from factory farms like this. No matter how an animal is farmed, humans need to ask themselves if it is morally right to take the life of another being. Pigs have been proven to be as intelligent and emotionally complex as dogs.

- Pigs are killed at 6 months.
- If pigs were to live a natural life, they would live until they were 8–12 years old.
- They are very frightened toddlers when they are killed.
- In the UK, 10 million pigs are killed each year.
- Globally, it is estimated that 1.4 billion pigs are killed each year, with almost 700,000,000 in China.

The German Nazis, confined, controlled, gassed and killed innocent beings… I can't see the difference Billy… can you?"

"I am fond of pigs, dogs look up to us, cats look down at us, pigs treat us as equal."

—Winston Churchill (1874–1965)

Billy was speechless; he had no idea of the suffering. He knew that pork was pigs, and that pork was bacon and sausage but he was not aware that they were so young. He was not aware of the horrid conditions. He was not aware of the mutilations. He was not aware of the huge numbers. Tears started to roll down Billy's face as he imagined all the things that Max had described.

"Max…" Billy said with a quivering in his voice and sniffing the embarrassing snot that comes out of our nose whenever we cry.

"Yes, Billy?" Max said softly.

"I had no idea, Max," sniffing snot again. "I want to help you, Max, this has to be stopped, and people need to know Max."

Max continued in a beautifully soft tone "Yes, Billy, that is one reason why I am here, to enable young people to know the truth about what is behind the meat on their plates, it's not meat Billy, it is a dead animal, not happily or willingly dead; confined, controlled, forced, abused, made to suffer and murdered Billy. They don't want to live like this, and they don't want to die Billy. They deserve to have a naturally long life, in the wild, free to do what they were meant to do in nature."

"I am never eating pork again, Max," Billy said sniffling snot again.

"Are you ready to see and hear about the next farmed animal, Billy?" Billy stared into space with the tears still falling down his face.

"I did say, that this is not pleasant knowledge, but it is vital that people know the truth, people need to wake up to the truth about these concentration camps that are all over the UK, Europe, the Americas, Australia, India, China and most other countries."

"Yes, Max, please go ahead and tell me everything you want to share with me, even though I might cry, I might have horrid images in my mind, please Max, I would rather know the truth, than carrying on my life not knowing."

"OK, Billy."

Chickens, Hens and Their Chicks

Once again they were in the rafters of a big barn full of chickens. "Wooooow, I didn't think there could be a worse smell than that pig farm Max, what is that smell?"

"It is chicken poop and wee Billy. Pretty bad eh?" The stench was a sickly sweet smell that was most unpleasant. Billy thought it was strange, that something so sweet could smell so bad. Billy could see below chickens in cages, it was very noisy with thousands of birds clucking.

"Here are some chicken facts for you, Billy, don't hold your breath too long, I need you alive!" Max laughed out loud, Billy's eyes started to water as it was so bad.

"Chickens bred specifically for laying eggs live inside big barns or cages called caged hens like this one. Outside Europe, the birds are often housed their whole life in tiny cages called battery cages that house one bird per cage, they can't move as these are around the size of an A4 piece of paper, and they cannot stretch their wings. It used to be the same in Europe, but those cages were banned and replaced with 'enriched' cages which house 10–80 birds per cage, they are the equivalent of an A4 piece of paper plus around a postcard size for each bird;

how generous of your lawmakers to give them an extra postcard size amount of space," Max said sarcastically.

"In theory, they can stretch their wings, however, as you can see it is overcrowded, so they probably don't, it is still far from a natural existence. Around 50% of UK hens live in these cages their whole life. Most of the cage has a metal wire bottom, not very comfortable or natural for their feet."

Max teleported them to another barn; there was a sea of chickens on the barn floor. "These barn hens are sitting in their own wee and poop which causes diseases such as foot rot and hock burns, where the bird's sensitive skin has been scorched by the ammonia-rich poop and wee covering the shed floors. They have a similar amount of space to the caged versions no more than nine hens a square meter in the UK, that is, pretty tightly packed, I don't think they move that much."

"What about free-range chickens, Max; is it the same as pigs?"

"Free-range is often the same as you see here; however, they have free access to go outside for part of the day, most do not as it is so crowded, they just stay put."

"What about organic, Max?"

"Organic just means they have not been given any antibiotics or vaccines and are fed organic food." Max touched Billy's shoulder; they were teleported into a clean factory with conveyor belts. Hundreds of chirping baby chicks were on the conveyor belt. Workers were picking up the chicks and putting them into different shoots leading to different conveyor belts.

"Where are the hens, Max?"

"There are no hens here Billy. Soon after the eggs are laid, they are put into a hatchery, which is a really warm cupboard simulating the mother sitting on the egg. Twenty-one days later, the chicks are born here in this factory."

"So they never get to see their mums?"

"No, Billy, this is factory farming, it is nothing to do with the animals' needs; it is all about efficiency and profit."

"What is happening down there?"

"They are being separated depending on their sex, males in one shoot and females in the other."

Billy's eyes followed one of the conveyor belts, the chicks entered into a chamber with doors opening and closing behind them after they had entered.

Max continued to explain to Billy what was happening "That is a gas chamber Billy; they are being killed in the gas chamber."

Stunned Billy couldn't talk, he just watched and listened. The gas chamber was turned on making a loud beeping noise for around 90 seconds. The other end of the chamber was another door, the conveyor belt started, Billy watched as the door opened, he could see dead chicks on the conveyor belt; they then disappeared down a hole on the conveyor belt.

"New-born male chicks in the egg industry are killed at 1 day old because they do not lay eggs and are not the best breed of chicken to be bred as meat for human consumption. They are gassed and then go into a macerator which chops them up into tiny pieces. In some countries, they are macerated alive. They are then sold as meat for feeding pet reptiles or used to make cat and dog food."

"Max, that is disgusting, what about free-range or organic chicks?"

"This happens in the entire egg industry even with organic and free-range, 99% of males chicks are born to die at 1 day old; they don't get a life. It is estimated that in the UK around 40 million male chicks are born, and then killed." Billy's eyes followed the female conveyor belt. They were being picked up by workers, their heads held for a second in a machine, then put back on the conveyor belt.

"They are being debeaked, without anaesthetic or pain relief; can you imagine Billy, having the tip of your beak cut off?"

"Why do they do that?"

"Because they will be housed in very overcrowded conditions, they start pecking each other and picking on the weak birds. In the wild, they would be pecking around in the ground, scratching the dirt searching for food, and they would not start pecking each other, even if they did try to do that, the wild chicken would be able to run away, chickens in factory farms are unable to run away. Once they are old enough, they are then used for their eggs just like their mums and are killed at around 18 months because they don't lay enough eggs to be profitable."

Billy was once again stunned at the unimaginable practices that are standard processes in mass animal farming.

They were teleported to another barn full of chickens. Max continued to talk.

"Chickens bred for meat are mainly housed in massive barns housing anything from 10,000–50,000 per barn. As with the hen layers, they are also selectively bred and many are fed steroids for fast-growing, they reach slaughter age in just around 40 days, about half the natural time it takes to become adult size. In essence, they are young chicks in an obese adult size body. As with barn hens, they are sat in their own wee and poop, next time you are at home Billy, take a look in the fridge at a whole chicken, you may see the skin is red and sore on the hocks from the hock burn."

Max teleported them just outside the sheds, there were rows and rows of these massive sheds, they must have been 100 meters long, 25 meters wide and maybe 20 sheds in all. At the end of each shed was a wheelie bin. "Take a look inside Billy, but cover your nose and mouth." Billy opened the bin, it was almost full of dead chickens, and the stench was their bodies rotting.

"Why are they dead, Max?"

"Due to the steroids in their feed, they grow so fast that their legs cannot carry them for long. Some cannot even stand; some are unable to get to the water or food so die of dehydration or starvation. Many die of heart and lung failure before they reach the slaughter age. When a worker sees that a bird is very weak and it's obvious it will die, they pick them up and dumped them in the bin, they die lying on top of their dead siblings and cousins."

Max teleported them back into the rafters, the barn door opened and some men came in, they were funnelling the birds towards the doorway, men just the other side of the door were catching the birds and chucking them into small crates that were then loaded onto a lorry. The men worked really fast, violently grabbing the birds, it was complete chaos. The birds were making a lot of noise, as were the men, they were shouting, laughing and swearing at the birds. Billy was as usual shocked and speechless.

"Due to the heavy-handed and fast-paced operation, many of the animals have their legs and wings broken or their hips dislocated, resulting in the birds being forced to endure relentless pain on their journey to death. The birds are transported to slaughter in these tiny crates, with no access to food or water, creating an extremely stressful environment. Poultry slaughter involves shackling birds by their feet and hanging them upside down before the machine carries them to an electric water bath where they suffer a painful electric shock, the purpose is to render them unconscious.

"Many birds do not get stunned as they hold their heads up and don't make contact with the water, some regain consciousness before they reach the neck cutter, meaning that they are fully conscious as their throats are sliced open. After the birds have had their throats slit, they arrive at the scalding tank, where their feathers are loosened prior to being plucked. In the UK, an estimated 8.4 million birds are still alive at this stage and are boiled alive in the scalding tank."

"Max, I have read that chickens dream as we do, they actually have REM sleep, and they cluck to their chick just before they start hatching to encourage them out and the chick clucks back to their mummy. They don't even get to have that very first natural experience, Max, hearing their mummies and calling back. I also read that they have different ways of communicating with each other; facial expressions, eye movements, postures and 24 different vocalisations. It is so sad that we have forced them to have such unnatural lives Max and then brutally kill them."

"That's one reason why I came to Earth Billy, to help you all to see what is going on. In the UK, humans eat around 30 million eggs per day. In the wild, chickens lay around 20 eggs per year, but due to man's interference, they lay around 300.

- Chickens are killed at either 1 day, 40 days or 18 months
- If chickens were to live a natural life, they would live until they were around 8–10 years.
- They are babies and young adults when they are killed.
- 975 million chickens are killed every year in the UK for their meat. 40 million hens are killed that are no longer able to lay eggs, as well as the 40 million 1 day old male baby chicks.
- "Globally, it is estimated that 50 billion chickens are killed each year.

"Chicks go from shell to hell, not all chickens are bred this way Billy, but the vast majority are. In the western world, people eat as much chicken on a typical day as they did in a whole year in 1930. Ask yourself this Billy, what right do humans have to take the life of another being?"

"The question is not, can they reason? Nor can they talk? But can they suffer?"

—Jeremy Bentham (1748–1832)

34

Chapter 3

"OK, Billy, time for some fun. How would you like to go flying?" Billy was still shocked from seeing and hearing about the pigs and the chickens. He wasn't sure he felt like some fun after seeing how much suffering the animals endure. He thought for a few moments and then agreed that perhaps that was enough horrid sights for one day.

"OK, Max, where are we going?"

"Well, Billy, I have also been visiting others around the globe. I would like to introduce you to a couple of them and I know that you happen to like the idea of going into space, so I thought that might make you feel a little better after seeing the pigs and chickens and hearing all those vile facts. Rather than thinking our way, we can fly!"

"Space sounds great Max, but I am not sure about meeting people, it's not something I am good at."

"You'll be fine Billy they will love you! Just be yourself and don't worry about what anyone else thinks. Remember that you have oodles of love inside you and compassion for animals, which is something that you will have in common. It will only be a short visit."

So, with that said Max and Billy went flying high into the earth's stratosphere, a dream come true for Billy. Max had surrounded Billy in a protective energy bubble and off they went.

"Max, what if someone see us or we are seen on radar?"

"Don't worry Billy, we are going so fast that anyone who sees us will take a second look by which time we will be gone, and they will think it's their eyes playing tricks on them and as for radar, we are not detectable by radar."

A few minutes later, they were floating above the earth. "We are now in what you call the thermosphere," said Max.

Billy could see the whole of the planet, the land, the clouds, oceans. He could see the shape of the boot of Italy, a spiral shape in the clouds which was clearly a storm as lightning was flashing every few seconds. Billy was once again mesmerised and speechless. Our planet, so wonderfully still, just hanging in the middle of space. Words just could not describe how he was feeling and what he was seeing. He noticed a strange shape, it wasn't land, it was in the middle of the ocean, an indescribable shape, beautifully swirling and shining, almost white, but for sure it was a bluey-green colour.

"Max, what is that beautiful shape in the ocean?"

"That is phytoplankton; we will talk about that sometime as it is a very important part of the ecosystem on planet earth."

They continued to float in the protection bubble for a few minutes to allow Billy to take in this moment, for him to stare in awe at the sheer magnificence of his home, planet Earth. Once Max had a sense that Billy was ready, he took them on a journey heading to Dallas, Texas, USA. On the way Billy realised they were surrounded by space junk, he hadn't noticed it at first because he was so mesmerised by the pure beauty of Earth, he thought how lucky he was in his bubble.

"The junk you can see Billy are bits of old satellites and rocket stages as well as the natural junk; asteroids, comets and fragments of meteoroids. There are around 3,300 operational satellites in the earth's orbit and around 18,000 bits of trackable man-made junk and it is estimated that there are 700,000 bits of natural debris between 1–10 cm and 170 million bits less than 1 cm."

Billy watched in amazement as they continued to fly as the bits of junk were bouncing off his bubble. Max dodged the satellites and the large junk, Billy imagined that it must feel like this to be a bird, swooping and swerving at speed. He couldn't get the smile off his face; he actually never wanted his smile to end as he was the happiest he had ever felt.

Lucy Broom was out walking near her home and was expecting Max and Billy to arrive. She was a very pretty girl, long blonde hair, blues eyes, slim. Lucy was a cheerleader for the gold stars football team. She was a bright girl; however, she was easily distracted by social activities, she was the most popular girl in her class.

She was always either chatting with friends, talking on her phone or on social media. Being a cheerleader took dedication as the practising was almost daily, so she didn't have a lot of time for much else except being with her dogs, she adored them, and they were her best friends. Lucy did have a brother and a sister but loved her dogs just as much as her family. Eating out and having BBQ's is a big thing in Dallas, there are more restaurants per person than in New York, Lucy and her family ate out a lot.

Max had already done the pig and chicken thing with her; she was as shocked as Billy was. Max also told her that the USA consumes 20% of the land animal slaughters in the world, whilst only having 5% of the global population. Americans were consuming such a large percentage of animal flesh, that it was really important that people's eye's our opened to the reality of what goes on and to how conditioned/programmed people have been for so long. She had also learnt that the USA also has the largest production of cow's milk in the world.

Lucy felt really terrible, as she had not paid any attention to the animals at all, she just ate what she had always eaten, without considering for a moment the animals, just like most people, she had been conditioned. They all three chatted for a short while, Lucy and Billy talking about the new information they had learned, then Max said that they had another place to visit. This time, they didn't fly; they went by Max's usual mode of transport; teleportation. The next stop was India.

Rohan Arya was born in New Delhi; he was a quietly spoken, gentle boy always doing for others, neighbours and family, actually anyone who needed help. Rohan would give you his last coin if you needed it. He was a very reliable character if he said he would do something he would be there, on time with a smile on his face willing and able.

He had a brother and a sister and lived with his mum and dad in an apartment in a block of 8 other families, they were like his aunts, uncles, brothers and sisters. Max had already had the pig and chicken conversation with Rohan too. Rohan was raised as a vegetarian, he learned that as many as 30–40% of people in India are vegetarian but they still ate eggs and milk products. Cows are so sacred in India that it is illegal to kill a cow in many Indian states; however, being sacred, the milk of a cow is revered, so it is consumed.

He had learnt that India has the second highest milk production in the world. Rohan and Billy chatted for a short while, Billy felt really comfortable with Rohan which pleased Billy greatly. Billy really had not met such a nice boy before, Rohan was comfortable too and didn't seem to give off the impression that he thought Billy was a bit odd. Max said it was time to go; Billy was disappointed and said that he looked forward to spending more time with Rohan.

Back in Billy's room, Billy thanked Max for taking him to meet both Lucy and Rohan and expressed his excitement at how much better the chatting was than he had expected.

Max smiled a knowing smile. "I knew you would be fine Billy. Life experiences don't always go the way your past experiences have gone Billy. Every time you feel fear about something Billy, walk into the fear. Know the fear is there, but just go right ahead as this will bring you more courage. Each time you walk into the fear Billy, you will gain more and more courage. Unless, of course, a lion or tiger is chasing you then be fearful and run for your life, Billy!"

Billy laughed out loud and then yawned. "Time for me to go, Billy, it's been a day full of excitement, shocking truths and walking into the fear! Get some sleep now; we have more to do tomorrow."

"See you tomorrow Max. Oh, and thanks again, it has been really terrific, a real eye-opener about the animals and a really special day up in space and visiting Rohan and Lucy, a day I will never ever forget."

The next morning, Billy awoke really late. His mum was in the kitchen. "Morning Bill's, you are up late, didn't you sleep well?"

"Yes, mum, I slept really well thanks, it was such a deep sleep, I slept through my alarm. Do I have to go to school today, mum? I really want to talk to you about school."

"Oh, not today Bill's I am working dayshift today, but I can drop you at school if you like, rather than walking, you can have an extra 15 minutes getting ready."

"OK, mum, thanks. Yes, please if you can take me that would be great." Billy desperately wanted to chat with his mum about school, he arranged with her to chat that evening.

After school, Max was waiting in Billy's room. "Hey!" They both said in unison. "Ready for more information Billy about farmed animals? Or would you like to go visit some more people?"

"Can we do both Max? I really want to know and learn what is going on in the world, not just to do with animals, but everything, I live my life in my bubble Max; school, home and out in the woods or in the garden. I didn't have a clue about what you shared with me yesterday and I feel really bad that the suffering is so severe and in such massive numbers. I do have some questions for you Max but I guess you already know that." Billy smiled.

"Go ahead Billy, ask away!"

"OK, so this morning I looked in the fridge to see what chicken and pork products we had. My mum buys free-range eggs and outdoor reared and red tractor labelled pork sausages, I asked her about it, she tells me that free-range means that the chickens are happy hens outside have a nice free life and that the outdoor reared and red tractor means that the pigs are looked after in a humane way and again are happy, free and outside. I asked her about the pigs being killed she said that there are regulations and standards in the UK and that the pigs don't suffer."

"Your mum is telling you what she believes to be the case. Food labelling like this, is really about making consumers feel better about what they are buying so that they don't feel bad about eating the animal or its products, in truth the industry has pulled the wool over the consumer's eyes by adding this label. It's there to ease people's conscience it's nothing more than marketing to sell the product and keep your eyes closed to the reality. The reality is somewhat different to what your mum and most people think Billy.

"Free-range eggs, like I said yesterday, just means hens are free to roam inside a massive barn and doors are opened for part of the day. They are free to roam, but many are unable due to the crowded conditions and size of their bodies, the same goes for the chickens that are reared for meat. Look at the numbers Billy, there are around 35 million hens laying eggs and around 160 million chickens are bred for meat at any one time, how many hens do you see outside? It's the same for pigs, free-range piglets are mainly born and reared outside until they are taken from their mums at 4–5 weeks old and reared inside, while the mum stays outside, ready for the next piglet to arrive.

"Even the outside space is cordoned off pens and for sure they have more space than the majority of pigs, but roaming is an exaggeration. An incredibly small number are reared outside, as one would imagine in woods, snuffling around with their snouts in the ground. Again, if we look at the numbers 10 million pigs are killed each year, they are killed at 6 months so that's more than 5 million at any one time; do you see many pigs outside, Billy?"

"No Max, we don't."

"So, do you want to know some more stuff about animals' lives?"

"Yes, I am ready Max, please share whatever you want."

"OK, the next are the other popular birds, it is a similar story to the chickens, so no need for us to go to visit them."

Geese and Ducks

"Geese and ducks bred for meat and are reared similar to chickens, they may have their wings clipped to prevent them flying. A duck's natural habitat is on the water, where their body weight is supported by the water. In the barns where they are intensively reared, they do not have any water to float in, their feet and legs can't handle the weight of their bodies because they are designed to spend a lot of their time floating. Some end up lying on their backs unable to get up, weak from lack of water and food, many die before the slaughter age.

- They are killed at ages 15 weeks and 7 weeks.
- If geese were to live a natural life, they would live until they were 10–25 years.
- Ducks would live until around 10 years.
- They are toddlers when they are killed.
- Around 14 million geese and ducks are killed every year in the UK.
- It is estimated that 3.5 billion geese and ducks are murdered every year worldwide.

In other countries, geese and ducks are also reared by being force-fed to produce a food that is considered a luxury called Foie gras, which comes from the birds' liver. They are killed at around 14 weeks old. This is illegal in the UK, due to welfare laws; however, this is crazy when you consider the lack of welfare for other farmed animals, it's not less welfare, it is just a different type of abuse. People in the UK decided that it wasn't moral to force-feed birds. What do you think Billy, is it moral to chop off body parts to baby animals?"

"Definitely not Max, I think it is disgusting that we do this, it is truly mind-boggling and diabolical, as you said, it is not different, it's the same and it is unthinkable abuse no matter how the animal is reared these mutilations and killings are not OK."

"France is the biggest producer of Foie gras and although it is illegal to force-feed birds in the UK, the bizarre thing is it is legal to import foie gras and sell it. What is the difference, Billy?"

"None Max, if it is brought in a shop, that's just the same, it doesn't matter what land in the world it was reared on. Ducks and geese do not have a nationality; they don't know if they are living in France or the UK; abuse is abuse no matter what land the animals are abused on."

Turkeys

"Turkeys are reared similar to chickens, but have other potential mutilations as well as the beak trimming, they may be de-snooded, de-toed, de-vocalised, have their spurs removed or their toes clipped.

- Turkeys are killed when they are around 4–5 months.
- If turkeys were to live a natural life, they would live until they were 10-15 years.
- They are toddlers when they are killed.
- 16 million turkeys are killed each year in the UK.
- It is estimated that 650 million turkeys are killed each year in the world"

"There will come a time when men such as I, will look upon the murder of animals as they now look upon the murder of men."

—Leonardo da Vinci (1452–1519)

"Max, I was thinking about talking to my mum about not eating animals and I know she would come up with all sorts of reasons why it's natural for humans to eat animal flesh. As an example, she would say; frogs eat flies, birds eat fish or lions eat zebras."

"Well, if you based everything you did on what other animals do, the world would be a different place; for starters, you humans would all go around sniffing each other's butts, as dogs do. Eating your own poop, like some apes do, burying your poop like cats or women killing men after having sex as spiders do."

Billy laughed. "OK, good points, thanks, how about this one? We are the top of the food chain and have been eating meat since we had tools to kill them."

"Precisely Billy, since you have had tools to kill them. If man had not evolved to make tools, you wouldn't be at the top of the food chain, wolves, tigers, lions and bears would be your predators. Also, if man hadn't evolved to make tools, how would you kill an animal?"

"I wouldn't want to kill it, Max."

"Imagine Billy, if you wanted to kill it, how would you do it?"

"Well, I couldn't Max, as I would need a knife or a gun to kill it, Max."

"Exactly, Billy, humans do not have the natural tools to kill animals, humans don't have talons or claws, humans don't have sharp teeth for ripping open flesh like lions."

"We have canines, Max; aren't they are for ripping open flesh?"

Max laughed out loud raucously. "Hippos Billy, have the biggest canines of all, and they graze on aquatic plants such as creeping grass, small green shoots and reeds. Anyway, you try and use your tiny teeth to open a pig belly, lamb leg, or cow flank, while they are alive and kicking, I really don't think that would be possible Billy. Lions and other carnivores have carnassial teeth at the back of their mouths which enables them to shear meat from the prey like knife blades. Lions swallow large pieces of meat whole; humans have to chew food.

"Humans have fingernails and teeth neither of which would be able to kill a live, kicking animal. Your teeth are for grinding vegetation and biting into fruit like apples. Also, humans cook or grind meat into mince, and you don't kill an animal and eat it straight away. There is nothing natural about how humans kill and eat animal flesh."

"So why do we all eat meat, Max?"

"In winter, when berries, fruits and nuts were sparse, early modern man needed to supplement their diets with meat because they were in survival mode, Billy. Humans can fully satisfy their bodies' needs with plants, the natural food that your bodies are designed for and in the world today, you produce food and ship it all over the globe. In cities, you can go to 24-hour supermarkets and buy pretty much any fresh food you care to eat, you are now not in survival mode, well some of you are not, the ability to have enough fresh food should be available to all humans but that is another subject we will cover later."

"If it's OK for animals to eat each other, why is it not OK for us to kill with our tools, we have evolved to have tools, so why not use them?"

"Along with tools, humans also evolved to have awareness, and you have a moral compass. Animals do not have the full awareness that humans have; however, they are sentient beings and are aware of their surroundings as well as having the ability to feel."

"What does sentient mean, Max?"

"Sentient beings can experience positive and negative emotions including pain and distress, joy and love. They are not consciously thinking about what they eat, they don't have the intelligence that humans have; humans have evolved into more intelligent beings than the rest of the animal kingdom, but that doesn't give you the right to have dominion over them.

"Animals eat out of necessity. Humans are able to sustain themselves without eating meat and animal products. Humans did have a necessity a long time ago to eat meat, that is the evolutionary process Billy, this is one of the next steps in human evolution to have the awareness that all sentient beings have the right to live a natural life, now that does include frogs eating flies, that is natural for frogs.

"Or even for wolves to eat chickens. Humans have compassion, humans have a moral compass, humans can decide if they want to eat meat or not; frogs do not have a choice and do not have that level of consciousness to consider what to eat, it is nature playing out.

"The other thing to think about is that animals are in harmony with nature, humans are so far away from harmony with nature. Lions don't catch zebras, lock them up, breed them and take away their babies. They catch and kill to eat; they are in survival mode. Humans are in profit mode; how much money can I make from raising the babies."

"Another one, I think mum would say is; we slaughter the animals in a humane way."

"That's just like saying humane massacre or humane holocaust; they just don't make sense Billy. Humane and slaughter is an oxymoron, the two words just don't go together. If you look up the word humane and the word slaughter, you will see the difference. Is there a nice way to kill a being that doesn't want to die?"

"No, Max."

"Anyway, they are not slaughtered 'humanely' Billy, they are stunned with prongs or gassed or electrocuted in water, these are not methods that would be used even for someone who did want to die."

"People often say that humans have always eaten animals, as if this is a justification for continuing the practice. According to this logic, we should not try to prevent people from murdering other people, since this has also been done since the earliest of times."

—Isaac Bashevis Singer (1902–1991)

Cows and Their Calves

"Next stop Billy is a modern dairy farm."

Billy was looking down at a large room that housed a massive round milking machine, which was slowly turning. At the entrance to the machine, a cow walked in, encouraged as there was food to eat. The cow walked into the individual stall where two workers attached the machine to her teats. The cows were like robots, eating grain whilst being milked.

Billy watched what was happening at the entry and exit of the machine, once the cow had completed a whole turn, the machine automatically detached from the cows' teats. The cow then backed out of the machine; clearly, she knew what to do as she had been trained. Billy counted how many cows were in the machine, there were 70.

Max teleported them to the roof, Billy could see calves in small pens with small hutches. The pens were individually fenced, so they were in essence alone. Billy thought they looked so young to be on their own, it was very sad to see them locked up just like prisoners. In Billy's mind, they should be running around a field with each other, having fun and suckling on their mothers' teats, instead of the mums being milked like robots and robbed of their milk.

"Max, when do the calves get to drink their mother's milk and be with her?"

"They don't Billy, they are given a substitute."

Billy was astonished. "But Max isn't cow's milk what the calves need?"

"Yes, Billy, but as always, follow the money, if they gave the milk to the calves, they wouldn't be able to sell it; they make more money from selling the milk as the substitute costs less than the profits made from the milk."

The last stop was a cowshed, where a man had his whole arm inside the anus of a cow.

"What's wrong with the cow, Max?"

"Nothing is wrong Billy, they are artificially inseminating her with semen to get her pregnant."

Billy watched in horror, it totally turned Billy's stomach. "Why are they doing that?" Billy whispered.

"It is the most efficient way to get animals pregnant." The man not only had his arm in her bottom but also inserted a long probe into her ladies' bits.

"What are they doing with that long rod?" asked Billy.

"It has bull's semen inside the end of the rod; they are squirting it inside her to get her pregnant."

Billy thought to himself, that it was OK for a vet to put his arm up a cow's bottom if she had a medical condition and he needed to feel what the problem was, but to do this just to get semen into her, to have a baby which will be taken away was just beyond belief to Billy. Max teleported them to another barn. As usual, up in the eaves, they sat looking down. Billy could see some cows with what appeared to be holes in their sides, with plastic rings integral to their bodies.

"A bizarre mutilation/experiment is going on here in Switzerland at a research company, as well as other places in Europe and USA. As you can see Billy, the cows have holes cut into their sides, the plastic ring is fitted to keep the flesh open and clean, the plastic is now part of the cow for her life. A lid is fitted to enable the researchers to 'open and close' the hole up, this enables them to put their hand into the cow's stomach, remove some of the contents to then measure the goodness that a specific field or feed has provided.

"The stomach contents have good and bad bacteria in them called microbes. The main purpose is to test different feeds to see what goodness they produce; in addition, they can then transfer the good stuff into a cow that needs the good bacteria. They are called cannulated or fistulated cows."

"Looks like crazy behaviour to me Max, I know you said it is to test what the goodness has been provided, but why do they do that?"

"Holy-e-cow takes on a new meaning, Billy." Max laughed his usual loud laugh, which, of course, only Billy could hear inside his head.

"Well, as usual, follow the money Billy, this has nothing to do with the welfare of the cow, it is to enable them to maximise on profit. The feed produces different qualities of meat or milk. They say that this does no harm nor bothers the cows; however, the procedure is a pretty big operation and takes the cow 4–6 weeks to recover, she would for sure suffer in that time. The suffering is a question humans should be asking themselves about; however, the other question each and every human should be asking themselves is; Is this morally right to do this to a cow?"

Max teleported them to a nearby hill for a chat. "Time for some more cow facts Billy, for a cow to produce milk she must first give birth to a calf. As you have just seen, this means dairy cows are generally artificially impregnated every year in order to keep a continuous milk supply."

"Why every year, Max?"

"Well, Billy, she will only produce milk for around 9–12 months after having a baby, so they impregnate her, again and again, to keep the milk supply coming. They are usually artificially inseminated within three months of giving birth to her first baby and each baby thereafter; this is so that she can continually produce milk.

"Calves would naturally feed on their mothers for around 9 months, but dairy calves are taken away from their mothers normally within 24–72 hours of birth, as we just talked about, this is so that as much milk as possible can be acquired from the mother. Separation of mother and calf is an incredibly traumatic experience and both will cry out for days or even weeks. Female calves are often separated from their mothers and are kept in solitary confinement as you have just seen.

"They will be following in their mother's footsteps to be milk-producing robots. Male calves are also separated, a large percentage are usually shot on site because they do not produce milk and are not the best breed for beef meat. This is another example Billy of following the money. The ones that are not shot are destined to be reared as Veal, which I will come onto in a moment. Some farmers do keep the males then sell them once they are 2–4 weeks, but this is more expensive for the farmer; he makes less profit than having them shot soon after birth, so it is a small percentage of farmers who do this.

"Dairy cows are milk machines for humans, robots being milked every day until they are around 4–6 years, then they are killed as they no longer produce enough milk to be profitable and are so worn out from being continuously pregnant and milked. Some even collapse through sheer exhaustion, if this happens, they are then dragged by their feet with a tractor and rope then scooped up into the tractors' bucket and dumped into a lorry to be taken for slaughter, it is estimated that 150,000 cows in the UK are pregnant when killed every year, the calf dying in her tummy.

"Most calves raised in the UK whether bred for dairy or meat have to endure painful mutilations such as castration and disbudding. Disbudding is a procedure where a calf is restrained and has a hot iron rod forced onto its horn buds in order to prevent the horns from growing which is an extremely painful procedure that is carried out without pain relief. Although banned in the UK, elsewhere cattle are also branded, this is done with a red hot iron which is held onto the animals' skin to burn and brand with a number or a symbol for identification.

"Other possible mutilations are tongue reshaping to prevent self-sucking, castration, ear tagging, nose ringing, and tail docking. Dairy cows have been modified to produce up to 10 times more milk than they would naturally, which means their udders are enlarged to such an extent it affects their walking, my guess is that it is pretty uncomfortable to have such enlarged udders. Around 30% of UK dairy cows have mastitis, a bacterial infection of the udder because they are continually being milked.

"Over 50% of dairy cows suffer from crippling lameness and pressure sores and some cows are forced to wear chains called hobbles for months at a time. These devices are used on mother cows who have suffered pelvic damage during calving, a frequently documented problem for dairy cows who have been selectively bred to ensure maximum milk production, these devices prevent the cow from laying down, forcing her to stand up when all she really wants to do is lay down and have a rest as she is in pain.

"Lastly, the 'humane' slaughter, most cows whether 'spent' diary or reared for meat are killed by first being stunned with a captive bolt pistol designed to render the cow unconscious without causing pain. The gun fires a steel bolt that is powered by compressed air into the cow's head/brain. They are then hung upside down by one rear leg and have their throat slit. It is estimated that 10% of cattle are not stunned effectively and will have to endure the experience of being shot repeatedly in the head or having their throat cut and their blood drained whilst still fully conscious."

"Max, I have read about the cows' diet if they were wild, they would eat a varied plant diet, with various herbs with medicinal benefits and soon after a cow has given birth, she will seek out stinging nettles to eat to replace her iron levels; they don't get any of this within the farming industry. They don't get to choose what to eat, but in the wild they are self-medicating.

"I also read that calves need a lot of sleep and don't graze as much as the adults and in the wild, one cow would stay with the herds' calves to have an afternoon nap, whilst the herd would wander off to forage. In essence, they have a natural nursery system. And, cows recognise up to 100 other cows in the herd, all of whom have unique personalities and have been known to show empathy to humans who are very sad or grieving. They are in essence emotional feeling beings just like us Max."

"Indeed, they are Billy. Human beings are the only species in your world that drinks the milk of another species, this never happens in nature, and in addition, not only do you drink another species milk, but also you do it in adulthood and for your whole lives, once again humans are the only species that drink milk in adulthood. If you really think about this, it really does not make any sense; adults don't need their human mothers' milk, so why would you need cow's milk? Raw milk is a dangerous product for humans, so dangerous that you pasteurise it to kill all the harmful bacteria, doesn't that tell you something, Billy?"

"When you put it like that Max, yes, it tells me that we really shouldn't be drinking it, not only from the point of view of the animal but also for our bodies."

"Some more cow facts for you.

- Cows bred for milk are killed at 4–6 years old.
- Cows bred for meat are killed at around 18 months.
- If cows were to live a natural life, they would live until they were 20–25 years.
- They are babies, toddlers and young adults when they are killed.
- Around 2.6 million cows are slaughtered every year in the UK.
- There are around 270 million dairy cows producing milk in the world, all of whom will be killed once they are 'spent' and replaced with their children.
- It is estimated that 300 million cows are butchered for their meat globally.

"Surprisingly, one of the biggest dairies in the world is in Saudi Arabia with seven fully automated milking machines; however, the biggest is in China capable of housing 100,000 cows. In China, they do not consume much dairy; however, the Chinese export most of the products to Russia."

"If you had to kill your own calf before you ate him, most likely you would not be able to do it. To hear the calf scream, to see the blood spill, to see the baby being taken away from his momma, and to see the look of death in the animal's eye would turn your stomach. So you get the man at the packing house to do the killing for you."

—Dick Gregory (1932–2017)

"Max, I have a question. Cows are artificially impregnated which is pretty gross. My question is where does the semen come from?"

"Well, Billy, the same but in reverse. Humans get involved rather than letting them mate naturally. Men collect the semen, by using a 'teaser' animal to get the bull aroused which entails him mounting the 'teaser'. Then the worker at the collection centre uses an artificial vagina that has thermal and mechanical stimulation to trigger ejaculation. Fancy a job, Billy?" Max laughed his raucous laugh.

"That is the grossest thing I think I have ever heard Max, why do we do that? Why not just leave the bull in the field with the cows?"

"The best bulls get the top money for their semen. One collection of sperm will artificially impregnate many cows, some have fathered over 100,000 calves. Also, there is no need to have males at each farm, it is cost-effective to have fewer animals to feed and rear. It's as I have said before Billy, follow the money.

"As you now know Billy, male calves are of no use to the dairy industry and less suitable for beef production, it is estimated that 90,000 male calves are shot soon after birth every year in the UK. Male calves that are not shot will instead be raised for veal a 'product' that is considered luxury either in the UK or in Europe. The calves have to endure, long traumatic journeys when they have recently been born, it is a very scary journey for them, babies are taken away from their mums, then put into a truck to be driven to a veal farm.

"Or they are driven a long way to the shipping port, transferred to ships and sent across to Europe, then they endure yet another long journey to the veal farm. Veal meat is a pale colour and very tender, to create this pale tender meat the process is solitary confinement in small pens and they are given food that is lacking in nutrients. It is a miserable short life for the calves; they are killed at 14 weeks when their natural lifespan would be 20–25 years. They are babies when they are killed."

"What about protein and calcium Max? Don't we need them from meat, dairy and eggs?"

"Billy, this is what you have all been led to believe; however, this is not the case. Animals get their protein and calcium from plants. If you eat a varied plant diet, there are plenty of proteins and calcium for your body. A human mother's breast milk is designed specifically to give a baby exactly what he/she needs, it contains 1% protein and that is for a baby that is growing at an extra fast rate.

"Cow's milk is over 3 times that amount. You can get plenty of protein from fruits, vegetables, pulses, grains and nuts. It's funny, Billy; most people will ask that question, but when they are all eating processed meat and dairy food, they don't ask themselves health questions. This is because processed food has slowly been introduced over many years, so people don't ask the question; processed junk is now normal. The idea of not eating animal products throws people into a panic about nutrition because it is considered not normal.

"Billy, it is more natural not to eat meat, processed food, dairy and eggs. Think about it, there is nothing more natural than eating fresh fruit, vegetables and pulses. Also, let us think about the animal world Billy, some of the biggest mammals are herbivores; elephants, rhinoceros, hippopotamus, bison, and wildebeest. These animals are all very strong and muscular, they eat vegetation. Humans are led to believe that you are meant to be omnivores, but this is another fallacy. Humans are naturally herbivores."

Chapter 4

Billy spoke to his mum about school. "Bills, you can't just stop going to school it doesn't work like that, anyway, school is compulsory."

"Mum, school isn't compulsory, that's just what we have all been led to believe, I have been doing some research on the internet and found that over 50,000 young people are being home-schooled in the UK, and it is rising every year. If I educate myself, I can still take the exams."

"What about the curriculum Bills, how will you be able to follow it?"

"Mum, this is also a misconception when home-schooled, you don't have to follow any curriculum, or do a set number of hours. There are loads of online resources to help. I promise you mum; I will study; and I will get good grades. I will share with you my progress as often as you like, so you can see that I am working towards getting the exams results."

"Let me sleep on it Bills."

"You said that the other day mum."

"Bills, this isn't a decision to make lightly, let me do some research and ask around and I'll need to talk to your dad about it."

"OK, mum, but please can we talk again tomorrow? I really want to start teaching myself as soon as possible."

"OK, Bills, my lovely boy, I really do love you and I am proud that you have come up with this idea. I will try to find the time tomorrow, I need to understand the process, then talk to you dad."

"Thanks, mum, I love you too, oh mum, I have something else I would like to talk to you about. I have decided that I am not going to eat animal products."

"Blimey Bills, that will make life a bit difficult, why have you decided that?"

"Because the animals are just as valid as we are mum, they deserve to live a natural lifespan. We kill them when they are so young and the farming practices are really horrible mum."

"Have you been on that internet again Billy, you know you can't believe everything you read."

"Something like that mum." Billy smiled to himself.

"People who don't eat any animal products are crazy hippies, they call themselves vegan, it is a very extreme diet Billy and I have read they like to set free caged animals and do criminal damage to farm equipment, it's not a diet or lifestyle to take seriously and it's a bit of an extreme fad Bills."

"Artificially inseminating dairy cows and taking away their babies is extreme mum. Killing most of the boy calves and sending the rest into solitary confinement to become veal is extreme mum. Sending the girls into solitary confinement to follow in their mums' footsteps is extreme mum. Stealing the calf milk to sell for a profit rather than giving it to the baby cow is extreme mum.

"Not only that, also, the cows have to go through that process every year, until they are exhausted, they are then sent for slaughter aged 4–6 years, that is extreme mum. If cows were wild, they would live 20–25 years. Then there are chickens, mum, in the egg industry, the boy chicks are killed at 1 day old because they don't lay eggs, that's extreme mum. The females get the end of their beaks cut off to stop them all pecking each other. That is extreme mum.

"They are housed in filthy barns, get diseases and sores and when they stop laying eggs at around 18 months, they are sent to be killed, if they haven't already died by then, that is extreme mum. Chickens in the wild would live 8–10 years. By me not consuming these products, a tiny bit less suffering and killing is happening. Each and every person who chooses not to be a part of such atrocities is reducing the suffering and killings, mum. I can sustain my body very healthily on fruit, vegetables, grains, pulses and nuts, I have researched it on the internet"

"When you put it like that Bills, that sounds horrific, but I am sure not all cows go through that and free-range eggs are all happily living outside Bills like I told you the other day."

"Yes, mum, all mass-produced dairy cows really do go through that, any mass-produced animal product, will have hidden suffering, behind closed doors. The farmers don't want us to know this stuff because we will stop consuming the dead animal flesh, milk and eggs."

"So how about you just stop eating eggs and drinking milk then Bills?"

"No, Mum, it's just as bad for the pigs, do you know what they do to pigs, mum?"

"No, Bills, all I can tell you is that the governing bodies will make sure that the standards are met and the pigs won't suffer and like I told you, I buy outdoor reared pork."

"Mum that is simply not true. That just means that the pig had some time outside. Only 3% of pigs spend their entire lives outside. Most pigs have their teeth clipped and tails docked mum and it doesn't say on the packet; this piglet was not mutilated during its life and spent its entire time outside—does it?"

"OK, Bills, sounds like you know what you are talking about, but I am not overly happy with it, but I know you are doing it for the right reasons and from your heart Bills, that beautiful big heart of yours and it is your choice, I won't stand in your way."

"OK, Billy, time to meet some more friends." Anahira lived in New Zealand, she was from an indigenous family. The Māori people originally came from Polynesian explorers who settled the Pacific Ocean more than 1,000 years ago by canoe. Māori's like to give their children names that have significant meanings, Anahira means Angel. Anahira lived in Auckland, which has the largest population, around 35% of all New Zealanders. Anahira lived with her brother and parents. Although the population in global terms is small and is sparsely populated outside of the cities, animal agriculture makes up two-thirds of the country's export goods, made up of mainly sheep and dairy farming.

Jiemba, pronounced Jim-Ba, is often shortened to Jimmy or Jim. Jiemba was 13 and lived with his brother, sister and parents. His mum was of aboriginal descent; his dad was born in Australia of English descent. Aboriginal people also had meanings for their names, Jiemba's name was really apt, as he laughed all the time—he was such a happy boy, his name means 'laughing star'. Australia is home to a variety of unique animals, including the koala, kangaroo, emu, kookaburra and platypus. Other than the usual farmed animals Australians also eat kangaroo and crocodile. Jiemba liked to play sports, go to the beach and hang out with his friends. He also liked to do parkour and had many scars to prove it!

They arrived together, meeting high on a hilltop in the Australian outback. The land around them was very flat, you could see for miles; in the distance were some other high hilltop peaks and it was very quiet and isolated.

"Where are we, Max?"

"We are on top of Uluru Billy, also known as Ayres Rock."

"No way, Max? That is incredible."

Jiemba and Anahira had already been here before with Max, so were a little blasé about it, but Billy was amazed, as he always was wherever Max took him. Seeing that Billy was impressed Jiemba wanted to share some stuff; "This sandstone rock is 3.6 km long, has a circumference of 9.4 km and it extends 2.5 km underground."

Jiemba laughed as he talked. Billy knew all these facts, as he had often read about it on the internet, but he didn't butt in.

Jiemba continued. "It is said that ancestral beings that are supernatural and creator beings reside in these sacred places so it is a really important part of the local people's culture."

Anahira joined in, "The other amazing thing Billy is that it started forming around 550 million years ago and Jiemba's ancestors are one of human's oldest continuous cultures and were probably the first to leave Africa around 75,000 years ago, a truly brave people who were great explorers and adventurers."

They continued to chat, but mainly about all that they had learned since meeting Max, it was just like meeting the others, a quick chat to start to get to know each other before they needed to start working together. When it was time to go, Max asked Billy to wait there, while he teleported Jiemba and Anahira back to their homes.

Jiemba spoke just before Max teleported them "Watch out for those supernatural beings Billy."

Jiemba was laughing as Max touched his shoulder to teleport him away. Billy was totally blown away to be sitting on top of this iconic rock. He was just stunned at the places he had been so far; The Himalayas, African Savanna, Florida Beach, Unity in a parallel universe, outer space as well as meeting Rohan, Lucy and now Anahira and Jiemba.

He took a few deep breaths, closed his eyes and just sat for a few minutes breathing, smelling the air, hearing and feeling the stillness around him. He wondered what was next, what places would Max be taking him to, who he would meet and how they were going to 'change the global thinking'. A few minutes later Max appeared.

"Hey, sorry for the delay, but I got chatting and I figured some time up here alone would be good for you."

"Thanks, it was nice to feel this place alone. Max, I spoke to my mum about not eating animals or animal products, she said that it is mainly crazy hippies that don't eat animal products, they call themselves vegan and sometimes do crazy things like setting free caged animals and are criminals. She said that it's just a fad diet and not to be taken seriously."

"She is right that it is called vegan when you don't consume any animal products, and they do have a reputation of being hippies with dreadlocks and loads of piercings and sometimes have crazily dyed bright coloured hair. People are judged by appearance, as they are not crazy people; they are very caring and compassionate people. Just because they choose to dress that way, doesn't make them any less valid than humans who conform to dress a certain way.

"Also, there is a growing movement of people in the world who are not dressed that way who are waking up to what is going on and are choosing to be vegan or choosing to call it eating a 'plant based' diet. Anyone who chooses not to eat animal products is doing it for many reasons Billy, but the main reason is that they feel it is morally wrong to take the life of another being. The vast majority do not do anything criminal; they are all very caring and compassionate and that is why they don't eat animals.

"Of course, some do act upon liberating the animals; this comes from their hearts, not from a place of wanting to do criminal acts. It is an act of love for the animals. If you like we can go and view a march or demonstration sometime Billy. You can meet and talk to the people, see for yourself what it's all about, why they are marching or demonstrating and what sort of people they are."

"OK, Max, that sounds good, thanks."

Max was keen to continue to show Billy the last of the popular farmed animals. "OK, Billy, ready for some more truths?"

"Yes, Max, what is next?"

"Sheep, goats and their lambs and kids."

Sheep and Their Baa Lambs

Once again in a barn, Billy and Max were up in the rafters, watching the farm workers handling baby lambs. The lambs were in the barn having some mutilations forced upon them.

"The boy lambs are having an elastic band wrapped really tightly around the base of their little scrotums, which obstructs the blood supply and after about 3 weeks the little balls shrivel up and fall off. This is called elastration and is the cheapest method of castration; it is done with zero pain relief. Billy, can you imagine the pain?"

"No, Max, it is making my eyes water watching and thinking about it, a band around my balls for 3 weeks, it would be beyond painful Max, why do they do that?"

"Males are castrated for a few reasons; it is believed that meat from castrated lambs is lighter in colour and, therefore, more desirable by the consumer. Another reason is that male lambs can become aggressive towards each other and it is believed that castration makes them more docile and easier for the farmers to manage. Lastly, it is done in order to prevent unplanned breeding, even though many lambs are slaughtered before they reach sexual maturity.

"It's not just their balls Billy, lambs also have their tails docked using the same method. Farmers perform this mutilation to prevent 'fly-strike' or 'blow fly', an infestation of maggots that occurs in the sheep's poop that gathers around the tail due to excessive wool. Sheep have been selectively bred to produce more wool than is natural to maximise profit, this disease is not as prevalent in wild sheep. They are also ear-tagged, as all cattle and pigs are. This is their personal ID tag."

"Why are they tagged, Max?"

"The reason this came into being is because of the BSE outbreak in the UK, also known as mad cow disease in 1987. The UK government had to slaughter 4.4 million cows and have their bodies burned and buried to eradicate the disease, which had infected 180,000 cows. Ear tagging had already been invented and used, but it was the BSE outbreak that caused the mass use of this system, to track animal movement, from farm to farm, farm to slaughterhouse.

"This was a new disease; it came about due to the animal feed having ground-up animal bones and other animal parts that are discarded in the slaughter process which is rendered down and called bone meal. Dairy cows were more likely to be infected, as the calves were given a highly concentrated protein substitute as they were not receiving their mother's milk, which contained this bone meal. Bone meal is now banned to feed to cattle, sheep, etc."

Billy interrupted "Max, it's not surprising, cows and sheep natural food is grass and plants, not other animals, no wonder they got sick. I guess that was mother natures' way of showing us that it was not good to feed herbivores dead animal parts."

"Not only that Billy, also, humans that ate the cow that had BSE, could be infected and die. In the UK, 177 people died from this disease and 52 in Europe.

Animal derivatives are in dog and cat food, it's no wonder your furry pets have so many diseases, it's in the food, Billy."

"But Max, aren't cats and dogs designed to eat meat?"

"Yes, Billy; however, they are not designed to eat processed food which is what you mainly give to your pets. All pets, hamsters, rabbits, guinea pigs, horses—you feed them processed foods, which are so far away from the animals' natural diet."

"Hmm, I guess I had never thought about that before Max."

On a field nearby filled with sheep and their young, Billy and Max sat on the grass to continue chatting about the sheep meat industry. "Baby goats, which are raised for their flesh and milk, are also subjected to the same mutilations as lambs."

"Max. I read that sheep are not as stupid as people think they are and are pretty amazing animals. They can recognise around 50 other members in a flock and the ewes have unique calls for their babies. They both have the same unique scent so that the mum can smell if a lamb is hers or not.

"They can sprint up to 25 miles per hour and have amazing eyes; they are rectangular and when they are eating grass the eyes rotate in the socket so that she can still see what is going on around her and she has a 320° viewing angle which is pretty outstanding when you think ours is around 190°, and most of ours is peripheral vision but a sheep has 320° perfectly clear vision. They have also been known to show empathy for humans, just like cows."

"Yes, Billy, they are amazing. Many animals have been known to show empathy for humans and other species other than their own. Sheep are generally reared outdoors; lambs are separated from their mothers at 4–6 months and generally are sent to be killed for meat. People see sheep in the fields and think it's all perfectly natural, even in the driving rain and snow or in the scorching heat.

"But wild animals do not stand about in fields in fierce weather as sheep are forced to do; they take cover under trees and in bushes but there are generally no shelters for sheep in the fields, so they have no choice but to suffer the extreme weather conditions. In the UK, around 4 million new-born lambs die within a few days of birth every year, mainly because of malnutrition, disease or exposure to cold weather.

"Diseases are rampant on sheep farms: mastitis, which is an inflammation of the mammary gland, is a bacterial infection, caused by intensive farming. Foot rot, also a bacterial infection, is present in over 90% of flocks in the UK with 5% of the sheep having the infection at any one time. This infection is passed to each other from the ground; mass farming is what keeps the disease prevalent because of the conditions and the numbers of sheep contained in fields and pens. Both diseases are caused due to mass farming and conditions in which the animals are living. If they were living in the wild and had a natural life, these would rarely be present.

"Both are painful and have to be treated with antibiotics and or sheep dips, where the sheep are dipped and held under the water in a chemical bath. Around 1.4 million sheep and goats are killed without being stunned each year in the UK using halal practices, which is a process of slitting the throat of the animal when it is fully conscious. Many people in the UK oppose this form of slaughter.

"In slaughterhouses across the UK, sheep are most commonly stunned using electrical prongs to render them unconscious; however, it is estimated that as many as 4 million sheep may be conscious each year whilst they are having their throats slit. So, people who buy lamb and do not agree with halal, are probably eating baby lambs that have been killed in the same way as halal, there is no real difference between halal and non-halal slaughter. It is the same for pigs and cows."

"Max, if we stun the animal before killing it, surely this is proof that they do suffer from fear and pain, otherwise we wouldn't go to the trouble of stunning in the first place. Or is this done to appease the consumer?"

"It is probably for both reasons Billy.

- Lambs are killed at 4–6 months old.
- If sheep were to live a natural life, they would live until they were 12–15 years.
- Lambs are toddlers when they are killed.
- Around 15 million sheep are killed each year in the UK.
- It is estimated that 500 million sheep and 400 million goats are killed each year globally.

"Not all sheep are treated this way Billy, but the vast majority are, sheep are no different to any other animal. They deserve to have a full and natural life, living wild, just as nature intended."

"I do not regard flesh food as necessary for us. I hold flesh food to be unsuited to our species. To my mind, the life of a lamb is no less precious than that of a human being. I should be unwilling to take the life of a lamb for the sake of the human body. The more helpless the creature, the more it is entitled to protection from humans from the cruelty of humans."

—Mahatma Gandhi (1869–1948)

Max continued, "Due to selective breeding, humans have caused the sheep to grow more wool on their body to maximise profit. The wool is for scarfs, jumpers, hats, gloves, carpets, lanolin for soaps and other cosmetics. Due to this excess wool, they now need shearing once or twice a year to prevent them overheating and to prevent Flystrike.

"Oh, let's not forget the main reason; for profit from selling the wool. The general public are led to believe that shearing is for the animals' benefit; however, wild sheep do not need shearing because they have a natural amount of wool on their bodies to keep them nice and warm without overheating, and they naturally shed the wool when the weather heats up. They are now sheared for their benefit, but only because of man's interference with nature.

"The biggest wool-producing countries are Australia, China, the USA and New Zealand. There is recorded an immense amount of violence towards the sheep when being sheared. Often the workers are paid per sheep, not per hour or day, so they work as fast as they can to earn as much as they can. The sheep really do suffer in this process, having their heads held down with the workers' boot or being thrown around and bullied."

"Max, you have mentioned selective breeding a few times, what does that mean exactly?"

"Farmers select the strongest and biggest or woolliest and use them for breeding. Over the years the animals have got bigger or woollier to enable them to command a higher price for the animal. Take a look in the supermarket Billy, small chickens sell for less; however, they would have all taken the same amount of time to breed, so the cost of breeding will be the same, but they get more money for the bigger animal. It is the same for cows, pigs and sheep but you the consumer would not see the difference, as you don't buy the whole animal."

Billy tried to imagine what it was like to be a farm animal, the only two conclusions he could come up with was what Max said, that humans are like the

Nazis' or that it would feel the same if aliens came to earth; They would forcibly take over power from humans, kill all people over 30 years of age because they would be of no use. Select the strongest and biggest men and women for breeding, murder the small and weak humans under 30. The 'breeder' humans would then be locked in sheds and small spaces.

The men and women would be separated, men would be forced to give their semen, the women would be artificially inseminated, the babies would be taken away and killed mostly for meat, some would be kept to be the next 'breeders'. As men would only be required for their semen, the population of adult men would be small in comparison to women, as just a few men would be required as they would be able to impregnate thousands of women from each breeder male. Women would only be required for the sole purpose of getting pregnant and producing milk, every year another baby.

From the age of around 15 until she was around 30, if her body could last that long, she would have 15 children! The women would be milked every day, hooked up to machines; they would be like zombies, swaying as they were sucked dry. Billy felt so helpless, 7 billion people acting just like Nazis/aliens unknowingly. It's not like people even realised it because it was normal, everyone did it so that's OK—well it's not OK, thought Billy and we are going to help people see that it's really not OK, most people have no idea of how horrible and horrific it is being an animal.

"Think about it Billy, humans love to eat animals instead of just loving and caring for them."

"Max, I know I have seen with my own eyes all these unimaginable things, but in the UK, we really do love our animals, is it really possible that we do all these horrid things to animals as standard practice?"

"If you love animals, the last thing you want is to have pain and suffering inflicted on them. Animals feel and inherently want to live and be with their mums, you wouldn't want to take them away from their mums so early if you really loved them. Every time someone buys meat, dairy or eggs this is what they are paying for. Even if the farmer gives them the best life possible in the fields, most will still carry out the mutilations, take away their babies and the animal will still end up at the slaughterhouse for a very fearful experience, the nightmare process of their death.

"The farmer cannot love his animals, that is not possible, it goes against what love is. Love is to look after someone, to adore them, to cherish them, to want them to be at peace and happy, not for them to die a painful scary death for profit. Sorry, Billy, you think you all love animals in the UK, but to truly love animals you wouldn't eat them or drink the milk that is made for their babies."

"Max, what about the animals we see in the fields having a nice life?"

"Of course, a very small percentage of animals do have a nicer life Billy, but it is a very small number. Some of them are in the fields their whole life. Even if they have had a life in fields, they are still loaded into big trucks for the first time in their lives, travelling sometimes a long way with no water or food, in all weathers, baking hot and freezing cold, squished like sardines in a tin and then forced into the kill zone; the slaughterhouse, which as we have discussed is a very scary experience for each and every animal no matter how nice their life on the farm as been.

"We can visit a slaughterhouse so that you can observe, rather than taking my word for it. It will give you the zeal to speak from your heart and a personal experience will be more powerful."

"OK, I will let you know when I am ready for that Max, thanks. Another thought Max, perhaps we should go back to the way farming was in the old days, not intensive factory farming, but more farmers with smaller farms then they won't suffer so much."

"Backwards isn't an option, evolution can't go in reverse like a car, evolution is forward. Humans need to see the mistakes they have made and come up with new ideas and systems to move forward Billy. Also, farms are now not just farms, they are big organisations, making a lot of money, they won't give that up, they want to maximise on profit. These organisations need to feed the demand of the people, if the people stop drinking dairy milk, they will just follow the money, they will start producing plant-based milks, this change has to come from within the people Billy it's the only way."

Billy had already decided that he was going to take responsibility for what he ate and now really wanted to spread the knowledge and show people what is going on in the world.

Max continued. "As we discussed mass-produced animals, are often artificially inseminated by man, so the animal doesn't even get to enjoy one of the most natural things any species can do... to mate! They are injected with growth hormones and antibiotics, which humans then digest when they consume the meat or the milk product. The mutilations and mass drug administration are carried out to stop behaviour or diseases that are only present because of the cramped conditions. If these animals had plenty of space and lived a natural life in the wild, they wouldn't be displaying the unwanted behaviours and diseases in the first place.

"Animals are crammed into lorries so tightly they cannot move and are transported for many miles to be killed. The experience at the slaughterhouse is a very unpleasant and fearful experience Billy, it's truly horrific and it is not humane. If people saw what goes on, they would be very shocked Billy and if factory farms and slaughterhouses had public viewing platforms or glass walls, they would soon be empty of animals."

"A man can live and be healthy without killing animals for food; therefore, if he eats meat, he participates in taking animal life for the sake of his appetite. And to act so is immoral."

—Leo Tolstoy (1828–1910)

Chapter 5

The next morning Billy was awake very early, keen to be with Max to go on some adventures and to learn. He was dressed and waiting in his room when Max appeared as usual from nowhere. "Morning Billy, today we are going to view other areas of food production, how do you fancy some more travel?"

Billy smiled a massive grin before he knew it, they were off!

Bees

"OK, Billy, next stop to one of the largest bee farms in the world."

Billy and Max arrived in a tree high up in the canopy; looking down on a vast area where thirty thousand beehives where located. "There are somewhere between 80 and 100 million beehives in the world. We are in New Zealand which isn't the largest economy of honey makers Billy that is in India and China; 12 million hives and 9 million, respectively. The USA also produces a lot of honey with nearly 3 million hives, honey bees are not indigenous to the USA that is another subject we will cover later.

"We are here in New Zealand for two reasons, one is that NZ is the biggest producer of Manuka honey, which comes from the nectar of Manuka flowers and is the most expensive honey you can buy and second because people of NZ have the biggest consumption of honey per person in the world. Bees are also suffering due to the huge demand for honey. Queen bees often have their wings removed to stop her swarming with her bees to make a new nest in the wild. Queen bees or the whole hive is often killed each year."

"That makes no sense at all, why do they do that, Max?"

"As always Billy, in mass production just follow the money; Bees only collect nectar in the summer months, it is cheaper to buy new bees than feed and keep them through the winter. To replace them, beekeepers often have new bees delivered in a box via the post. Can you imagine Billy, being put inside a box, it would be totally dark, like a cardboard coffin, then the coffin-like box would be moving whilst it is shipped from place to place to finally arrive at the destination address. Some bees are dead on arrival."

"If they are not, I bet they have a really bad headache," said Billy, with a sad look on his face.

"Many Queens are artificially inseminated, she is stuffed in a tube and held in position whilst she is prodded and poked to get the semen inside her from a drone bee. The drone bee is killed in the process of removing his semen."

"Wow, that is unimaginable with such a small creature, why do we do that, Max?"

"In the wild, honey queen bees mate in flight with around 15–20 drones, so it is impossible to control the breeding unless done in the laboratory using instruments. Do you know how honey is made and why?"

"Yea, the bees eat nectar and turn it into honey but I don't know why they make it."

"OK, Billy, as you say, bees eat the nectar, they suck up the nectar through a long tongue like thing called a proboscis and store it in their first stomach. They visit 50–100 flowers per trip and around 10,000 per day. The bee then goes back to the hive and vomits into the mouth of another bee. They then play ping-pong with the liquid back and forth in their mouths several times before it gets spat into the hive."

"That's gross Max."

"To make 1 pound of honey, which is around 2–3 jars, bees have to visit 2 million flowers and fly 55,000 miles, that's further than going around the earth twice Billy, all for a couple of jars of honey. Bees are pretty cool as they do a waggle dance when they are in the hive to tell the other bees where the good flowers are. Bees make the honey for themselves and their family to eat and it lasts them through the winter."

"That's a bit unfair Max, they do all the hard work of flying, collecting nectar, storing it and then we go and take it away from them."

"Yes, Billy, and what is worse is that humans steal the honey, then either kill them or give them a substitute called sugar water, which does not have all the nutrients that honey does, so now the bees are not as healthy and have diseases that were not present when they were wild, which means they now need antibiotics. There are other yummy products that are in the shops, honey isn't the only option. It really does go to show, that for life to thrive, life needs to be balanced. The bees don't thrive on their own now because they are dependent on humans to treat the new diseases."

"What would happen if we stopped tending to the bees, Max?"

"Well, Billy, it would be a process of allowing nature to take over. To start with, humans would need to stop taking the honey, which would give the bees all that they need, which over time would restore the balance, the diseases would stop, then once you were sure they could survive, humans would then stop beekeeping and the bees would make natural hives in the wild. Not all bees are treated in this way, but vast majority of mass produced are."

Fish and the Oceans

On the roof of a fishing boat, Billy and Max sat taking in the sea air and watching the fishermen at work. "These are sea 'factories' that are emptying out the seas at an alarming pace. Some nets are 5 miles long; everything in its path gets scooped up. The sea creatures are all squished together in the net and when the net is lifted out of the sea, they are all lying on top of each other 'suffocating'. Dolphins, sharks and many other species are flung back into the sea, either dead or nearly dead from the experience.

"They are merely by-catch. Target fish is what ends up on the dinner plate, by-catch, also known as by-kill is the fish that gets caught in the nets that either they are not allowed to keep due to local fishing laws about what fishermen are allowed to catch or they just don't want it because it has no monetary value. By-catch is estimated to be from 20 to 40 times the weight of the target fish. I'm sure you already know Billy that fish breathe by taking water into its mouth and forcing it out through the gill passages.

"The gills are feathery organs full of blood vessels that take the oxygen from the water and into the fish's cells. So, in essence, they are breathing, it's just not how you know it on land. Seawater acts as hydration for the fish's gills but when out of the water and all that air is flowing by their gills, it is essentially like something is blow-drying the fish's gills. The gills dry up and can no longer function properly, which is why they 'suffocate' and die out of water.

"Humans used to say that fish couldn't feel pain but fish really suffer when they are caught; they have sensory receptors and do feel pain. They may not have a voice to scream, but trust me, Billy, as you can see, they are not having a good time. There are many ways that fish are slaughtered, depending on the species and the boats' onboard facilities. Common slaughter methods are: a blow to the head or two or three if the first one doesn't kill them outright.

"Decapitation with or without electrical stunning, tearing of the fish's gills by slicing a knife through them, immersion into iced water, carbon dioxide gassing; the fish enter water that has been saturated in carbon dioxide, this rapid change in conditions irritates the fish's gills, they struggle for oxygen for several minutes before dying or having their gills cut. Some fish take up to 10 minutes to die. The last method of murder is what we are about to witness, Billy."

Billy looked down to the deck of the boat. A really big fish had been caught. "Is that a tuna, Max?"

"Yes, Billy, it is indeed a mighty fine example of a tuna fish. Some people don't realise how big these beautiful fish are; they just eat a small amount from a tin, or a small tuna steak not having a clue that these majestic fish are very large."

Billy continued to watch as the man hauled the fish to a clear space on the deck. The man put the tuna between his legs holding it still; he then took a metal mallet and what looked like a really large, thick and long nail and bashed the nail into the head of the tuna. Billy gasped. The tuna was trying to escape by thrashing around. Next, the man took a long metal cable he put one end into the hole that the nail had made at the top of the head and rammed it into the tuna forcing three feet of cable through its head, brain and into its spine.

Billy nearly had to look away. At the moment the cable was inserted, the tuna's mouth opened suddenly really wide, its eyes looked like they were going to pop out of the sockets and if it had vocal cords, it would have been screaming in immense pain, it continued to thrash around. Billy was almost speechless but was curious.

"Why do they go to all that trouble Max, why not just use one of the other methods you just described? Is it a case of follow the money?"

"Always Billy, some commercial operations go to even more trouble, once the fish is caught, they rope the tuna's tail and allow the tuna to swim alongside the boat for a while allowing their heart rate to drop and for the fish to cool down, this is because when they are being caught their heart rates are very fast and a build-up of lactic acid is thought to spoil the quality of the meat. Next, they slice their arteries located just behind the pectoral fins and allow the fish to bleed out in the sea for 10–15 minutes.

"The killing you just witnessed is because it is quick and considered more humane, also it stops the heart beating which stops the blood from circulating and coagulating in the body and spoiling the meat. Fishermen have different ideas about what is the best method for the best quality of meat. The global fishing capacity could catch the worlds' catch four times over, in other words, there is not enough fish for the fishing fleets to fish.

"Longline fishing fleets set 1.4 billion hooks each year, it is estimated that those lines would go around the planet 550 times. The mouth of the largest fishing net in the world is large enough to accommodate thirteen Boeing 747 aeroplanes. The scale of it is totally out of control Billy. Around 40–60% of Bluefin tuna is purchased by one Japanese company, Billy this is big money and this company has frozen many years' worth of Bluefin. Once tuna is extinct, they will be able to command whatever amount of money they like.

"If they care about the oceans or about humanity, they would stop buying the fish, use up the frozen stocks and allow the tuna numbers to recover, but as always Billy, follow the money, it's all in the name of profit for a relatively small number of people on the planet, they are only thinking about the profit, not the future of humanity or the sea life. The knock-on effect of the large species almost dying out, in some cases creates an increase in other species because their main predator has almost disappeared.

"Lobster populations have increased as they are eaten by tuna. Rays have also increased as they are eaten by sharks, and jellyfish infestations on beeches have become more of a problem, as their predators are tuna, sharks, swordfish, turtles and some species of salmon. The ecosystem of the oceans is a delicate balance, it is now totally unbalanced. Losing species; what does that mean?

"Massive reduction of food for other species, declining water quality and stability of the ecosystem that will be a road of no return unless humans decide to stop taking from the seas very soon. For generations, humans have been taking from the sea, which until recent years has had little or no impact. However, the last 50 years of industrial-scale fishing has had a catastrophic impact. What can your generation do to stop reaching mass extinction?"

"We have to stop this, Max; humans need to wake up to the damage that we have caused."

"Predictions are that the oceans will be empty of fish by the year 2048. That may sound like a long way away Billy, you will be in your forties, which I know at 12 is impossible to imagine, but trust me; it will be here soon enough. Time really does go by quickly; I am sure you have heard adults saying so. That is one thing that is true for every human being Billy, before you know it, you will be your dad's age and there will be no fish left in the seas."

"Truly man is the king of beasts, for his brutality exceeds theirs. We live by the death of others: we are burial places!"

—Leonardo da Vinci (1452–1519)

Kemala Lin lives in Indonesia with her sister, which hauls the fourth-biggest tonnage of fish in the world, behind, China, Peru and America. She loves to play badminton. She too had no idea about what is going on in the seas and with land animals. Billy met her on the beach. Kemala had beautiful long flowing hair and eyes that Billy couldn't stop staring into. He was mesmerised by her, she was truly beautiful, and like no other girl he had ever seen. He had actually never even fancied a girl before, he felt like he was under a spell, he couldn't stop staring at her while she spoke to him, he didn't even hear some of what she was saying as he was so captivated.

Max interrupted the gaze that he was holding. "Two to three trillion fish are killed every year, which is four times what it was in 1950. Up to 40% is discarded as by-catch. One-third of what is kept is used to feed land animals; the small fish are ground up and manufactured into pellets to feed pigs, cows and chickens. An example of why eating land animals is not good for the planet, you are feeding them fish, if you all stopped eating land animals, the amount of fish that is taken from the oceans would dramatically reduce.

"It is estimated that as many as 650,000 dolphins, seals and whales are killed each year and 40 million shark as by-catch. The ocean is dying, and you know today what you didn't know 50 years ago. If you wait another 50 years, it will be too late; your decisions and your actions as individuals and as nations will shape the future of the oceans, the planet and your existence."

Billy wanted to stay longer than usual and asked Max if he could come back for him in a while. Max was cool with that and disappeared to leave them on their own. Billy wanted to know as much as he could about Kemala, her favourite food, what she did with her time, about her family, friends and the school she went to.

To his surprise, Kemala also seemed very interested in him, asking many questions about his life too. They had a little in common, mainly the love of nature and all the things that Max had been sharing with them, the adventures, the horrors and the other friends around the world they had been meeting.

Max reappeared after about 30 minutes, Billy gave Kemala a hug, which lasted a moment longer than she was used to, they both smiled at each other whilst holding a long gaze and said bye as Max touched Billy's shoulder to take him home. "She is special, isn't she, Billy?"

"Max, I couldn't take my gaze away from her eyes, I have never experienced that before, it was truly a wonderful time, just chilling and chatting with her. Is it possible that you can take us on an adventure together sometime Max? I would really like to spend more time with her. That is, of course, assuming she would like to."

"Sure Billy, we can do that no problem. See you tomorrow."

Whales, Dolphins and Sharks

The next day Max teleported Billy and Kemala to the roof of a tourist boat. "Wow," said Billy excited.

He could see a pod of whales 100 feet away. He wasn't sure, but he thought he counted 12. They could hear the whales blowing water out of their spouts creating a fountain of water to rise above them. Billy watched in awe, the sea air was fresh and salty. Kemala and Billy sat next to eat other, their arms were touching, Billy had never been that close to anyone before but he was enjoying this new experience.

In his usual style, Max started commentating; "Although the international whaling commission prohibited commercial whaling in 1985, some countries still kill whales for meat. They are hunted and killed using harpoons, firearms, blunt hooks and explosives or they are driven into whaling bays where they end up beaching on the shore; they are then killed with knives. Japan, Norway, the Faroe Islands and Iceland still sanction whaling. I thought you would like to see these magnificent beings having a nice time, rather than be hunted and killed in such horrific ways."

"Thank you, Max; this is truly an amazing experience, another one I will never forget."

"Me too Max, it is wonderful and inspiring to see them in their natural habitat," said Kemala.

"Dolphins next," said Max.

Without another word, they were teleported to another boat. This time it was a private pleasure boat cruising fast alongside a massive pod of dolphins. They were flying out of the sea, twisting, somersaulting and squealing with joy. Billy wasn't sure how many there were, but he guessed around 40–50, it was a truly wonderful sight to see.

"As much as I don't want to dampen your experience, it's really important you know that in Japan, dolphins are driven into kill zones where there is no escape. They are caught by their dorsal fin, strung up then dumped onto the back of a pickup truck, driven to a kill area, where their throats are slit; they are left to bleed to death. It's not a quick slice of the knife; it is a painful and slow death.

"Dolphins are also hunted to be used in the human entertainment industry in 'wildlife' sea centres. The clue is in the name, they are wild creatures and should be left to live a natural life in the wild, but more about that later. For now, let's focus on the big mammals in your oceans."

The next stop was another boat, this time a commercial fishing boat. "Around 50 million sharks are hunted, savagely caught and killed for their meat or fins, as many people in Asia like to eat shark-fin soup and the meat. Shark finning is the act of removing fins from sharks, often while the shark is alive. The sharks are often discarded back to the ocean, still alive but without their fins and unable to swim they sink to the bottom of the ocean and die of suffocation or are eaten by other predators.

"Shark finning at sea enables fishing vessels to maximise profitability by increasing the number of fins harvested, as they only have to store and transport the fins, by far the most profitable part of the shark. Some countries have banned this practice and require the whole shark to be brought back to port before removing the fins, but this does not make much difference as the sharks are still been hunted almost to extinction. This is a demand-driven industry, people of the world need to stop buying this soup and meat.

"This is a tradition that dates back to the fourteenth century; initially, it was a rare delicacy only enjoyed by the nobility and aristocracy; however, nowadays, it is big business. Shark-fin soup can be sold for $100–$200 per serving."

"Damn these human beings. If I had invented them, I would go hide my head in a bag."

—Mark Twain (1835–1910)

Max continued, "There is only one way the oceans will recover; for everyone all over the world to wake up and stop killing fish, it is a demand-driven industry. Sustainable fishing is not viable. Laws are not viable. The earth's people have to realise that they only have one sensible choice; to leave the oceans to repair and regenerate; it is very simple, the ocean is not yours; it is the home of all the fish and mammals that live within it and humans are either going to see how simple it is or continue and be the cause of the next mass extinction, including humans ."

Keiki Yamamoto lives in the Fukuoka area of Japan with her brother and parents. She loved baseball and Karate. Living on one of the biggest of almost 7,000 islands that makes up Japan, she also loved the beach and swimming and was interested in earthquakes and volcanoes, due to Japan having 1,000 small earthquakes a year and over 60 active volcanoes. Billy and Kemala met Keiki on the beach just to meet and chat, as with all the others, no surprise to Billy to hear that she too had no idea about the unnecessary suffering that goes on to get food on our plates.

Living by a harbour, she had seen dolphins, whales and sharks on the harbour floor, but had never really given it any thought, as it had always been that way, but now she agreed with Max, that the people of the world needed to change their daily habits to start to reverse the damage that humans have done to the creatures and the oceans. After they chatted for a while, Max took Kemala home, Billy was disappointed, but he trusted that Max had a reason and didn't ask questions, he just accepted it and was grateful that he got to see her again.

"OK, Billy, next stop—the great barrier reef."

"What? Are you joking me?"

"No, Billy, I know you often daydream about all these places, which is why I want you to experience them, if only for a short time."

As usual, Billy was speechless but had a great big grin on his face. Max surrounded Billy in the protective energy bubble, and they were off flying high into the earth's stratosphere and beyond.

"I thought we were off to the ocean Max."

"First I wanted to show you the reef from space Billy; I imagined it would be cool to fly to it from here."

Billy gazed at the sight before him, he knew where the reef was, stretching 1,400 miles along the northeast coast of Queensland; he had studied the map many times. The turquoise blue seashore he could see was stunning. To be in space and see the outline of the land and the colours was just as mesmerising as the first time he went into space with Max. He knew he would never tire of being in space or being with Max.

They started to slowly float down to earth, Billy had tears in his eyes at the sheer wonder of being in space and of the earth, how beautiful it was, he wanted every human to experience this, he wanted to share his experiences with his mum but knew that she would think he had gone crazy and wrapped up in his own imagination. For a second, he did wonder again if he was still in a very long dream or maybe he had actually gone crazy or in some sort of a coma.

They reached the reef at the southern end; he saw all the creatures he had dreamt about; hump head maori wrasse, manta rays, spaghetti worms, white humpback whales and so much more. The colours and sea life were better than he had imagined it to be, although he was aware that 50 years ago it was even more stunning, as he had read that the coral reefs have suffered in recent years and much of the coral was dead or dying.

They floated along towards the north, along the way they saw sea snakes, sea turtles, seahorses, striped surgeonfish, dugongs, clownfish, red throat emperor fish, snappers and coral trout.

"What is that white coral?" asked Billy.

"That is very recently dead coral Billy, sudden temperature increases in the sea causes the coral to rapidly die, we will talk another time about sea temperatures and the impact it has on Earth."

Eduardo Gonzales lives in Peru with his dad they loved to go fishing together. The Peruvian commercial fishing fleet catches the second-largest tonnage of fish in the world, second to China. The meeting of Eduardo was like the others, a brief chat to start to get to know each other before Max spoke and as Billy expected Eduardo had no idea about the oceans dying and the devastating impact commercial fishing is having on all the species.

"From the usual food creatures to the weird, human's even farm, kill and grind up cochineal beetles to make a red, pink and purple dye for food such as frozen meat, fish and fruit. Also, energy drinks, powdered and alcoholic drinks, yoghurts, ice cream, dairy-based drinks, sweets, syrups, fillings, chewing gum, canned fruits like cherries, jams, dehydrated and canned soups and ketchup. It is also used in artificial flowers, paints, red ink, rouge, eye shadow, lipstick and medications.

"It takes 70,000 of these tiny critters to make 1 pound of dye, which is ½ a bag of sugar. Peru alone produces 200 tons each year, which equates to 28 billion of these little bugs being bred to be killed in Peru. There are natural, none insect dyes available. By the way, if you want to avoid consuming these little critters look out for carminic acid, carmine, cochineal extract or E120. As a food dye, it has been known to cause severe allergic reactions and anaphylactic shock in rare cases."

Billy and Eduardo said goodbye and both said they looked forward to seeing each other again soon.

Billy slept like a baby that night, dreaming of all the things he had seen recently.

Max arrived as usual in Billy's room. "I have shown you the most popular mass-produced/caught animals, but there are many more, either bred to be killed or caught in the wild like grouse, dogs."

Billy looked horrified "DOGS?" Shrieked Billy.

"Yes, Billy… dogs, in China and other Asian countries dogs and cats are bred and eaten. Horses."

"OMG, horses Max, surely not?"

"Yes, Billy, horses are eaten in many countries, such as the USA, Mexico, Kazakhstan, Mongolia, Argentina, Italy, Brazil, China, Russia, France, Switzerland, Germany, Belgium, Japan, Indonesia and Poland. Donkeys, rabbits and hares, kangaroos, guinea pigs."

"GUINEA PIGS?" gasped Billy.

"Yes, Billy, apparently, they taste a bit like chicken, it is eaten in Ecuador, Peru and Colombia which is where they originate from. Deer (you call that venison), quail, pigeon and frogs.

"Incidentally, it is illegal to farm frogs in Europe; however, 90% of the frogs farmed in China and Indonesia are exported to Europe. Another crazy law that is laughable as it is legal to import frog's legs, really what difference does it make? In China, the frogs' legs are chopped off with a pair of scissors or knife, the frog is left to die, unable to move, they bleed to death.

"Squid, octopus and shellfish like lobster, prawns, oysters and mussels. Oh, and If you don't know Billy, lobsters are boiled alive; perhaps you have seen them in tanks in restaurants. Camels are farmed for their milk. Ostriches are farmed for their meat and eggs and emu's for their eggs.

"Guinea fowl and grouse are farmed for shooting for fun and for their eggs and sometimes the meat is not edible, as it has been obliterated from the shooting. Yaks are farmed for their bone and meat, it is highly revered and is said to be medicinal in places such as Nepal, Himalayan India and Tibet. Buffalo/Bison are used for their milk and meat and peacocks for their feathers and meat.

"Reindeer and elks are shot or reared for their velvet antlers, the meat, their whole heads as trophies and for live Santa grottos at Christmas time. I could go on Billy but the list of unusual animal exploitation is very long. You even eat insects on TV game shows, so why horses and guinea pigs are abhorrent is down to your conditioning/programming. What difference does it make Billy, fish, pig, chicken, dog, horse or guinea pig or insect? They are all the same, Billy. They all have eyes, hearts, blood and brains.

"They can all feel pain, feel fear, feel love and many have compassion. They communicate with each other and have intelligence. Dogs, dolphins, cats, elephants and horses all understand commands that you teach them, this shows their underlying capacity to understand, if they understand this, they understand what is about to happen to them in the slaughterhouse Billy.

"If humans were to see all animals as the same as the treasured companion animals, they wouldn't want to eat any animal. That's where humanity needs to get to, to treasure all living things, to respect them, to look after them. Not farm, kill and eat them. It is mankind's responsibility to look after these animals, give them back the earth, it is their home too. If you were to ask any animal, does it want to die, it would say 'no thank you very much I would like to be with my mummy and my brothers and sisters.

"Isn't it odd Billy how human beings really love and cherish some animals, your companion animals, but eat others? This is all down to religions, cultures, traditions and conditioning/programming Billy. In many nations, humans pay for their dogs to have haircuts and buy plush beds, toys and even jackets, yet you continue to eat other animals as if they are completely different. All animals have intelligence, all animals have language, all animals feel pain, all animals are capable of love, and all animals feel fear."

Dogs and Cats for Food

Billy and Max were in a small side street in a Chinese city; it was noisy from the traffic in the main street and lots of people talking very loudly and bartering with each other in the shops. Billy took a moment to look around him, he could see some dogs in small cages, there were five or more of them in each cage all different colours and breeds, they were squashed in tightly and couldn't move. They didn't look like pets; they were skinny and grubby from the dust off the street. It was really hot, and they didn't have any water in the cage. As always Billy was shocked by what he was seeing.

"As already mentioned, Billy, dogs and cats are eaten in Asia, but this festival takes it to another level, due to the extra abuse. The Lychee and Dog Meat Festival, commonly referred to as Yulin Dog Meat Festival, is an annual celebration held here in Yulin, Guangxi, China, during the summer solstice in which festival goers eat dog/cat meat and lychees.

"The festival began in 2009 and spans about ten days during which it is estimated that 10,000–15,000 dogs are consumed. Throughout the 10 days of festivities, dogs are paraded, squashed on top of each other in wooden crates and metal cages and are taken to be killed and eaten. Many dogs suffer before being killed, there are videos of dogs being beaten to death with metal bars, skinned alive or boiled alive."

"Seriously, Max, they are skinned and boiled alive?"

"Yes, Billy; the Chinese officials say that these dogs are killed humanely, but the evidence is clear that this is not true. The people believe that the meat tastes better when the animal has suffered."

"The thought of that actually makes me feel sick, can we rescue the dogs over there?"

"Billy, our job is to share the information; there are local charities that do rescue some of the dogs. Rescuing is great for the few that are rescued, but education and awareness are what will really create big change, Billy. Perhaps the people in the UK would prefer it if these dogs were killed in the same way that you kill pigs in the UK?"

Billy didn't answer; he was stunned at the thought of that too.

Max continued, "I think that people in the UK love dogs and would not want them killed in slaughterhouses, they would not want them killed full stop. It begs the questions Billy, what is the difference between a dog and a pig or a sheep?

It's not just the festival time when dogs are eaten, Billy; it is estimated that 10 million dogs and 4 million cats are eaten in Asia every year.

"Dog flesh can be found on the menu in North Korea, South Korea, Vietnam, China and in some African countries. In Hong Kong, Taiwan and the Philippines dog meat is now banned and in the early 1900s, dog meat used to be eaten in some parts of America and Europe too. The great news is that it has been changing, slowly but surely people around the world have stopped eating dog meat, this is evolution Billy.

"It is a slow process in your reality, but it is moving in the right direction, in the future, all over the world, it will be considered immoral to eat dog meat. In fact, in the future, it will be considered immoral to eat any animal or exploit any animal if humans wake up in time. Animals will be free, once people start feeling, thinking and acting differently. It starts with each and every one of you, making a decision not to be part of the demand."

"The greatness of a nation and its moral progress can be judged by the way its animals are treated."

—Mahatma Gandhi (1869–1948)

That evening Billy spoke to his mum about school. "OK, Bills, I have looked into this in detail, it appears to be quite a simple process; however, I am concerned that you won't get your exam results."

"Mum, I promise you, I will study hard, I won't let your down, mum; have I ever let you down or broken a promise?"

"No, Bills, you are a wonderful son, you are respectful, caring and thoughtful, and you have never broken a promise, but this is your future we are talking about Bills, it's serious stuff."

"Yes, mum, exactly, I really do believe that I will have a better future if I self-study mum, school is a 'one size fits all', but I don't fit that one size."

"OK, Bills, here is the deal. You can teach yourself; however, I need you to keep me updated with anything you are struggling with, any extra help you need and I would like you to document your learnings and progress so that we can use it as a discussion tool on a regular basis."

Billy couldn't believe it. He was so thrilled that his mum agreed he just hugged her tight and kept repeating, "Thank you, mum; thank you, mum; thank you, mum."

With all that fresh air and the early morning, Billy was asleep before his head hit the pillow. As always, he dreamt of adventures around the world. The next day, Billy's mum wrote a letter to the school advising them that Billy would no longer be attending school.

Chapter 6

Max arrived, as usual, the next morning. "OK, Billy; time to buckle up for some serious fun. Do you trust me, Billy?"

"Errrr… depends Max."

"What we are about to do will blow your mind and I really need you to keep calm. Just breathe, Billy; everything will be fine."

Billy couldn't imagine what was going to blow his mind more than travelling in space and going to Unity. In a blink of an eye, they were in a jungle. The grasses were really tall, maybe 500 ft. high and plants even taller. Billy thought 'this place was seriously weird' everything he could see was massive.

"Where are we?" Billy asked.

"We are in your back garden, Billy."

"WHAT? In my back garden, don't be daft Max. Seriously where are we?"

The grass in front of them started to rustle loudly and then came through the grass what appeared to be a giant ant… Billy started to step back.

"Stay still… stay very still… if you move, he will see you and decide that you might be tasty. Ants are excellent at detecting movement, but they don't exactly receive a high-resolution image of the world around them."

OMG! Billy thought. He could not believe his eyes, there before them was an ant, the ants that he admired, the ants that he spent hours and hours watching. He could now see this gigantic ant in magnified detail, it was breath-taking. Billy was in the ant world. He felt a sneeze brewing; what a time to sneeze, he thought. Max had said to stay still, so he couldn't even pinch his nose to stop it from brewing and coming out. "AAA–CHOO! Sorry." Billy whispered.

The ant came rushing toward them, its mandibles ready for action. As it approached them it seemed to bounce back from them and fall onto its back. The grass started rustling again and six more ants appeared.

"Don't worry, Billy; I surrounded you with a protection bubble," Max said, laughing.

Billy didn't say anything, he just stared, with his eyes and mouth wide watching the ants, he was in amazement at the movement of the ants, the sheer size of them; they were the same height as Max. Billy wondered how this was even possible and again was questioning whether he was still in some epic dream that was never-ending.

The ants were making a clicking noise, they were talking ant language, how utterly amazing that Billy could hear them 'talking'. More ants arrived before long there were dozens of them surrounding them, they all kept trying to get closer but the bubble was impenetrable. They stayed for a short while and then Max took them back to Billy's room.

"That was absolutely awesome Max, how did that actually happen? You miniaturised us? That just blows my mind, Max… I know… the human language can't explain how it is done and maybe one day you will show me."

Billy smiled at Max and continued, "Thanks, that was really terrific, I love ants and to be that up close to them was truly amazing."

"My pleasure Billy, I knew you loved ants, and wanted you to really experience them up close and personal. Let's think about the ant world for a moment Billy, the ant world is very small; as I am sure you know they will forage up to 100 yards away from the nest. They have no concept of further than that, no idea about the earth and how tiny they are, no idea of the universe. This is the same for humans Billy.

"Before mankind had the technology to further explore the stars, your awareness was limited, but your awareness is slowly increasing as more discoveries are made; and your evolution continues. Your awareness does not extend to that of a parallel universe. You have many theories; however, you do not have the awareness or a knowing."

"So, what was that 'bubble' you mentioned?"

"It's is an energy protection bubble, the same as when we are in space. Maybe I will teach you one day, Billy."

Max smiled as Billy looked excited at the prospect of learning things that as far as he was aware, no one on the planet knew how to do.

"So, Billy… getting back to animals, it's not just the animals you eat that are suffering, you exploit so many animals in the name of entertainment or profit. The suffering is immense. Once again you have all been conditioned/programmed to think that this is normal and acceptable."

Entertainment
Bullrings

Billy was teleported to a big round stadium packed full of spectators. Inside the stadium was a bull being chased by men on horses. The crowds were shouting and cheering, it was very noisy. Billy felt really uncomfortable, he knew what was coming, but he had never experienced such a cruel scene.

"It is assumed by the people that bulls are aggressive creatures and want to fight with the men in the arena when in actual fact they are quite calm and peaceful animals. In the wild, they will only fight to defend themselves or their territory, but when they do, they are pretty ferocious. A man would not survive such an experience, for this reason they are selectively bred to be slow, and predictable.

"They have to endure a miserable existence, there are many possible standard practices that are inflicted on them and some may be unlucky to have all of these awful tortures forced upon them; weeks before a fight, heavyweights might be tied to the neck of the bull to weaken him. Petroleum might be rubbed into his eyes, to reduce his eyesight. He may be beaten in the kidney which further weakens him.

"He may be given tranquilisers to put him in a hypnotised state. They may feed him excessive amounts of salt, causing him to drink lots of water becoming bloated and thus, slow. Most bulls have their horns shaved or cut off as this prevents the bull from defending himself as he would in the wild and thus injuring the horses and men.

"For many hours or a couple of days before the fight, the bull is held in a tiny dark isolation cell and he is not given any food or water. Just before the bull is released into the arena, he is harpooned causing him pain and bleeding. When he is released, the daylight blinds him. He is confused, he has no idea what is going on and why this is happening.

"The men on horses you can see here are called Picadors', they chase him and spear him repeatedly with a spiked lance into his back, neck and shoulders, he suffers blood loss. He may fall and get too weak to raise his head or walk or he may try to crawl away. Due to fear and lack of control, he might poop or wee himself. He feels every stab, he is scared for his life, he really doesn't want to fight, and he just wants to be left alone."

Billy could see the fear and the helpless look in the bulls' eyes. The Picadors backed away as the matador stepped in, Billy continued to watch as Max continued commentating.

"As you can see the matador steps in and attempts to stab this beautiful creature in the heart, however, often misses the heart and stabs him in the lungs, which can cause blood to come coughing out of his mouth and nose. After stabbing him again and again, they might cut off his tail and ears; he is then sometimes dragged around the ring to show the cheering audience and may still be conscious at this time.

"The horses are also suffering as they are often routinely drugged, they may have wet newspapers or cotton wool stuck in their ears so that they cannot hear so well, which prevents them from getting distracted by the cheers from the audience and the roaring bull. They are often blindfolded to stop them from seeing the bull and running away, as they too are very scared.

"Sometimes their vocal cords are cut so that the crowds will not hear the horses screaming in fear. Horses are regularly injured from the bull charging into them and have to be killed as they are no longer able to participate and no longer of use. This barbaric 'sport' is still legal in Spain, Portugal, parts of southern France, Mexico, Colombia, Ecuador, Venezuela and Peru.

"It's not just in arenas, there are bull festivals where hundreds of people chase the bull through the streets before taunting and killing it. They call this entertainment and cultural tradition! The only way that this suffering will stop is if the people of earth stop attending these horrific events."

"Max, this is not entertainment."

"No, Billy; it is not; it is, however, part of the culture and tradition which needs to change, humans need to change their traditions, create new traditions to honour the animals, to remember the animals that have suffered in the past, have a celebration that you have freed yourselves and the bulls from this savage behaviour."

"We are acting like zombies Max."

"Indeed you are, Billy."

"All of the creatures ever made—human is the most detestable. He is the only creature that inflicts pain for sport, knowing it to be pain."

—Mark Twain (1835–1910)

"OK, Billy, time to meet some more friends."

Jack lives on a very small farm in Spain. He lived with his older brother, his grandparents and parents. All the animals got along together, hens, cockerel, cats, dogs, donkeys, horses, sheep and pigs. They all got along because their only enemy was the humans. The family used the animals for breeding and for eating their flesh. The dogs churned out puppies litter after litter, as did the cats. The family earned some good money from the puppies and kittens.

The cats and dogs were very used to seeing their babies being taken away in a stranger's car but they were very sad about it. The hens were used for eggs, for flesh and breeding. The male baby chicks were not of much use to the humans, as male cockerels can fight, and they don't lay eggs so they were mainly used as food for the dogs and pigs. The dogs and pigs really didn't like to eat the little chicks, but if they didn't they would go hungry.

The farm was very small; the animals had very little space; however, the chickens were able to be free, scratching around. The animals on the farm did not go through the same horrendous life as factory farms; they had a more traditional life. However, it was still not a natural, happy life; they were still being exploited for money and killed for food. Jack was born on the farm and also went to the local bullfighting ring.

A lot of places in Spain have stopped the bullfighting; however, some are still in use. Jack had never really given a thought to any of the animal sufferings; to him, it was just normal. Billy was starting to see a pattern, that the new friends he was making were all the same as him, they just hadn't thought about it because they had been eating meat since they could chew and in Jack's case, he had been going to watch the bullfight as far back as he could remember and had seen all the animals being killed since he was old enough to walk. Billy wondered that perhaps most of humanity were 'asleep' to how humans had dominion over the animal kingdom.

Circuses

Sat at the back row of a large round covered arena, Billy could see below an elephant sitting on a small chair waiting for instruction from the trainer. It made Billy feel really sad that such a magnificent creature was lowered to do such things and all in the name of entertaining humans and making a profit for the circus owner.

"Circus owners, intimate the animals and beat them to do acts for the laughing and cheering crowds. Elephants and tigers do not want to be here, and they do not want to be beaten or drugged. They just want to be left alone in the wild to live their lives the way nature intended. Some 'owners' are also reported to remove the claws and teeth of the animals to render them harmless.

"This is outdated entertainment and is banned in the UK and in other countries; however, the easier way for this to be an entertainment of the past is for the people to stop going. There are much fewer traditional circuses around nowadays; however, they would soon stop owning the animals if the people stopped attending the animal part of the show.

"I am not suggesting Billy that circuses should stop, just the animal part of it. Many elephants arrive within the circus community at a very young age; they are easier to train as they are less defiant as a fully grown adult that has been in the wild its entire life."

"When I look at animals held captive by circuses, I think of slavery. Animals in circuses represent the domination and oppression we have fought against for so long. They wear the same chains and shackles."

—Dick Gregory (1932–2017)

Tourist Selfies

Max teleported them to meet another friend. They met on a beautiful beach with turquoise water and fine white sand. They were in Thailand, the sun was hot and it was a beautiful day. "Billy, meet Pingpong Amudee, Ping for short." Billy discovered that Ping likes to practice Thai boxing, a form of kickboxing.

When she was younger, she would watch her three older brother's practice, which is how she became to have a passion for it herself. She lived with her mum and her brothers. She had learned from Max that 100 years ago there were 100,000 elephants in Thailand and that it is estimated that there are now only 2000.

They walked into the tourist area and before them was a big queue of people, Billy peered through the window to see what everyone was waiting for. He could see a tiger laying down, a man grabbed the scruff of the tigers' neck and pulled his head up whilst ushering the person next in line to come and sit to hold the tiger around the neck. Billy was shocked, he couldn't believe his eyes. He heard Max's voice in his head.

"The tiger is drugged Billy, as you can see he can hardly move."

The tourist smiled for the camera and then joined another queue which was for an elephant shot, another docile sentient being that was forced to comply to have tourists sit on her tusks all for a selfish selfie. Flabbergasted Billy asked, "This is considered cool?"

"Yes, Billy, some tourists love to have selfies with beasts. Once again, a very simple one to resolve as the tourist chooses where to spend their money, if they say no, I do not wish to have my picture taken with this beautiful sentient being as it should be free in the jungle, the suffering would end. The change has got to come from each and every person to make a decision what to spend their money on.

"Thinking, I am just one person and cannot make a difference so I may as well join in is not being authentic and will not change anything. People need to become more aware Billy, aware of their actions and aware of the right thing to do. If no one wanted a selfie, the oppressor that is holding them captive won't want to keep them as they will be costing them money."

"Max, what would then happen to them?" asked Ping.

"That would be down to the oppressor, perhaps they would sell the animal, but if people share their views with these people that the animals belong in the wild, there is a chance that they will be liberated back into the jungle or if they have had teeth removed, then they would be re-homed into a real animal sanctuary."

As usual, they didn't stay for long, just enough time for Ping and Billy to share a few experiences. As they said their goodbyes, Max put his hand on Billy to teleport him to a new destination.

Rodeos

The scene before him was breath-taking, standing on the edge of a mammoth river he was surrounded by lush vegetation so thick he couldn't see through it. The sounds coming from within the forest were very loud, shrills from animals, squawking birds, insects of many different species, making a kaleidoscope of sounds.

"We are in the Amazon, Billy."

As Billy looked out across the water, he could see what appeared to be dolphins swimming and propelling themselves out of the water with total ease.

"They are boto's, also known as the Amazon river dolphin."

"They appear to be different colours, Max."

"Yes, they change colour as they grow older, babies are grey, then changing to pink and finally fully grown adults become white. This is Pedro Santos."

Billy turned to see a boy the same size as him, slim and very muscular for his age. They chatted, which Billy found surprisingly easy, he felt like it was getting easier and easier to talk to people. They walked away from the river's edge through the forest, Billy was in awe of the forest and he caught sight of monkeys swinging in the trees, he stopped to watch for a few moments.

They arrived at a small village, Pedro explained that this was his home; they lived a simple life with his two brothers and sister, parents and both sets grandparents. They lived off the land growing a few vegetables and foraging in the forest for fruits and nuts, such as camu camu, passion fruit, acai, bacaba and many more. They chatted for a while, then Max jumped in.

"Some interesting facts for you, Billy, about the Amazon rainforest and Brazil. The name Brazil comes from a tree named Brazilwood and the Amazon River is the second longest in the world and around 60% of the rainforest is located in Brazil. Brazil is home to a wide range of animals, including armadillos, tapirs, jaguars and pumas. Human activities such as logging, mining, fishing and agriculture are important to the Brazilian economy but are also a serious threat to Brazil's diverse environment.

"I don't need to tell anyone how important the Amazon rainforest is to the natural balance of the earth's environment; this is a very well-known fact that has been reported for many years by your environmental experts. It is estimated that 10% of animals and plant species live in the Amazon and that the whole canopy might be as much as 50% of the global life forms on Earth."

The next moment they were teleported to an arena where a rodeo was in full play. Billy wasn't sure he wanted to watch any more horrid scenes of animal abuse but at the same time, he felt he must witness what was going on around the world.

"Rodeos are held in North America, Australia, Brazil, Canada, Mexico and the Philippines. Bulls and horses don't buck just because they are wild it is because they are in pain. A belt called a flank strap is secured around the body and around the penis and balls. The animals are worked up by being slapped, teased and may be given electric shocks by rods and tormented to bolt out of the shoot in a frenzy.

"As the bull leaves the shoot a sharp tug on the rope that controls the flank strap is enough to cause the animal to start bucking in pain and the animals often suffer broken legs. Roping involves lassoing a baby cow whilst it is running away at full speed, the lasso jerks the animal backwards stopping it dead in its tracks causing it to fall onto its back; it gets up, but is caught by a man and slammed back to the ground. This is not entertainment, but because people take their young children to watch, it is normalised and has become part of the culture and traditions.

"This is incomprehensible in a civilised society like Unity. The same rules apply, if the people stopped attending this 'entertainment' would stop. It needs to stop with your generation, Billy. In years to come, if humans don't go extinct, they will look back on this and all the other horrendous acts towards animals and be in shock and horror that it was considered entertainment and that people actually paid to watch these horrific events."

Pedro looked ashamed that his fellow Brazilians were involved in this barbaric 'sport'. "Max, I am sharing as much info as I can with people I meet, as we do all need to become aware and see if for what it really is and realise that we can choose not to join in," said Pedro.

Gambling

Back in the UK, Max and Billy were at a dog race track. The race was just about to start. The bell rang, the doors opened and the dogs were off.

"Dog and horse racing is only in existence for one reason; profit. Many dogs and horses fall; brake bones and even die when racing. Dogs are trained on running machines perhaps 4 times a day, but for the rest of the day, they are caged prisoners. They are normally either in solitary confinement in dark sheds or sometimes two per shed and often they are muzzled.

"They do not choose this life and it is not natural for a dog to be caged for 23 hours a day. Dogs are starved before the race and have lots of pent-up energy as they are also not exercised prior to the event. People think that the dogs enjoy racing; this is simply not true, they have miserable lives and are hungry which is why they chase the mechanical lure. The only thing that keeps this business going is demand.

"If people stopped attending and stopped betting at the betting shop or on your internet, racing would become obsolete. Horses and dogs were not put on this earth to race each other. Competition like this is a man-made desire, not any animal in its natural environment would do such a thing as race. They would run for fun, not to win, just for the pleasure of running and racing is simply not pleasurable for the animal.

"The noises of the spectators, the music, the commentators over the loudspeaker, not to mention the injuries or death they endure; all for profit and entertainment of man. Horses are given legal and illegal drugs to improve performance, they are frequently lame and suffer many injuries and often have to be killed as the injuries are so severe.

"At fairgrounds throughout the USA, animals are used to race in crowded areas such as pigs, ostriches and more.

"The unfamiliar surroundings, the noise and the crowds are confusing and the animals often fall and break bones at which point they are slaughtered as they are no longer able to compete for this pointless contest that they are forced to participate in. They really didn't want to compete in the first place. The racing of many different animals goes on all around the world.

"I am repeating myself Billy, but if people stopped the desire to gamble, the suffering would be a thing of the past. It really is as simple as that and for people to stop attending, first they need to wake up, get in touch with their hearts and feel compassion and empathy for the other species on planet Earth, not just think about their own gain or entertainment."

Wild Sea Mammal Entertainment Parks

"OK, Billy, you have seen dolphins and whales in the wild, now let's see more of what humans like to call entertainment."

Sat in an arena, Billy could see dolphins performing tricks to receive a reward of fish to eat.

"Sea lions, dolphins, whales and other sea life creatures are stolen from the ocean, imprisoned, drugged and held captive in tanks, not for their good, not for conservation but for profit and 'entertainment'. These wondrous creatures should be swimming in the oceans, not in small tanks, where all they can do is go around and around, going totally crazy.

"Once again, if people just stopped going to these so-called attractions, they would close and the suffering would stop. Human's need to re-write what entertainment is. The definition of entertainment is the action of providing amusement or enjoyment. Knowing that these creatures are lonely, sad and trapped in a tiny space surely cannot provide anyone with amusement or joy?"

"Seeing creatures in their natural habitat, this is the real joy, Max."

Zoos

Next was a Zoo, Billy and Max arrived looking down at a gorilla alone in an enclosure.

"Zoos, safari parks and aquariums where animals are captive in small cages, pens or tanks are just not enough space to give the animal its natural needs. Especially nomadic animals like giraffes and elephants or long-distance swimmers like sharks, dolphins and whales. Elephants in their natural habitat walk up to 12 miles per day, in zoos and safari parks they have a tiny area to walk up and down in.

"Dolphins, whales and sharks swim 80–150 miles a day, in aquariums they live in small tanks where they can only swim around and around. Look at the animals, Billy, they have cage madness, they either circle or pace; this is because there is nothing like the area required for them to display their natural behaviour, they are trapped and literally going insane being locked up.

"In the UK, there are over 50 zoos/safari parks and it is estimated that there are over 10,000 worldwide. The zoos say that they are helping conserve the species, this is just a smokescreen, do not believe this, it is mainly marketing. Even if a zoo is doing conservation work, really it should be done in the country of the origin of the animal, in a national park that has thousands of miles of land with only one plan; to release these animals back into the wild. In the UK, they are not able to release back into the wild elephants or gorillas, so they clearly do not have plans to release them. Just ask the zoo when do they plan to release the animal back into the wild and you will find the answer.

"A radical thought Billy; better for the animal to be in their own habitat and become extinct than be held captive in a cage or a very small pen to eventually die in captivity, whilst their children suffer the same miserable life. Extinction is a natural occurrence; however, it is humans that have caused most of the extinctions in recent times mainly due to deforestation.

"In some zoos in Asia, terrified cows, donkeys, pigs, and chickens are dropped into the lion and tiger enclosures as live prey as 'entertainment' for the crowds. Once again, if people did not visit the zoos, they would be forced to close. They are nothing more than prisons holding innocent being's captive."

"But Max, with all these closures of businesses wouldn't that create a massive meltdown of the global economy?"

"As with many changes in your past history, new ideas and ways of doing things would replace the old Billy. Everything in life is impermanent Billy, nothing stays the same, evolution and what you call progress is constantly changing. Billy, I would like to show you something."

As usual, the next moment, Billy was in a place far away, in the jungle. "Where are we, Max?"

"In Nepal, Billy."

Billy could see several tourists sitting on top of an elephant, and across the other side of the river, he could see what appeared to be a couple of crocodiles basking in the sun. Several long boats full of tourists were being driven upriver to see crocodiles and other wildlife. Neither Billy nor Max said a word, a few moments later; they were teleported to what appeared to be a crocodile zoo.

"This is a conservation breeding centre, Billy."

There were hundreds and hundreds of crocs in different enclosures; each enclosure housed the same size croc, from tiny babies in one enclosure to adolescence in another all lying on top of each other, with very little space. Max teleported them to an elephant enclosure. The elephants were chained up.

"This is also a breeding centre, Billy."

Billy could see young elephants next to their mums; they were all chained on one leg. One youngster was rocking forwards and backwards trying to get to his mum, he couldn't quite touch her, it was so sad to watch, Billy just starred, and he could feel the anguish of the youngster, just wanting to be free of the chains to touch his mother.

A tear welled up; Billy wiped his eyes with the back of his hand. There were ten elephants with their young. He couldn't understand why the elephants were not in the jungle, surely, the babies were now old enough, and they should now be released to the wild to live a natural life, to roam.

"Max, why are they not in the wild now?"

"Well, Billy, the fact is that they make too much money from tourists who come to see the elephants, many people are very disappointed as they don't expect to see the elephants chained up, but the reality is, that these are being bred to bring in the money, always follow the money, Billy."

"So, are they being bred to become the next generation of tourist rides?"

"Yes, Billy, that is exactly what is going on here, as well as just to be here, people pay money to come to 'conservation breeding centres'; however, in reality, they are often no different to zoo's."

"And the crocs Max, what about them?"

"They are destined to become handbags and shoes Billy. A small number are released into the wild, the park needs some crocs in the water to attract the tourists to pay for the long boat rides, but there are not that many in the wild, there are hundreds in the enclosures, so there is only one conclusion to make, remember Billy follow the money."

"The wild, cruel beast is not behind the bars of the cage. He is in front of it."

—Axel Munthe (1857–1949)

Hunting

The next scene was a man having his picture taken with a dead lion in front of him. He was holding a long gun and grinning, clearly very happy to have shot the lion.

"Lion hunting, now this one really gets me going, Billy. A lion is at the top of the food chain. If you didn't have guns to kill them and drugs to calm them, you would be very scared of these enigmatic creatures. Lion hunting is purely for man's pleasure to shoot. What right do humans have to kill another animal Billy, just for entertainment?"

"We don't Max, I don't get it either, I don't even like killing ants! I know in the UK fox hunting is now banned, but it still goes on due to a loophole in the law that means they can continue to hunt but under the guise of 'trail' hunting which is just a cover-up for the fact that they are still hunting, the government need to remove this ridiculous loophole to stop this barbaric and cruel 'sport'.

"The other thing we do in the UK is to cull Badgers, I know this is nothing to do with hunting Max, but we actively trap and kill badgers as it is thought that they spread TB to cows, which has a financial impact on the farmers. The reality is that in the areas where they do cull these timid animal's they report that the number of incidences of TB in cows does not reduce. I bet the badgers probably don't even go near the cows and now that I have seen that most cows are in sheds, this makes even more sense to me."

"As always Billy, it is your generation that will make this change, if you don't go hunting, this industry will stop it really is as simple as that. Many species are hunted throughout the world, too many to mention, but as you are from the UK, one to mention is deer hunting in Scotland. People pay big money to go hunting for wild deer, if people of the UK ask themselves what is the difference between a lion and a deer, I am sure that most people will come to one answer."

The Ivory Trade

Lying before them was a dead elephant, its tusks removed. A young elephant and the herd were mourning over her carcass. Billy couldn't hold back the tears; he was so sad to see such a beautiful animal dead, all for the greed of man.

"Despite a ban on international trade thousands of elephants are killed every year for their tusks; they are used to make carvings, ornaments and jewellery for the wealthy man's pleasure. The biggest demand is in China. Some new dyes are now being painted onto the tusk, which means the tusks are then worthless, this will help; however, this industry is easily stopped; if the demand for the Ivory went away there would be no need to kill these magnificent animals."

Billy was now sobbing, his heart felt heavy, all the things Max had shown him had been building up inside him and now there was no stopping him from having a really good cry.

"This is what others need to feel Billy, it is feeling that will change the people's thinking. You cry Billy, as much as you need to, it is very therapeutic to cry and one of the most natural things any human of any age can do. Unfortunately, many humans have become detached from these deep feelings, we need to spread this empathy and love, Billy."

After about ten minutes, Billy felt a lot lighter, he was still snivelling snot and wiping his face with his hand, but the release of the tears made him feel calmer.

"Let's talk about the last of the entertainment examples here Billy rather than witness any more monstrosities, but before I do, I just wanted to mention a less known ivory. The helmeted hornbill is hunted for its solid bill; it is sold as 'hornbill ivory'. They can be found in Malay Peninsula, Sumatra, Borneo, Thailand and Myanmar. They have become very rare, so the price increases which means it is even more wanted by the rich. These birds do not deserve to be hunted and killed just as no other species does."

Fun Rides

At a nearby hill, Max continued, "The next two exploitations we do not need to visit Billy, all over the world, camels, elephants, donkeys and horses are used for tourist attractions; animals are working to make money for humans. Animals were not created to work and to be held captive like prisoners. They were created to be free. Once again, this is quite simple; the people of the earth need to simply refuse to ride the animals or horse-drawn carriages.

"Even riding your 'own' horse is no different to the working animal, except perhaps they are treated as pets rather than working animals. Animals are not yours to own Billy, people say they love their horses but they ride them for pleasure. What does the horse get out of it? Horses were not born to be ridden they were born to be wild and free. Ever wondered why the horse has to be 'broken in'?"

"I guess because it doesn't want to be ridden?"

"Exactly, the term 'broken' is exactly that; the horses' spirit is broken to the point he just gives in, it is the same with the circus elephants"

"What about the people that say their horse loves to be ridden?"

"I am sure if the horse had the choice, he would be wild and free, he probably makes the best of a bad situation and appears to enjoy the riding, as he is not stuck in a field or in a stable; this is the only reason why they seem to enjoy the riding, nothing to do with what the horse actually wants to do. If humans imagine what it is like to be any captive animal, they would soon come to the conclusion that the animal would choose to be free. The definition of a captive is 'a person who has been taken prisoner or an animal that has been confined', what do you think, Billy?"

"I think that humans are deluded Max, humans think that they are superior and have the right to do as they please with animals, to have dominion over animals and to use the animals for profit. Once you see the scale of the situation, it is easy to see the delusion."

Angling

"Fishing as a sport I am sure you know is called 'angling'; it is barbaric as it is often just for fun. The fish get hooks stuck in their mouths or down the throat, which anglers remove often damaging the fish's mouth, sometimes the fisherman has to get his fingers or a pair of pliers to remove the hook from deep in the throat causing immense suffering. The fish will sometimes die of shock once it is put back in the water or be so weakened by the experience that other fish attack it.

"Being handled by humans can cause damage to the fish's delicate fins and cause a loss of their protective scale coating which makes them vulnerable to disease. All in all, the fish suffer and if they don't die, they get caught again and have to endure the suffering over and over. In addition, not only do the fish suffer but also other aquatic animals and birds get caught in fishing lines and other fishing debris left behind by the angler."

Exotic Pets

Arriving on a farm, high on moorland, Billy could see many animals around. Pigs, geese, ducks, sheep, goats, donkeys, horses, chickens, lamas and peacocks.

"This is an animal sanctuary and animals are brought here for many reasons; unwanted pets or found injured or have been treated badly by their owner. That goose was born with deformed wings, she cannot fly, the pigs were brought as micro pigs to be house pets, but they didn't stop growing, you can see how big they have grown…that is not a pet that you want on your sofa."

Max and Billy laughed. "The species that I want to show you today are inside Billy."

Inside there were many tanks with snakes, turtles, terrapins, bearded dragons and tarantulas.

"Pet stores who sell exotic pets are the root cause of this problem Billy, as well as the demand. If they hadn't been imported in the first place, no one would want one. People see these beautiful creatures and decide they want one as a pet, then get bored or don't realise how much it costs to keep such pets, or they grow so big that they can't keep them. They end up somewhere like this Billy.

"Animal sanctuaries are funded by donations only and are restricted by how much space they have as to how many animals they can home. This is about ownership; other species are not yours to own. They are shipped halfway around the world sometimes in really bad conditions, maybe even smuggled in, just for the human ego to say they own a pet snake or spider, it is considered 'cool'.

"These exotic animals need extra special care, as they often require heating and lighting. Bearded dragons are the most popular lizard to be kept as a pet in the UK, they come from Australia and live 10–15 years, so it is a long commitment to 'own' one of these. Corn snakes are another popular 'pet', they originate from Northern America, they also live for around 10–15 years and require special food and environment.

"This is, as always, a money-driven industry and a demand-driven industry, if people didn't feel the need to own pets, these beings would be left in the wild to do what they are meant to do. Whenever someone really stops and thinks and asks themselves; Is this really OK, to capture a wild animal, ship it around the world to sell for a profit so that I, a human being, can have some enjoyment or kudos, if they really stop and see it for what it is, there is only one conclusion; it is not justifiable just for their pleasure.

"And actually, all animals were originally wild, it's not just exotic animals that need a deep thought about the moralistic view, any animal that is not in their natural habitat that is 'owned' is being exploited."

"Max, what about cats and dogs that have been domesticated who share love and a deep bond between owner and animal?"

"Humanity is where it is at and do need to move forward; however, you can't now just discard all your dogs and cats out into the woods to fend for themselves. If you have paid a lot of money for the animal, then it has been exploited and you are satisfying your desire and enabling someone to make a profit.

"If you rescue an animal that needs a home; and you pay a small fee to an animal rescue centre to help with their operation, then you are showing compassion and love. You treasure your cats and dogs like your children, most of them live luxurious lives, they will be the last of the animal kingdom to be liberated, there are so many other animals that are suffering and need to be given back to the earth before cats and dogs.

"On Unity, all animals are wild and there is enough wild land that gives the animals natural space. I guess Billy, humanity needs to look at what really needs to change now, change that and the rest will unfold. Marine aquatics are also suffering, as they are shipped around the world to end up in someone's house in a fish tank, which really does not meet its needs.

"For each one that survives the gruelling stressful journey, it is estimated that around nine others die. Other exploitations occur to feed the exotic pets. Worms are farmed as feed for captured birds and fish. Crickets are farmed as feed for captured reptiles, and in some countries, people eat the crickets too, they are deep-fried and are apparently a tasty crispy little snack."

"So, what should people do who already 'own' captive pets, Max?"

"It is highly unlikely you will be able to get them back into their natural habitat, so continue to care and look after the animal and make its life as comfortable as possible and if you feel that it is not morally justifiable to keep captive any animals do not buy anymore and tell your friends and family that you will not buy pets in the future."

"Take sides. Neutrality helps the oppressor, never the victim. Silence encourages the tormentor, never the tormented."

—Elie Wiesel (1928–2016), a concentration camp survivor

Chapter 7

The next couple of days Billy had time off from gallivanting with Max to study on his home school work. Max arrived on the third morning since they had last been together. "OK, Billy, we don't have that many places to visit before we get to work with your friends, so let's get through them as quickly as we can.

"If people stopped eating meat, dairy, fish, honey and eggs all other bi-products would also disappear, people who consciously choose not to consume animal products would also consciously choose not to buy the bi-products."

Clothing

Feathers for Our Luxury Comfort

Billy found himself up in the rafters of an open-walled shed in the countryside. It was hot; thank goodness it was opened walled Billy thought, as with this heat it would be very stinky. Billy knew they were in China, as he recognised the language. There were a lot of geese in the shed honking.

Lots of people were sat on small stools with a goose between their legs, knees gripping the body of the bird; with one hand they were holding the neck and head down to stop the bird from moving. Using the other hand, they were violently plucking out the feathers. You could see spots of blood on their skin, where the feather's had been ripped out.

"OMG Max, why are they doing that?" Billy whispered.

"Geese and ducks are bred for their feathers to go in jackets, duvets, sleeping bags and pillows. Around 80% of the world's feathers come from China, where often the feathers and down are plucked alive and the birds suffer a lot of pain."

"Why don't they wait until the geese are dead, Max?"

"Well, Billy, as always follow the money, the feathers grow back at which point they are plucked again and again for around 6 times until the feathers stop growing. They are then killed as they are no longer a profitable commodity. This is a demand-driven industry, the only way that this suffering will stop is if the people of earth stop buying products filled with feathers and down."

Coats That Evolved to Keep the Original Owner Warm

In a dark, smelly damp barn, Billy and Max could hear all sorts of animal noises.

"Fur coats are made from furry animals, their fur coats, not humans. Over 100 million furry animals are killed each year, 25 million in the USA. These animals are either obtained by hunting, trapping or they are farmed just like the animals you eat but killed for their fur. Animals like foxes, rabbits, minks, muskrats, beaver, stoat, otters, seals, cats, dogs, coyotes, chinchillas, possums and opossums.

"Once caught or bred they never see the daylight or feel the earth under their feet. Wild animals get cage madness as they are used to being free to run, roam and hunt but they are in small cages, they are frightened, frustrated and stressed. They end up going crazy, they scratch to get out, pace up and down or go around and around in circles endlessly. Dehydration, malnutrition and other seriously painful ailments cause much suffering as well as exposure to freezing temperatures.

"As always, the least expensive are the most appealing ways to kill these furry animals; Carbon monoxide poisoning, strychnine suffocation, breaking of the neck and anal electrocution are the common methods used. After being skinned the carcasses are often ground up and fed to the animals that are still caged."

Max teleported them, they were standing on ice, as far as the eye could see was a frozen expanse of water all around. A seal pup was not far away with its mum.

"Harp seal pups live in the Atlantic frozen waters and in the Greenland seas, they are bludgeoned to death and skinned. Carcasses are left to rot on the ice. Fur is sold under a different name to hide from the shopper what animal it came from."

"OMG, Max, they brutally kill these beautiful innocent babies?"

"Yes, Billy, fur coats sell for thousands of dollars; the most expensive was in 2015 and was reported to be sold for $1m. In the UK, fur farms are banned, but importing fur coats, hats and boots is legal, so the ban doesn't actually stop the suffering. Another example, Billy, of a crazy law that was brought about to appease the people and make people in the UK feel like they are kind, compassionate animal lovers; however, if people in the UK are buying fur products, they are deluding themselves."

"Surely if a law is in place, it should cover the importing and selling as well as the hunting, trapping and farming?"

"You would think so Billy, once again, this is a demand-driven industry, and if the people of earth stop buying these products it will eliminate all the unnecessary suffering."

"Max, we have been wearing fur coats since we were cavemen that is a very long program to change."

"I agree, Billy; some programming doesn't just go back to when you were children; sometimes it is thousands of years of programming; however, now is the time for a change. In caveman times, it was the only choice available to survive; you now have the technology to make clothes out of something else other than dead animal skins."

Skins for Sale

In a very hot and dusty location, Billy found himself looking at a truck full of cows that were lying on top of each other with no room to move.

"Demand for leather mainly comes from the USA and Europe. Little or no thought of where it came from, you all wear it; coats, gloves, wallets, belts, shoes, bags, sofas and even on car seats, dashboards and doors. Every year around 1 billion animals are killed for their skins. Leather comes from many animals; horses, cows, calves, goats, lambs, pigs and even dogs and cats but a big percentage comes from cows in India.

"We talked earlier about how the cow is sacred in India. India has the biggest cow population in the world estimated at 283 million and as you know it is illegal to kill cows in many states of India. Men who do not care about the tradition of the cow being sacred force them to the ground to be shoed and roped for the first time in their lives which is a terrifying experience.

"Then they are forced to walk sometimes for several days in the heat and dust without food and water, many animals faint and fall to the floor. Once they reach the arranged transport collection area, they are forced into trucks, having never been in a truck before this is also very frightening for the cows.

"Often there isn't a ramp, so the men manhandle the weary cows into the trucks, causing injury, sometimes broken bones. The cows often have to lie on top of each other as you can see there isn't enough room in the truck. The men don't show any kindness to the animals and completely lack respect.

"The noise and the motion of the truck is also a new experience which is very stressful, after a few days in the truck with no water or food they reach their destination; just on the other side of the border of India or in Indian states where it is legal to kill cows. As many as half will already be dead by the time they reach the slaughterhouse. For the ones that are still alive, they are forced to the ground, then all four legs are tied together to stop the cow from moving and kicking the men, their throats are then cut in front of each other.

"The throats are generally hacked and sawed off, as often the knives are not sharpened. The skins are sent to tanners where toxic substances are used such as chromium which is a carcinogen and gets into the water table, rivers and seas. Leather is dead skin that naturally decomposes unless potent substances are used. The people working in these tanners don't have special clothing to protect them from the harmful chemicals; they stand in the 'baths' full of this substance probably with zero knowledge of the danger they are putting themselves in.

"The other big country for leather tanning is China, where they have very little laws for animal welfare. Leather from both India and China is in most of the high street shops in the USA and Europe. If people stop buying leather products, the suffering will end. Other exploitations of the animal kingdom for clothing/cloth include angora goats that are farmed for their wool as are llamas and alpacas.

"Silk comes from the caterpillar of a moth; they are farmed and when they are two months old, they spin a cocoon of silk to contain themselves until they metamorphose into a moth. Soon after they finish spinning their protective shelter, humans heat the cocoon which kills the caterpillar, the silk is then harvested. This is by no means the total list, there are many more, Billy."

"Because the heart beats under a covering of hair, of fur, feathers, or wings, it is, for that reason, to be of no account?"

—Jean-Paul Richter (1763–1825)

Ting Wu lives in China, she was an only child, something she and Billy had in common. Her parents were brought up mainly on a vegetarian diet, any meat used was in very small quantities to add texture and flavour to a meal; however, people in China have become far more affluent and westernised which means they consume a lot more meat than in the past. Pork is China's favourite meat along with chicken.

Ting didn't have any knowledge of the suffering or have any awareness of the massive numbers of animals that were being reared to be killed. Max had shown her two seven-story and one thirteen-story pig breeding facilities that looked like massive hotels, certainly nothing like farms. She learned and shared with Billy that the thirteenth-floor facility is the world's tallest building of its kind and has the capacity to house 30,000 sows, birthing up to 840,000 piglets annually. He had also taken her to a dairy facility that housed 100,000 cows.

"This is not farming Billy, this is big business," said Ting.

Max decided he wanted to take them both together to learn about Rhino's horns and why they are sought after.

Crazy Beliefs
Horns or Toenails

In front of Billy and Ting was a dead rhino. "Rhinos are killed for their horns in Africa; the horn is exported to China, Vietnam and other countries in Asia where ancient Chinese medicine is practiced, and it is believed that ground-up horn has medicinal properties to treat fever, rheumatism and gout. There is also a new belief that having a rhino horn is a status symbol and is even given as a present.

"The horns are composed largely of the protein keratin, also the chief component in human hair and fingernails, and animal hooves. So, grinding up one's own fingernails is tantamount to the ground horns. This industry is easily stopped; if the demand for the horns went away there would be no need to kill these magnificent animals. It is simple, people just need to grind up their own fingernails.

"There are some areas where the national park keepers are actively dehorning, this is where they give the Rhino a general anaesthetic and remove the horn in a safe way. If this is not done, the risk is that poachers will drug the rhino, cut off the horn below the blood supply line to maximise on the amount of horn to sell and leave the animal to bleed to death. It is great that the keepers are dehorning; however, it would be far better if the demand was to disappear so that the wonderful beasts could be left with their horns intact and in no danger from poachers.

"Rhino populations have reduced by 90% in the last 40 years which is exclusively due to the demand for Chinese medicine. It really is the same as everything we have spoken about Billy, once the demand is gone, the animals can live in peace and free of suffering at the hand of man. Pangolins are also a prize catch for keratin and meat. The scales on its skin are believed in China and other Asian countries to have medicinal properties, due to the keratin.

"They have been hunted so much in Asia, that there are very rare, so now they are imported from Africa. They command a lot of money; so much so, that they are the most illegally hunted and killed animal on the planet, making up an estimated 20% of all illegally killed animals. Both the rhino and pangolins would thrive if the human demand was to disappear. It is really easy, once the demand has gone, these animals will be left in peace to live a full and natural life.

"Other animals hunted for the ancient medicinal beliefs and as a status symbol are tigers and leopards. Around 8,000 tigers are also illegally farmed in Asia for their body parts exclusively for ancient medicinal beliefs. Another absurd tradition is extracting bear bile. Around 12,000 bears are held captive to have bile extracted from their gallbladder. They are often locked up in small cages their whole lives unable to stand on all fours or turn around and never allowed out.

"The Chinese people believe that the bile has medicinal properties and perform surgery on the bears to have a permanent open passage from the gallbladder to the abdomen for easy extraction. The really old bears that are no longer producing bile are sometimes left in their cage to die, with little or no food and water. Many other animal parts are used in Chinese medicine such as cow gallstones, leeches, scorpions, horns of antelope or buffalo, deer antlers, testicles and penis bones of dogs, snake bile, turtle plastron, seahorses, shark fins and gill plates of mobula and manta rays.

"Traditional Chinese medicine also includes around 35 human body parts including bones, fingernails, hair, dandruff, earwax, impurities on teeth, poop, wee, sweat and organs; however, most are no longer used. If people ask themselves why the use of human parts in Chinese medicine has declined, they will realise that clearly, people have changed their opinion on the effectiveness of the medicine or how grose it is. If they really think logically and critically, they will also come to the conclusion that it makes no sense that parts from another species are medicinal for humans as it really is a crazy notion that has been passed down generation by generation"

"Those who can make you believe absurdities can make you commit atrocities."

—Voltaire (1694–1778)

"OK, time for a small gathering."

They all appeared at the same time, Lucy, Rohan, Anahira, Jiemba, Kemala, Keiki, Eduardo, Jack, Pedro, Ping, Ting and Billy. They were on top of the Great Wall of China, not the tourist part near Beijing which has been re-built and maintained; they were in a very rural location surrounded by nature. There were mountains in the distance all around them; it was truly a magnificent sight.

The air was sweet with the scent of flowers, it was warm with sunshine and birds sang their songs. It was amazing that the wall was not maintained, as they could really imagine what it was like when it was built, what the surrounding area was like, how hard it must have been to be there building the wall. The wall was overgrown with nature, vines, trees and plants with beautiful purple flowers everywhere.

Pedro was curious to know how Max managed to get them all to appear at the same time when Max was just with him.

"How did you do that, Max?" Pedro asked.

"Do what Pedro?"

"Get us all here when you were just with me?"

"Ooh, you all really do like to know how I do stuff, it is one reason why I chose you all! I can be in more than one place at a time Pedro. Actually, I can be in many places at the same time. Remember everything is energy, so once a being has evolved enough to learn how to manipulate the energy; you can do almost anything you like.

"My teacher back home has taught me so much since I was a boy. You see, school on Unity is not like school here on Earth but that is a story for another time. I brought you all here, just to let you all get to know each other a little more. I am in touch with many more young people around the world; in fact, I have friends in every country; however, it is important that you all get to know each other over a period of time, as you will have a stronger bond with each other which will be very important in our future work together, more of that another time.

"For now, I just wanted you all to sit and chat and get to know each other a bit, before you all meet more new friends. I will be back shortly, chat amongst yourselves."

He disappeared into thin air. They all chatted about what they had learned and wondered how they were going to change the world. They exchanged information about where Max had taken them. It seemed, that Max had taken them all to destinations that they had in their minds to one day visit or in their wildest dreams. Billy wondered what other places Max might have planned to take him.

He discovered that they had all been to Unity and seen the animals and children playing. Rohan had been sat on the top of Big Ben in London and the leaning tower of Pisa in Italy, as well as being on the moon. Lucy had been to Machu Picchu in Peru, the Amazon River and on top of the Statue of Liberty in New York. Ting had visited the ancient Angkor ruins in Cambodia, the Antarctic and Table Mountain in South Africa.

Jack had also been into space to float and view planet earth, on top of Mont Blanc mountain in the French/Italian border and the Grand Canyon. Anahira had been to Niagara Falls, Mount Everest and the lost city of Atlantis. Jiemba had visited Greenland, Patagonia and the pyramids in Egypt. Kemala had been to Stonehenge, The fjords in Norway and The Colosseum in Rome.

Keiki had been to Kailasa Temples in India, The African savanna and on the top of the statue of Christ in Rio. Eduardo had been to the leaning tower of Pisa, he also went into space and the Angkor ruins. Pedro had also been to Grand Canyon, Mount Everest and big ben. They all hoped that they would visit all the places mentioned in the future. No one had been to any slaughterhouses but had visited factory farms.

They discussed the idea of seeing the slaughterhouses with their own eyes and all agreed that on the one hand, they would like to see it, just to know it from their own experience; however, they also agreed that they really didn't want to because they would be polluting their minds with the pictures of mass suffering and fear and not just words from Max, but actually with their own eyes. Lucy suggested that they could just view it on the internet, rather than being teleported with Max. They had all come to the decision that they did not want to be the demand that paid for the suffering and killing of innocent animal babies and toddlers.

The atmosphere between them was electric, they were all excited to share their experiences and opinions about what was going on with Max and how they were all now connected to each other. They talked about Maxs' 'special powers', what he could do with energy and how they were all looking forward to the continued adventure.

After around half an hour Max returned.

"This, the Great Wall of China was started in 220 BC and took 10 years to complete by over 1 million labourers. Sadly around 300,000 died during construction, many were buried within the 13,000 miles of wall. Messages were relayed by smoke signals, lanterns and beacon fires between the many turrets. This relic should be a great reminder to humans that war and seeing other humans as enemies does not work, but more about that later. So, you all want to go see some sites together now?"

"Where to, Max?" asked Rohan.

Rohan was scared that they were about to visit some slaughterhouses, knowing that Max was somehow earwigging in on their conversation. He didn't feel ready to see what goes on inside the houses of death.

"Don't worry, not to a slaughterhouse."

They all instinctively held hands and were teleported to a rural area, the sky was clear with the sun beating down, it was very hot. They were in a clearing in the woods.

"We are in Australia. Not far from here is a really large factory farm, I wanted you to see the scale of the mass breeding that is going on. Typically, these really large factory farms are out of sight with a lot of land surrounding them, which means the general public do not get to see this. We are going to all hold hands and go flying together, you need to see this from up above to really get an idea of how your farms have been turned into factories."

They all held hands and created a ring of people, just like skydivers. They slowly started to float up, all looking a bit pensive as they rose 500 feet up in the air. Billy was astounded that they were stable as if they were still standing on the ground.

"OK, guys allow your legs to float out behind you so that we are horizontal, whilst still holding hands."

Once horizontal, they started moving south towards the big factory farm, they arrived seconds later. Jiemba was laughing his head off as he was really enjoying the flying experience with everyone. The buildings were very long and identical, rows and rows of long large buildings, too many to count, they just went on and on row after row. There was one big square building at one end, and rows and rows of smaller buildings, miniature in comparison to the long large units, again too many to count.

"What you see below is a large dairy factory farm, the long buildings house the cows, the small solitary pens house the female calves and the square building is the milking house."

Billy couldn't believe the scale of it; it was way bigger than anything he had seen when visiting with Max the other farms. Max started a decent at one end of the long buildings; they landed to see the numbers of cows inside the sheds. There were many hundreds of cows inside the shed, all standing around, in their own poop, huddled up together, the smell was pretty gross and it was noisy from hundreds of cows mooing.

Next were the pens, hundreds of babies in solitary prison cells they were mooing constantly, crying for their mums. It was just horrid; Billy's heart was pounding, as he started to feel a little angry, as he knew that the babies were being fed substitute milk and that they just wanted to be with their mummies. As always with Max, it was a short visit and next they were in a new location.

"OK, now let's look at the cattle that are bred for their flesh."

Once again, they slowly ascended high into the sky and flew over a cattle ranch. It was much bigger than the dairy factory, penned in, not fields, as there was no grass, just dirt and poop. There wasn't any shelter for the cows to escape the hot blaring sun. Thousands of cattle, pen after pen.

The last stop of the day was in a beautiful rural area with lush tree-covered hills all around, mist was in the air but the smell was not sweet as you would imagine such a beautiful place to be. Billy could see 4 massive white buildings, 7 stories high, 18 windows across, they looked like hotels, and not a farm.

"We are now in China. Believe it or not, this is a pig farm. It is what they are now calling a mega farm or breeding facility. As Ting knows, this is the largest of its kind in the world; the people of China love eating pork."

They all said goodbye and hugged each other, as Max took them all home at the same time. Billy thought it was weird to think that Max had 'split' himself into 12 to teleport everyone individually home.

Birds That Cannot Fly?

The next day, Max teleported Billy to a café that was on the edge of a town with stunning views of mountains and hills as far as the eye could see. It was a beautifully hot day; they sat outside in the shade. There was a delightful sound of birds singing. Billy looked up into the trees to see if he could get a glimpse of the birds but he became aware that they were just behind him; he turned and saw beautiful small colourful birds in cages. They were solitary cages about one-foot square each, housing one bird, twelve cages in total, hung up on the wall of the café.

"People keep birds in cages, what are these people thinking Billy? Birds have wings and were born to be free, flying high in the sky not stuck in small prisons. This is all about ownership; actually, a lot of issues on earth are about ownership. You do not own birds, you do not have the right to capture and cage them. People hear their 'songs' and think they are singing for joy, they are shouting 'will someone please set me free, so I can fly'."

"Shall we Max? Let's do it."

Max smiled and thought for a moment before replying. "I am not sure that is the answer Billy, the café owner will just buy more birds."

"But Max, if enough people were to release caged birds perhaps, the 'owners' would come to realise that this is not right, it's not fair to house a bird in a cage, perhaps they will come to think like you and me that the birds should be wild, flying free, perching on branches and playing in the air with their friends and families."

"OK, Billy, let's do it, we need to wait until the café is very quiet."

A little later Billy and Max got to work freeing the birds, the café owner was inside cleaning up from the last customers. Billy was so excited, he had never done anything like this in his life, his heart was pumping fast and his mouth went dry with fear of being caught. He opened a cage as Max opened another, two birds flew out together, Billy felt overwhelmed to be liberating the birds and his whole body was alive with excitement.

Cage by cage they let all the birds free just in time as the café owner stepped outside as Max touched Billy's shoulder to get them back to Billy's room. Billy couldn't stop laughing, he laughed so much his belly started to hurt.

Finally, he could speak, "Max that was the best thing I have ever done in my life, words just can't express how brilliant it felt to free the birds."

Billy was talking really fast and was the most animated Max had ever seen him.

"I am glad you enjoyed that Billy, perhaps we will free some other birds and animals another day. Time for me to go Billy see you tomorrow."

With that, he vanished, leaving Billy alone with a massive grin across his face, thinking about the twelve birds flying into the nearby trees.

"Housing animals in more comfortable, larger cages is not enough. Whether we exploit animals to eat, to wear, to entertain us, or to learn, the truth of animal rights requires empty cages, not larger cages."

—Tom Regan (1938–2017)

The next day Max arrived as usual, "OK, Billy. Today is going to be a tough day; I don't want to sugar-coat it for you. The next scene Billy saw was a big crowd of people in the street; they were all cheering and shouting. He could hear what he thought were dogs fighting, but he couldn't see anything as the crowd was so dense. Max teleported them to a nearby roof.

"I took you first down into the crowd so that you could feel the energy down there, Billy."

"It didn't feel good Max, it felt ferocious."

He could now see that it was two dogs fighting, he wanted to scream at them to stop the fight. He just couldn't comprehend why people wanted to watch such a horrid scene. They all seemed to be egging on the dogs to rip each other apart. The two dogs looked like they had been fighting for a while; they were covered in blood and looked in a really bad way.

Billy could see they both had old scars, so were clearly not new to this 'game' that humans had taught them and forced them to participate in. He thought to himself, dogs don't fight for fighting sake; they would only fight to defend themselves, this is totally wrong that humans are making money and enjoying this grotesque show. Billy was disgusted.

"Dogfighting is still legal in Japan and Russia. Although outlawed, it still remains popular and held openly in parts of Latin America, Pakistan and Eastern Europe and clandestinely in the USA and in the UK. Cock fighting is still popular in Cuba, parts of India, Peru, Mexico, South East Asia, Pakistan and Iraq. Ram fighting is popular in Nigeria, Uzbekistan and Indonesia."

Vivisection

Born to Be Experimented on
and Tortured

"OK, Billy, I would like to take you to a place that will be dark when we arrive, don't be scared, I will be with you and it is inside a modern building, so no danger."

It was pitch black and Billy could hear animals gently making grunting noises. Max created light from his hand which was like a really bright torch beam.

"Wow, can you teach me that one day, Max?"

"Maybe Billy, Maybe."

Max shined the light down the middle of the room, it was a long slim room with no windows Billy could see there were cages running down either side and the light made the animal's eyes shine and lit up their cute faces, he knew instantly it was small monkeys. They looked so much like humans, just a little hairier. Billy's heart sank, having seen monkey's in the Amazon in their natural environment, Billy knew it was just wrong that these beings should be held captive in prisons.

"Household products including cleaning products, paints, dyes, inks, petrol products, solvents, tars, pharmaceuticals, perfumes, cosmetics and hair/body products are tested on animals; mice, monkeys, dogs, cats, rats and more. These animals are bred, held captive, often they never see the light of day or touch the earth and have unspeakable things done to them to test products before they are released for humans to use.

"In these experiments, animals are forced to eat or inhale substances or have them rubbed onto their skin or injected into their bodies. The animals are then subjected to further monitoring and testing before often being killed so that researchers can look at the effects on their tissues and organs.

"There are alternative ways of testing products nowadays; in vitro testing, which uses human cells and tissues in a Petri dish and in silico models which is computer modelling techniques. This barbaric testing does not need to continue. Products are available to buy that have not been tested on animals, they are known as 'cruelty-free'. However, most of the public have their heads in the sand about these tests, they all know it goes on but they choose to ignore it, they think that testing isn't that bad and that the animals are well looked after.

"This is not the case Billy. Humans can stop this simply by refusing to buy from the companies that test on animals. If everyone did this, the companies that test on animals would soon have to change their methods or they would simply go out of business. The power is with the people Billy; individuals just need to vote by spending their money with ethical businesses.

"All the information is on your internet, it isn't hard to make this change. Another fact is that in China it is the law that all products have to be tested on animals, so any company that does not test on animals, but wants to sell in China, need to have their products tested in China on animals. They sell the ethics all over the world, but when the largest populated nation has a law that requires the test, they go along with it. Once again, it's all about money Billy, if they really had ethics, they would just refuse to trade in China."

"The reason why I am against animal research is because it doesn't work. It has no scientific value. One cannot extrapolate the results of animal research to human beings, and every good scientist knows that."

—Robert Mendelsohn (1926–1988)

In a forest nearby, Billy met some more friends, Czar Smirnov from Russia, Oskar Fischer from Germany, Ava Bisset from France, Nicole Ricci from Italy as well as the 11 friends he had already met. Billy was starting to realise that Max had some big ideas and was creating an army of young people all around 11–14 years of age each one from a different country, Billy was so excited to know how the coming days and weeks would unfold.

Once everyone had a chance to meet and chat, Max spoke.

"There is global devastation going on right now in the sea and on the land on a scale that is mind-boggling. I could go on and on as there are a lot more examples, but you now all have enough of a picture to understand what needs to happen. The big question is how we influence the 7 billion people on your planet? Tell me, how do you think it looks from the more evolved being's perspective in the universe, looking at what humans are doing to animals?"

"It doesn't look good Max," said Billy.

"Humans think of themselves as superior to the animal kingdom which leads to mass exploitation," said Ting.

"Yes, Ting, this is called speciesism," replied Max.

"Humans are far from superior, humans are primitive," replied Rohan.

"To most of the animal kingdom, human beings are no different than the Nazi's," Oskar replied.

"I would go as far to say that this behaviour is actually madness, when you really stop and think about it, examine all that is going on; it really is lunacy on a mass scale." shared Nicole.

"Max, what about all the people that are working in farms, working within all these animal industries? Don't get me wrong, I agree with everything you say, but I am also thinking of the knock-on effect, it would cause so many people to be out of work."

"Very good thinking Billy, you see academia isn't necessarily required, critical thinking is just as important as any exam paper, actually it is more critical! Not that I am suggesting that you don't take exams, your mum wouldn't be very impressed; however, there are many very successful people who did not take their education all the way. Well, of course, a lot of changes will be required, with no mass animal farming new areas of natural habitat will be required to accommodate the animals.

"Not like zoos or safari parks, proper natural habitats that really meet the animal's needs. You already have national parks that do meet the needs of the animals, so you can utilise these and create new areas. There is plenty of land that has not yet been built on; actually, around 1–2% of the land on Earth is defined as 'artificial surface'; there is a lot more land that can be shared with the animals.

"The land 'owners' just need to come around to realising that the land is not theirs. It is everyone's, not just every human, every creature; you are custodians of the land. It is your responsibility to look after the land, look after the animals. So, once these new areas have been created, new fences will need to be erected and then these new areas, let's call them Earthling Wild Zones EWZ for short, would need to be managed in some way. The animals would be left to get on with their lives, but it will still require some human management."

"And where will the money come from for all this, Max?" asked Ava.

"Another excellent question, later we will cover another subject one which will create a diversion of money, but also from the people, there is enough wealth in the world to make this change, once the people of the world change their thinking, it will be easy to fund these new changes that need to take place. Once people see the enormity of the global issues, more about that later, they will be happy to contribute.

"All the animal charities in the world, especially the animal rights charities, will be able to divert their efforts to help create this new way of being. The people that are already donating billions every year would continue to donate and the money usually spent on fighting for animal rights would be spent on looking after the animals. Economies have changed in the past, they are always changing, and new industries are always emerging, just as old ones did.

"Let's look at the music and film industries. Music used to only be listened to in clubs and people gathering together to sing, then came radio, then vinyl records, then the tape recorder, then the CD, then the mp3 player and now it is streaming online. Same as the films, it was originally only live plays in theatres, then came cinemas, then TV, then video, then DVD and again now it is streaming.

"Typewriters became computers, the horse and cart became the car, so you see everything changes, like I said before you live in a life of impermanence. Industries come and go, people adapt, and human beings are very resilient and very adaptable to change when faced with new situations. Farmers could change their fields into solar farms. Another revenue is new inventive food made from plants, which would be supported by the farmers that have diverted their business from animal exploitation to growing plants.

"For example, already you have available milk made from oats, soya, coconut, almonds, cashew, rice and more. The dairy farmers can change production from cows' milk to plant milk. This gives the consumer a healthier option and more choice than they ever had without any suffering, fear or death.

"Perhaps a 'change grant' could be given to the farmers and other people in animal industries to pay for the change of production or change of job on a temporary basis until they were again earning a living. Sure, there will be some changes for many people; however, things don't ever stay the same as life is like a river going one way, changing with every moment. Nothing in life is permanent.

"Do you know how many land animals are killed just for food each year?"

"No, Max, but I don't think I am going to like the answer," replied Ozkar.

"It is estimated at around 57 billion per year. I repeat that is 57 billion every year and that doesn't include sea life."

"I can't get my head around that number, Max," said Nicole.

"It is 57 and 9 zeros'," replied Max.

"Thanks, but that doesn't really help, I guess I just need to know that it is massive!"

"Maybe this will help you, Nicole. It is around 1,800 animals per second or around 156 million per day. Another way of understanding how big a number is to look at it in seconds. 86,000 seconds is 1 day, 1 million seconds is around 12 days, 1 billion seconds is around 32 years, 57 billion seconds is around 1,800 years."

"So, if one animal was killed each second, it would take 1,800 years to kill the same number that we kill in 1 year?" asked Billy.

"That is correct," replied Max.

Everyone looked shocked, and they were still trying to fathom the numbers.

"How will we continue to look after 57 billion animals that are not being killed?" asked Jack.

"Great thinking Jack, it's very simple. Around 7 billion people won't stop eating meat overnight; the ripple effect will take some time, just as the drop in the water on a lake takes time to get to the land. The demand for meat will gradually decline, as this happens the breeding will decline and eventually there will be a manageable number of animals, for the Global EWZ foundation to organise re-introducing the animals into the wild."

Slaughterhouses

"OK, everyone, it is time we went to see a slaughterhouse in operation. This really will be one of the worst experiences for you all; however, I feel that to know the truth, you need to experience it for yourselves. If at any time you have had enough and want to leave, just raise your hand and I will teleport you back here to wait for us. Is there anyone who is totally against seeing the truth?"

No one raised their hand but they all looked a little uneasy. Billy took the hand of the friends sat on either side of him; they followed his lead and held each other's hands.

"We trust you, Max; let's do it," said Rohan bravely.

"As we all know, this is not a happy place. You are misled into thinking that the animals are killed in a 'humane' way."

Arriving outside they saw before them around 35 people standing outside holding up protest banners and placards with various messages: *Friends, not food; Their bodies, not ours; We cherish dogs but kill pigs, chickens, sheep and cows; Our planet, theirs too; Stop animal exploitation go Vegan; End all animal oppression now.*

The protest was very peaceful. A Lorry arrived with a mixture of pigs, lambs and cows. Some of the protesters walked slowly ahead of the lorry in a procession, almost like a funeral march. Some were taking pictures of the young animals, some held their placards up to show the people in the cars and passing pedestrians, why they were demonstrating.

Inside the building, before them, several cows were lined up. They were inside a high walled alley, with no room to turn around. In front was a door which opened and closed automatically. Men were prodding and pushing the next cow to go through the door. Clearly, the cow instinctively knew what was coming, Billy could smell death, so he felt sure the cows could smell it too.

Once the door was closed, you could still see the hooves of the cow that had been pushed through. The cow waiting in line was backing up and trying to escape, trying to turn around but it was impossible, there simply was no room, the alley had been designed to keep the animal forward-facing and unable to escape.

Billy could see the fear in her eyes, she knew what was coming, she was scared for her life, desperate to escape, she just kept trying to turn around and even tried to get her front legs up on the wall to escape, but it was no good, it was just too high, she didn't want to die. Billy thought to himself; what human would want to die like this, they are no different to us, we are animals too.

"Employees at these murder houses are reported to have a very high rate of depression, drug and alcohol abuse as well as suicide. The workers are either violent or have become numb to the fact that these animals feel pain, have emotions and suffer. The slaughterhouse is just a production line, care is not taken to ensure they do not suffer; actually, it seems that it is quite the opposite and some workers take pleasure in abusing the animals. Even if this was not the case, the animals are still murdered purely for your taste buds. If human toddlers that could not yet speak were in line at the slaughterhouse, they would show the same fear as the pigs, sheep and cows."

The cow beyond the door suddenly fell to the ground, it was difficult to see, but she then appeared to roll out of the trap she was in and disappear, the door opened for the next one in line to be forced through the door.

Max continued, "She is not dead yet, they stunned her with the air gun I have told you all about, she will for sure be stunned, but may well still be slightly conscious, if not, there is a chance she will come around whilst having her throat cut when she is strung up by her back leg."

Billy felt sick, he started to cry, he looked around at the others and could see that everyone was crying, even Max seemed to have tears welling up in his eyes. Max knew that was enough and that they didn't need to see the actual killing, he teleported them all back to the forest. They all breathed a sigh of relief, smelling the fresh air, seeing the beautiful green trees and plants. They all instinctively took some deep breaths to calm their emotions.

"OK, one more time everyone."

Max teleported them all and they all stood on a footpath that went along the side of a building that was heavily fenced and gated. The sounds coming from the building were horrifying, pigs screaming, not just one pig, many pigs constantly screaming. They didn't stay long maybe a minute or two, Max just wanted everyone to hear for themselves the screaming, the fear and the suffering that the six-month-old piglets were going through when being sent to their death by gassing.

"Humans share the planet with all sentient beings, for humans to realise why they should give all sentient beings their freedom, they must first see the similarities you have with them.

- You all need food and water, desire freedom and are aware of your surroundings.
- You all seek companionship and love your babies.
- You all have personalities and love to play.
- You all make friends and communicate.
- You all feel pain, experience fear and joy.
- You all cry and want to live.

"Once you all see these similarities, surely you can only do one thing; give them their freedom and give them back to the earth."

"Max, it is clear to me that we don't need more knowledge, we just need to be responsible for our own actions and stop eating fish, animals, dairy, eggs and honey," said Ava.

"The thing is Ava, most people do not know exactly what is going on, they are led to believe that animals don't suffer and that they are killed in a 'humane' way and this is simply not true. Also, the conditioning/programming runs really deep within people as it is their culture and traditions. People don't like a change of this type so they really need to feel something for them to change, just as all of you are feeling.

"On Unity, if such a thing as factory farms or slaughterhouses existed, everyone would know what went on because nobody hides anything, no one lies, no one covers up, everything is all out in the open, but sadly humans are not yet evolved enough to be completely open about everything.

"If humans do take action and change their ways, in the future there will be museums of farming, slaughterhouses and of other animal exploitations. People of the future will be shocked and sickened by what was done in the past."

"Auschwitz begins wherever someone looks at a slaughterhouse and thinks: they're only animals."

—Theodor Adorno (1903–1969)

Chapter 8

Billy didn't sleep well that night, Max arrived as usual and said that he would be back the next day and that Billy should take a day off. Billy took his bike and went for a ride in the countryside, in the woods and across fields of arable farmland. He passed various animals in fields, he felt angry that most people would see them and think they were having a natural and nice life and his mind was troubled, as he wanted to help the animals, not just watch all the suffering.

He knew that he would not be causing pain and suffering by not consuming any animal products, but he wanted to take action in some way to actively get others to know what was going on behind the walls of farms and slaughterhouses.

Billy woke the next day to find Max at the end of his bed.

"OK, Billy, I know you are very keen on nature so I thought today we could go for a walk and chat." They arrived on some hills and started to walk along a path.

The Environment

"The environment is key to the survival of nature and all life on Earth Billy. Everything is co-existing and is dependent on something, for example; plants and trees release oxygen that you breathe, you breathe out carbon dioxide, which the plants need.

Around 10,000 years ago, wild animals made up 99% of the total biomass of planet earth, human beings made up 1%. And, the land looked very different, much of it was covered in trees. "Today, human beings and the animals that you have dominion over make up 98% of the total biomass; wild animals make up 2%. Humans have stolen the earth from the free-living animals and much of the land has been cleared to grow food and keep animals. Why is this important?

Well, the balance of the environment has been altered by humans and mainly in the last 50–70 years.

"As I have mentioned before there are 500 dead zones in the seas around the world, equalling 95,000 square miles of the sea completely devoid of life, these zones will increase in number and size, if humans continue as they have been in the last 50 years. The planet's seas are great regulators of temperature and movement of heat around the world, affecting life on the land.

"The oceans are unbalanced due to many reasons, all of which are caused by humans. You all have the opportunity to save the oceans and save humanity but humans across the world have to change their daily habits. It is a very complicated and long story, to tell you everything about the oceans would take too long Billy, but here are some highlights of what is going on within your oceans. Around 70% of the earth is the ocean, and around 70% of all species on the planet are aquatic.

"Humans are dependent on the ocean for their survival because more than 50% of the oxygen you breathe comes from the oceans, imagine, Billy, more than 5 of your breaths out of 10 have been generated by the oceans, without it, there wouldn't be enough oxygen in the air to breath, the oceans are more important than most people realise. The oxygen coming from the sea is created by algae, seaweed and phytoplankton. To remind you the phytoplankton is what you could see from space Billy, the beautiful swirling shape.

"Phytoplankton are microscopic marine plants that live in oceans all over the planet. They can't be seen with the naked eye, but as you know they can be seen from space cameras when vast blooms of them are drifting in the seas. They are the life force of the oceans, so vital you cannot live without them. Not only do they produce oxygen, they also absorb carbon dioxide and are food for the zooplankton and small fish. The small fish are the food for the bigger fish."

"What does Phytoplankton eat, Max?"

"Great question Billy, you must have read my mind," Max laughed his usual raucous laugh.

"The ocean is one big circle of life Billy. The Phytoplankton feed off the poop of all the bigger creatures. Blue whales for example expel around 3 tons of poop each day; it is rich in iron and nitrogen and is basically a nutrient-rich fertiliser. So, you see Billy, the whales need the phytoplankton and the phytoplankton needs the whales. Humans and all land creatures need the whales, the phytoplankton and all the other sea life to prevent the air from reducing in oxygen.

"Oceanic PH levels and flows are essential for these invisible life forms to take in carbon dioxide, create oxygen and survive. The healthier the oceans, the more phytoplankton, fish and mammals there will be. So, where do humans come into this you might ask, one is very obvious, you take a vast amount from the sea and don't put anything back.

"In fact, you take and add a whole load of pollution, causing the oceans to be unhealthy. Fishermen complain that the whales and seals are stealing their fish, but what they don't realise is that with more mammals, there would be more phytoplankton and more fish, which in turn would make the oceans healthier."

"And surely, it's not their fish Max. It's the mammals' breakfast, lunch and dinner."

"Absolutely Billy, 70 years ago, the sea was in really good shape, the oceans were full of life and bursting with colour and in total balance; however, the sea has been depleted by up to 90% for many species. Estimates are 650,000 whales, dolphins and seals are killed every year and 90 million sharks. Sharks have been around for 400 million years, but are set to be extinct, all down to recent human devastation of the seas.

"Not only are sharks hunted for their fins that sell for $400 per pound, it is estimated that 40 million sharks are pulled out of the seas as by-catch, by so-called sustainable fishing methods. Around 90% of the top predators have gone. Around 95% of cod has gone. Around 96% of bluefin tuna has gone; they are now so scarce that in 2013, one bluefin tuna was sold in Japan for $1.7M.

"Sea turtles are one of the earth's most ancient creatures, the seven species that are around today where around 110 million years ago, unlike other turtles, they cannot retract their heads or legs so get caught in the fishing nets, they are on the endangered list, however, continue to be injured and die every day that the fishing vessels are out at sea. Shrimping has a massive impact on other sea life due to the by-catch; it makes up to 1/3 of the global by-catch and in some cases for every kg of shrimp caught there is 20 kg of by-catch. All of these big changes in aquatic life forms are having an impact on the health of the seas, which in turn has an impact for life on land.

"Fish farming was designed to be a solution to depleting fish stocks; however, it has had a knock-on effect of another kind; Fishermen target 'trash' fish, which are juvenile fish not worth catching for humans as there is little flesh on them, but they are fine to be ground up and fed to the fish on the fish farms. Four tons of wild 'trash' fish would be used to produce just 1/5 a ton of shrimp reared on a fish farm.

"Five kilos of anchovies would feed 1 kilo of salmon. The major problem with this is that the fish species that are caught as 'trash' doesn't get a chance to mature and multiply; this is devastating news for future fish numbers. Emperor penguin numbers have declined because their food 'krill' has been fished to feed farmed salmon. Each species in the ocean plays a vital role in the oceanic life cycle and is an important part of the symbiotic relationship keeping the sea in total balance.

"It's ironic Billy, the more fish farms you have the less fish you will have in the seas. More than 50% of seafood for human consumption was produced by fish farming of which China has 60% of all fish farms in the world. Around 33% of European Union fish is imported from outside the EU, where regulations are none existent, so people in the EU all think fishing is sustainable because of your local regulations but it is not, this is not a local problem, it is global.

"In the Atlantic coastal waters, menhaden fish are the 'kidneys' of the oceans. They clean the oceans and are also food for the bigger fish. They have been hunted since before Europeans landed in America; however, in more recent times, they have been caught in vast numbers to be used in food for farmed animals, dog/cat food and human health fish oil supplements."

"Why would we feed fish to animals that don't naturally eat fish?"

"For the omega 3 Billy, it is great marketing! The bizarre thing is, that the fish don't produce omega 3 naturally Billy, they get it from plants in the sea that they eat. One-third of all global fish caught is for animal feed. If you stop eating animals the demand for fish reduces immediately.

"If humans also stop eating fish, the seas have a chance to repair and to once again flourish. The Menhaden fish are at a critically low number, humans really do need to leave them, to enable them to flourish, as they help keep the oceans clean.

"Then there is dredge fishing which is destroying the seabed. This type of fishing is targeting scallops, oysters, clams, crabs and sea cucumbers that all live on the sea bed. A dredge is a big heavy steel-framed scoop, covered in metal mesh, open at one end, which scoops up whatever is on the seabed. So not only are you taking the fish you are destroying the seabed, where the plants grow.

"You dredge the same area over and over again until the seabed looks like a dessert not a flourishing sea forest as it should. In some places, you have created marine parks, these protected areas are wonderful, and they really do work when they are funded and manned, massive recovery has been achieved; however, only 1% of the ocean is protected.

"More regulations and laws will not be enough to aid the oceans to repair and thrive. If humans really want to turn it around and get the oceans back to being healthy, one thing that has to happen is that fishing has to stop; there is no such thing as sustainable fishing. It is really simple; humans need to stop eating/buying/catching fish.

"Coral reefs are vital to the overall wellness of the seas and oceans; they are the nurseries of the sea world. They make up less than 1% of the seabed but are home to around 25% of all sea life. They are dying for many reasons, as you know, the water temperature is a major reason; however, there are a few more human causes; coral mining, organic (animal poop) and nonorganic (chemicals) pollution, digging canals to gain access to island bays for tourists. Once again, humans need to leave them alone to regenerate and prosper.

"Here is another fact about animal agriculture; it is causing a big percentage of some of the world's biggest environmental issues.

"Cows burp a lot! They burp methane into the atmosphere, it is estimated that 14.5% of global CO_2 emissions are attributed to livestock burping! That's larger than the transport sector combined for all air and road. Around 20% of the Amazon rainforests have been destroyed, that's around 200 million acres since 1978. Each year another 5 million acres are being lost. Around 80% of that land is occupied by livestock or grain is grown to feed the livestock.

"The world's cattle eat enough grain to feed 9 billion people whilst there are around 1 billion malnourished people in the world. Just using a portion of the grain would feed every hungry human mouth on the planet. Around 70% of USA arable land is used to grow crops for animals, not humans. If you buy beef raised on land, it is more land-intensive, eating grass rather than grain takes up a lot of space, and they burp a lot more when eating grass, producing 40–60% more methane. There is another job for you, Billy, catching the burps and measuring the content!"

Max couldn't help himself sometimes, such a serious subject but he still liked having a joke, to make Billy laugh or turn his stomach.

"In North Carolina, USA, there are 10 million pigs, they produce the same quantity of poop and wee as 100 million humans. This poop and wee is not treated; it goes into the ground, which seeps into the water tables, in turn spilling into the rivers and seas causing massive pollution which kills the life that is living in the rivers and seas.

"Sheep dips have been found to cause soil contamination and water pollution. They contain chemical insecticides that are highly toxic to aquatic plants and animals.

"It takes over 10 times the energy of fossil fuels to produce a calorie of animal-based food than it does to produce plant food. Ten times as much water and 10 times as much land is required. It takes 2,400 gallons of water and 12 lb of grain to make 1 lb of beef. One acre of land can produce 40,000 lbs of tomatoes, 53,000 lbs of potatoes and only 137 lbs of beef.

"So you see Billy, it's not just the animal exploitation that vegans are concerned about; it is about the planet too. If the world went vegan all of the above problems will disappear – all of them.

"Everything humans are doing now is having a knock-on effect and until things change it is only going to get worse.

"If you were in a boat with many holes, all different sizes; and you were sinking which hole would you deal with first, Billy?"

"That's easy Max, the biggest hole."

"Precisely, which is why animal agriculture and fishing is the first thing mankind needs to focus on to slow down the pollution as quickly as possible. It is quite simple; humanity needs to wake up and stop eating animals and animal products."

"Max what about other industries that are responsible for pollution?"

"We will cover the environment in more detail another time Billy; however, your topic of choice was animals, so I am just giving you the animal side of the environment story. The single biggest thing an individual person can do to have a positive impact on the environment is to stop consuming animal products, it is also the easiest thing to change."

Chapter 9

Health

Max and Billy continued to walk. "It's not just about animal abuse and the environment. Eating animal products is having a negative impact on human health. Discoveries prove there is a direct link between food and health. Billy, I know at 12 years old, health is not something you think about but if you look at the massive rise of the chronic diseases that are taking people's lives very early or causing long-term pain and suffering, the rises coincide with the increased meat, dairy, egg and processed food consumption.

"Bear with me on this subject Billy as it is very relevant and important to why humans need to stop eating their animal friends. It also coincides with the increased use of antibiotics and pesticides in addition to the pollution that is now in the water tables and air. Diseases that I am sure your family have experienced, or maybe your family friends or neighbours, such as heart disease, cancer, diabetes, obesity, high blood pressure, strokes and dementia.

"Around 40% of Americans are obese and 50% of Americans are on prescription drugs and the UK and many other countries are following right behind the footsteps of the Americans. The answer isn't another pill or moving the responsibility to your doctor, the answer is the food that you eat. Eliminate refined, processed and all animal foods, as well as other toxins you can prevent and sometimes reverse these diseases.

"Your medical systems are treating disease, it needs to evolve to prevent disease through diet, exercise and lifestyle as this will save trillions of dollars, which is another revenue stream that can support the future changes on planet Earth.

In the USA, pharmaceutical companies put more money into political lobbying than any other industry. Why?

"Because they make so much money from the drugs given to the animals, and the diseased people, they have to bribe the political system to keep things under the radar of the general population. By eliminating heart disease in the USA, it would save over $300 billion, in the UK it would save around £7 billion. Around 80% of antibiotics that are manufactured in the USA are made specifically for animals—animals that are perfectly healthy. As I have said before, they are given antibiotics because disease spreads easily when so many animals are kept in such filthy facilities and in close proximity. Animals in the wild do not need antibiotics.

"Diverting spending from expensive medical procedures to the education of eating what Mother Nature provided would create a healthier and happier population.

"Eating a plant-based diet the world over would cut healthcare costs by 70/80%. In addition to medications in the USA, people spend $50 billion on vitamin and mineral supplements. That's a huge amount of revenue for the supplement manufacturers, which people would not need if they just ate the right foods, because all the vitamins and minerals are found in plant foods.

"Imagine Billy what could be done if that money was diverted to new ideas, new systems to make the world a better place. And, it would feed the hungry people of the world.

"Let food be thy medicine"

—Hippocrates (460 BC–370 BC)

"The doctor of the future will no longer treat the human with chemical drugs but rather cure and prevent disease with nutrition."

—Thomas Edison (1847–1931)

"All those years ago both Hippocrates and Edison were correct, there are some doctors who are now looking at food and lifestyle choices and working closely with patients rather than giving another prescription for medication and they are having remarkably positive results with patients coming off medications and diseases going into remission.

"Seafood is portrayed as the healthier option compared to land animal flesh. However, seafood is contaminated with so many chemicals and waste. The fish are full of mercury and PCBs which humans then consume."

"Why is that bad for humans, Max?"

"Mercury is toxic which gets into the sea from pollution in rivers from human activity. Algae absorb mercury, algae is the bottom of the food chain, tiny fish eat algae, then fish eat the tiny fish, bigger fish eat the fish that has eaten the tiny fish and so on. The toxic cocktail in the bigger fish is compounded as they absorb the toxins that were in their dinner. Tuna for example will have higher toxins because they are larger predatory fish. Humans then absorb the mercury and other toxins."

"Max, I read once that mercury is deposited from volcanoes, so I guess it gets into the rivers and seas too?"

"It does, however, natural releases of mercury are not within the control of humans and anthropogenic releases have increased mercury quantities in the oceans threefold in recent years."

"What does anthropogenic mean?"

"Originating in human activity."

"So why is mercury bad for humans?"

"Mercury consumption in all ages of humans can result in peripheral vision loss, weakened muscles, impairment of hearing and speech and deteriorated movement coordination. Infants and developing children face even more health risks because mercury exposure inhibits proper brain and nervous system development, damaging memory, cognitive thinking, language abilities, attention and fine motor skills. Max continued.

"Farmed fish are given antibiotics and pesticides, due to the overcrowded conditions and salmon are given a synthetic pigment to turn their flesh from grey to pink. Humans that eat fish are absorbing the antibiotics and pesticides.

"The impact of these toxins builds up slowly in humans, and the symptoms may be subtle and gradually get worse, so no one would ever consider it was the food slowly poisoning them."

"I want to show you the potential futures ahead of your generation. Would you like to go to the future, Billy?"

Billy's eyes widen and he was grinning, "Are you kidding me; of course, I would love to experience that Max."

"I thought you might like that, Billy." Max was grinning too.

"OK, here we go." Max put his hands on both of Billy's shoulders, a bubble appeared around them, and they seemed to be floating just off the ground. They slowly started spinning, they went faster and faster until they were spinning so fast Billy couldn't even tell they were spinning, the spin became stillness, a bit like in the eye of a storm, you would never know there was a storm happening. A few moments later they were in the future.

"What year is it, Max?"

"2053."

"What is that smell?"

"It's the smell of death and disease, Billy."

The wind was strong and the sun was burning very hot. Billy could see people and animals that looked like they hadn't eaten in weeks. Cars were abandoned everywhere, windows in the buildings were all smashed, the land was arid, the trees were bare and dying. Billy sat down to observe the ground, he was looking for ants.

"The ants are still alive Billy, but they have had to dig deeper into the earth and come up to the surface less often."

"This is devastating Max, this is all because man has continued on the same path of consuming all the creatures and abusing the earth?"

"Yes, Billy, as well as other damaging industries, that have been polluting your home which we will talk about another time. This is what happens if man does not wake up to the harsh reality of your collective actions."

Max took Billy into another spin, they arrived in the identical spot they had just left, Billy knew it was the same place as he could see the hills in the distance. He could see happy smiling faces, chilled out people having fun and laughter, the sun was shining and the land was bursting with plant life. Max teleported Billy to a hillside, he could see animals in nature, many different species all living in harmony together.

"This is a new EWZ, it was a wonderful transition from abuse to compassion, but this is only a potential future Billy, there is much work to be done for this to become a reality. OK, Billy, let's go further into the potential future."

The spin lasted a little longer than the last two, but moments later they had arrived. They were in a city.

"This is London, Billy."

The only sound was the wind; there were no people, or cars or police sirens. Windows and doors were all open or smashed, the pavement had plants and trees growing up through the cracks, there was rubbish flying around everywhere. London was totally deserted. They started walking along the road.

"Where is everyone?"

"They are all dead, Billy; humanity ate themselves to extinction. People didn't take personal responsibility, they didn't think they could make a difference, many thought it was the government's responsibility to fix things. People got sicker; they expected expert scientists to come up with new medications. The animals got sicker too, it was awful to watch the poor innocent animals, they got sicker because of the long-term effects of the intensive farming practices, the antibiotics, and the processed feed with the ground-up fish.

"What they needed to eat was nature's menu, not a man-made product. Life in the seas continued to decline, as did the nutrients in the soil and the water became more and more polluted which made it harder and harder to grow fruit, vegetables and grains. The seas eventually became totally empty; the water was foul and polluted. Without the sea life keeping the water balanced, it became toxic for people to swim in. Industry all around the world collapsed, people lost their jobs with no new industries to follow because everything around was dying, it was a downward spiral.

"The natural disasters became more violent and regular, water and food became scarce which led to people's behaviour to change towards each other and all of humanity was once again in survival mode. It was a long road to the demise of all earthlings. Humans saw themselves as separate from the animals, more advanced, more important.

"So, you see Billy, you are animals, that's what you are, not different to cows or pigs, you all need nature to survive, you all need the air to breathe. Without nature or air, you all die; you are all one, you are all part of Mother Earth, not separate."

Back in Billy's room. "Humans are the only species that does not live in harmony with nature. Change is perceived to be difficult, but it is liberating. If humans liberate all beings, you will in turn liberate yourselves. Humans are stewards of the planet, not owners, it was the past generation's responsibility to pass it on to you in good shape but sadly they have made a really bad job of it.

"So, it's tough for your generation, but at the same time, it will be an amazing time of change, which will bring new prosperity, new health and happiness to the people of the earth if people wake up. This is the next step of evolution Billy, for humans to realise that it is the responsibility of each and every one of you to be good stewards of the planet, the animals and each other."

The next day Max arrived as usual. "Yesterday we went to possible futures Billy, how would you like to go to the past?"

"Of course, Max, I would love that, where are we going?"

"It's a surprise, Billy," Max repeated the process of slowly spinning around gradually getting faster and faster, except this time, they were spinning in the opposite direction.

Before him, Billy could see the pyramids in Egypt, as always, he was speechless, eyes wide taking in all that he could. It was just as he expected, the women in long white linen dresses, men in loincloths. The towering carved stone statues of gods and the buildings with grand columns and entrances. There was a festival taking place, people were sitting on tables playing board games, children were juggling balls and running around laughing having fun.

Many faces were covered in green and black makeup. The women wore lots of gold jewellery. The atmosphere was like nothing Billy had ever experienced. Unusually Max didn't talk, he just sat quietly while Billy watched all the people, singing and laughing.

"Max, I have a question. If we can visit the past, surely can we change some events that would stop the animal exploitation and change the course of humanity?"

"This is not possible Billy, even if we did change some things, animal exploitation has been growing since the days man invented tools, so the only way to really stop it, would be for man not to have evolved at all. The only way forward is for man to continue on the evolutionary path. The only way is to change the present and as you know, that means man evolving emotionally and to feel the immorality of the domination and exploitation of the animal kingdom."

"Nothing will benefit human health and increase chances for survival of life on Earth as much as the evolution to a vegetarian diet."

—Albert Einstein (1879–1955)

Chapter 10

The next day, Max gathered everyone on a hilltop with stunning views far and wide. It was a beautiful day, not a cloud in the sky, the air was fresh and a slight breeze was blowing. Billy felt they were high up and he could smell a sweet floral scent coming up from the valley below. Billy felt free when he was in nature, especially when he was with his new friends.

"As you all know, I have many more friends here on planet earth, I would like to now bring you together with another group that has been getting to know each other."

Appearing from nowhere was a group of smiling young people all standing together—everyone started mingling and introducing themselves to each other. Billy met many more new friends. Tala was from the Philippines; she was very beautiful and had long flowing hair. Tuan was from Vietnam, he was short with a beaming smile. Zeynep was from Turkey, she was very chilled out. Min-Seo was from South Korea; she wore glasses and had a bobbed haircut that was beautifully shiny and jet black.

Sven was from the Netherlands he was tall with blonde hair and bright blue eyes. Dinis from Portugal had shoulder-length brown curly hair and beautifully bronzed skin. Rina from Israel had a beaming smile. Freja from Denmark had short dark spiky hair and a few freckles across her nose. Dimitrij from Slovenia was very stocky, Khayone from South Africa was very tall and slim and had big beautiful deep brown eyes, Lars from Norway was also tall and slim and Alice from Canada had very long red hair tied in a ponytail.

"Humans have been evolving for thousands of years. What was acceptable and normal in the past is now considered unacceptable and barbaric in many nations." Max waved his hand, a bubble opened up, like a big cinema screen.

It was a man being hanged, there were crowds of people cheering and shouting. The man was standing on a wooden platform around 6 feet above the ground. His hands were tied behind his back with the rope around his neck which was tied to the gallows above him. The trap door that he was standing on suddenly opened; he dropped a couple of feet through the hole and shook for several minutes before becoming still.

"Humans could be hanged not that long ago in the UK—the last hangings where in August 1964, it was then banned in 1965. In Australia, it was 1985; however, it is still used in some countries as a standard form of capital punishment, which goes to show how the ripple effect takes time, these countries will eventually follow the lead of the countries that have outlawed this barbaric killing."

Max waved his hand again, a woman was tied to a wooden pole, her hands were high above her head and her feet were also fastened. There were lots of logs around her feet, a man started lighting the wood, the flames started rising licking at her feet, and after a few minutes, the flames were surrounding her whole body as she screamed and writhed in pain.

"In the UK, women were burned at the stake until 1790 for being found guilty of witchcraft. This still goes on in your world; however, it is rare, and generally, it is murder rather than capital punishment. Not only were women burned at the stake, in Europe in the Middle Ages, but also cats were associated with the devil and witches and were also burned at the stake. By the beginning of the fourteenth century the cat population was very low, some scholars noted that the depletion of the cats is what caused the bubonic plague to ravage humans in Europe because the cats were not around to eat the rats, it was the fleas on the rats that spread the plague."

The last wave of Max's hand depicted the American slave trade; many African men and women were chained at the feet and were forced to work very hard and long hours in the cotton fields.

"Until 1865, people actually bought human slaves, they 'owned' them. They gave them meagre food and shelter, and they were often whipped and tortured for not doing exactly as they were told. You now all consider this absolutely immoral, utter madness and unacceptable behaviour. It is a very similar treatment to animal slavery in your farms, circuses and other animal exploitation all over the world.

"Underworld criminal human slavery and other barbaric acts still happen in your world today, but more about that another time. Humans are still evolving, in 100 years many things that are normal and accepted today will be considered immoral and primitive. As I have explained before cultures and traditions have changed in the past and will continue to change.

"Many humans do not think about evolution and think that 'this is how it is', that you have reached the finish line into what you are. That is not correct, nothing is permanent; the universe is expanding and changing; the earth is evolving and life on earth is changing. However, it is changing so slowly that in your reality you cannot see it or feel it changing. This time on planet Earth is at a critical point, the changes that have been occurring over the 60–70 years are having a massively detrimental effect and if things don't change, you won't have another 60 years.

"Humans are a very young species; modern man has been around 200,000 years. The big bang was almost 14 billion years ago and if the universe had been around just 1 year, humans turned up on 31 December at 11:59:59 and in less than 100 years humans have done an immense amount of damage to other humans, to all other creatures sharing this beautiful planet and the planet itself. Something has to change, if not, humans will be extinct. It is out of control, but if you all start taking responsibility, then humans can turn this around."

"So Max, how do we get people to stop being the demand that is creating all this suffering?" asked Nicole.

"Well, it starts with awareness and the only way to create more awareness is to share your own. What I need you all to do is to speak to people. Open their eyes, their minds and hearts to allow them to reprogram themselves and change your cultures."

"How do we do that Max, I don't know anyone?" asked Billy.

"You have 1,200 people at school, Billy."

"Oh yea, how am I going to talk to them, I am the weird one, remember." Everyone laughed, with Billy.

"And once you have done that Billy, you need to talk at events where there are many people."

"WHAT? You want us, to talk to big groups of people?"

"Billy, you can't force people to change their thinking, but what you can do is to show them what's really going on in the world, show them the lunacy and the only way to do that is to talk to them."

"But Max, I don't talk to people, I have not got a clue what I would say."

"Don't worry about that Billy I have a plan, the secret is sharing everything, through love and compassion."

"Billy, you came across as confident when I met you," said Kemala.

"Yea, I agree," said Ting.

"Why can't someone just put it on TV? Everyone watches TV Max?" asked Lucy.

"Because what goes out on TV is highly controlled, our messages will not be 'approved' by TV bosses. Also, if I hack into the TV channels which I can do, I could easily get a message to broadcast to all TV's across the world, but people will think that it is the message of one crazy person and will not be taken notice of. However, a bunch of teenagers like yourselves, that can see what is going on and reach the hearts of the people will have more of a chance of waking people up to what is going on."

"OK, Max, I trust you." said Billy.

"It will be fine Billy, what's the worst that could happen? Billy all you need to do is to invite people to stop and think about the information you are sharing with them. Sharing vital information for everyone to consider and discuss together to conclude if you should all observe your individual and collective behaviours, which for the most part have been conditioned/programmed into you from a very early age.

"We talked about the ripple effect earlier, the more people that are talking about this, the more that people will start to wake up to the fact that this is what is happening and will want to join in. We haven't really talked about the collective consciousness that much, imagine that humans are like mobile phones constantly uploading and downloading information. Everything is energy; you are all connected to each other energetically, just like when I take you to places around the world.

"So, everything you think is being transmitted to the collective energy stream, let's call it the energy matrix. So, the more people that are seeing and hearing what is going on in animal agriculture and other animal exploitations, the more those thoughts are being transmitted, the more other people will be starting to think about the subject or will be ready to have their eyes opened.

"It's the same for anything, everything is happening in the world due to the collective thoughts of everyone on the planet. It's very complicated and I know it is hard to get your heads around this, but trust me, your awareness isn't yet at the extent of understanding that your individual thoughts create your reality and the sum total of 7 billion people's thoughts are all creating what is happening in the world. Some people are aware of this, but the vast majority of people are not."

That night as Billy was drifting off to sleep, he kept repeating the names of the new people he had met and imagined their faces, he really wanted to remember everyone's name when they met again and was looking forward to seeing how they were going to communicate to the world, even though the thought of himself talking filled him with dread. He smiled himself to sleep that night, thinking about all his new friends and the up and coming events.

The next day, Max gathered everyone together. Billy couldn't believe his eyes, this time there were many more young people, he guessed around two hundred in total. He was standing with his new friends whom he had personally met.

"OK, we are now ready to start working together to communicate to the world and to your individual countries. There is one of you from each country; however, we have three of you from both China and India because you make up around 40% of the global population. The United States of America consume 20% of the killed animals and have the highest production of milk in the world, closely followed by India, so the USA also has three of you to spread the message.

"This isn't about blaming the biggest consumers of pigs or fish or milk, you are all in this together; human beings on planet earth, you all need to stand together, think about the impact you are having on the future and come up with new systems to ensure the world's people are fed and watered without continuing to decimate the planet and murdering other sentient beings. There are too many of you to get to know each other, which is why we have many groups. You can support each other within your group, sharing ideas and knowledge.

"We will organise many appearances at many sporting events, music concerts, festivals and cultural events. From the information you have recently learned, each of you need to come up with speeches to share with your people. Working within your groups, you will all have slightly different messages to deliver as your countries have different traditions, although many of the issues are global, such as the depletion of the seas and the death of animals for food.

"Practice with your family and friends, talk at your schools; share with them what you have learned.

"If your generation does not change the direction of humanity, world disasters will get worse and more frequent. Water will become more scarce; the soil will become more nutrient-poor; food will become scarce; more people will die; more fighting will happen; and so your behaviour will become more primitive as you will all be in survival mode. There are nearly 1 billion people suffering from hunger in the world and 350 children die from starvation every hour; that is every hour of every day, 350 children hungry then dead.

"That's over 3 million children dying every year, through lack of food and water. Is that the world that everyone wants? You feed 57 billion animals that you will eat when there are a billion people hungry, does that makes sense to any of you?" No one said anything. "To change everything, everyone needs to change and I know that you all are going to make some pretty amazing changes in the world.

"You may all feel that it is a mountain to climb, influencing 7 billion people, but it will happen, it's already happening, all you need to do is to speed up the process. I have been working on this for some time now and I know that you are the right team to do the job, so please, all of you, trust in yourself and in each other—KNOW that you WILL make a difference in the world."

The next day, Billy got dressed in his school uniform. He had decided that he had to overcome his fears and speak at the assembly class first thing in the morning. Max arrived as usual.

"I see you have decided to go to school, Billy?"

"Yes Max, it has to be done, as you said; what is the worst that can happen? They already think I am weird, so I have nothing to lose, only something to gain."

"You will be brilliant Billy, see you later."

Billy arrived at school early and hid behind the school curtain on the stage of the main hall. Everyone started to arrive and as the hall started to fill, Billy's tummy tightened and his heart started beating fast, his thoughts going around and around about the reaction he thought he might receive from his peers at school. He imagined them all booing him off stage and laughing at him. As his thoughts went all over the place, his mouth was getting dryer and he even started to feel a little shaky and sick.

He heard Max's voice, "Billy, breath deep and slow. They will love you. Just be yourself."

Billy looked around but couldn't see Max anywhere. "Where are you, Max?"

"I'm with you, Billy, you just can't see me, I am always with you. Rather than worry about the outcome which is a fear of 'what if' of the future, think about what it is you are going to say or think positive thoughts, positive thoughts create positive outcomes, just as negative thoughts create negative outcomes. Remember to mantra."

"OK, Max, thanks."

Billy started a mantra in his mind 'this will be fine, they will be nicely surprised, this will be fine, they will be nicely surprised' Billy repeated this many times until his heart rate lowered, his tummy felt better and he was calm. It was something Max taught him to do in preparation for speaking. Once the hall was full, a teacher walked in and up the steps to the stage. Billy walked out in full view of everyone. He stood at the front of the stage and just started talking.

"Good morning everyone. Some of you may know me, I am Billy. I am a bit of a loner and don't have any friends here at school. You may have noticed that I have not been around recently, that is because I am now home-schooling as I want to learn about things that are not on the curriculum. I am studying the planet, the creatures and the way the world really is. I have come here today to share some of what I have learned with you."

Billy looked at the teacher as if asking permission to continue, the teacher nodded in acceptance, Billy continued. "The planet is our home; it is also the home of every living thing, from ants to elephants and everything in-between. Humans are causing devastation all over the globe, from deforestation to polluting the seas. The oceans are dying for many reasons, one of which is that 90% of the fish stocks have all been fished which has a massive impact on the ecosystem. It's a long story, but 50% of our oxygen comes from the oceans, which will, in the future be massively reduced due to the ecosystem failing.

"Once oxygen levels in the air that we breathe get to below 10% we won't be able to breathe, we will all die and take all other species with us. Another major impact on life on earth is the animal holocaust that is happening all over the world right now. Around 1,800 animals are being killed every single second, I repeat, that is 1,800 every second.

"For every word, I speak another 1,800 gone, bred into existence to be murdered when they are still toddlers; all for our taste buds. They live miserable existences and very often have painful mutilations carried out when they are babies; teeth clipped and tails chopped off to name just two and some animals don't even meet their mummies, some are taken away soon after birth. They all have a very fearful often incredibly painful death.

"We are told that they are killed 'humanely' this is not true. I ask you all today to think about whether you feel it is morally right or justifiable to confine, torture, mutilate and gas or violently stun before killing any other living creature; just for our pleasure.

"Let's think also for a moment about our cats and dogs, you love them, you cuddle them, they love and cuddle you back, they are no different to piglets, lambs, calves or baby chicks.

"If the world stopped eating animals, the planet would start to heal. We are polluting the earth with the animal's burps, this is methane, there are so many animals on the planet that have been bred to feed us, and they are the single biggest contributor to the bad gasses in the earth's upper atmosphere. Animal poop is one of the biggest pollutants going into our rivers and seas, causing 500 dead zones in the rivers and seas all around the world.

"A dead zone means where nothing exists, zero life. We are eating ourselves to extinction. You may ask yourself 'what can I do? I can't make a difference I am just one person'. If everyone thinks like that, we will become extinct. If everyone takes responsibility for their actions, then it will make a massive difference. We have a chance to change the course of our future each and every one of us, we have to try.

"This is a revolution; a revolution for life; a revolution of evolution. We can make a difference, our generation needs to be the change; and you can be the change you want to see in the world. Until very recently I ate animal flesh, milk products, eggs and honey.

"I then learned everything I have shared with you and more and I just could not be a part of it anymore. It really isn't that big a deal to remove these from your plate, please stop eating fish, meat, dairy, eggs and honey. Go vegan as a step towards the change that our planet desperately needs."

Everyone started clapping and cheering, they all stood up. Billy had his first speech and his first standing ovation. His body was tingling all over with goosebumps. He smiled, he looked into the eyes of his classmates, they looked at him with admiration, not fear. Billy couldn't believe how easy it was; it just flowed out of him as if it wasn't even him.

The teacher walked over and shook his hand, smiled and said, "How would you like to come back another day to share more of what you are learning, Billy?"

Billy almost could not speak but managed to say, "Yes sir, thank you, I would like that."

Billy left the hall buzzing, his body felt light, he couldn't stop smiling, his head was held high.

Later that day Max gathered Billy's group together to enable them to talk and help each other prepare themselves for the communications. They all spent a lot of time discussing which specific area they would focus on outside of the main message.

"OK, guys and girls, who wants to go first?" Max asked.

For a few moments, no one raised their hand; eventually, Lucy did.

"Great, thanks, Lucy. What do you want to focus on?"

"Well, Max, as you know in Dallas we eat out a lot, so I thought I would speak about how vegan food is just the same as our traditional food nowadays, I have been doing some research and it is pretty amazing what food is available. I would also like to include that we are eating ourselves to extinction and destroying nature and all other creatures as well as the animal holocaust that is going on every second of every day."

"OK, great, I would like you all to stand behind Lucy. I am going to open a holographic portal to an event in your home town, everyone at the event will be able to see you all, and you will be able to see the event, but you will actually be a holographic projection."

Everyone started chattering excitedly about how incredible this sounded. Moments later they were ready for their first holographic event. The event was at an American football match in Dallas, Texas, where over 90,000 people were expected to attend.

"OK, Lucy, are you ready?"

"As ready as I will ever be Max."

"Great, I will count you down from 3, OK... 3, 2, 1 you are live."

The portal opened up, it surrounded them all, they could see in front of them the stadium and the audience. The game hadn't started yet.

"Hello, Dallas," Lucy called loudly. "My name is Lucy; my home town is Dallas. Today we are here to share an important message with you all. We are eating ourselves to extinction. That sounds dramatic, but trust me it is the truth. The fish in the world's seas are almost gone; we have taken 90% of the fish in the world's seas.

"This has a dramatic effect on the ecosystem, which we are all dependent upon for 50% of the oxygen in our air, if we don't do something about it soon, we will not be able to stop the inevitable; that our air won't have enough oxygen for us to breath, we will all die. Added to this the 57 billion land animals the world breed for food are polluting our water tables with toxic waste and our atmosphere with harmful methane. I ask you all to go home and research it yourself, look it up there is plenty of information on the internet.

"Animals feel pain, joy and fear just like we do, so please ask yourself, is it morally right that we take the life of another being for our pleasure? So, how can we personally impact the biggest challenge that human beings will ever have to face?

"To start, it really is quite simple. Remove meat, fish, eggs, milk and honey from your plates for good. Instead, buy vegan food; there is so much choice here in the USA for vegan food. We can have everything we like, milk that is made for humans not calves with many choices of flavour, oat, almond, coconut, soya, cashew and the bonus is that it is healthier for humans than cow's milk; it has zero lactose, zero cholesterol and is lower in fat and sugar.

"We have burgers that really have the same texture as ground-up cow flesh, nothing like the original veggie or bean burgers that came out many years ago. We have scrambled egg that tastes just the same as egg made from mung bean. Mac and cheese, spaghetti bolognese, lasagne, stir-fry's and many other Chinese dishes, curry's, burritos, nachos, fajitas, tacos, cupcakes, muffins, cheesecake, chocolate cake, chocolate and sweets.

"It is surprising how these vegan versions are really rather lovely. Meat is not good for our health or the environment, we all need to stop and consider the impact we are having on the planet.

"Reasons to go vegan:

- Zero animal suffering that you as an individual are paying for
- Less pollution in our water tables and atmosphere
- Increasing fish quantities in our seas which will in time once again flourish
- It is better for your heart
- You will prevent or even reverse diseases and maybe come off medication
- You will have more energy
- Less water usage, it takes an enormous amount of water to feed and raise animals

"Be a part of saving our species, if we all do nothing, we will become extinct. There is no plan B, we do not have another planet to go to."

Lucy and the group started chanting:

- Go Vegan for the animals
- Go Vegan for the planet
- Go Vegan for your health
- Go Vegan to save humanity
- Go Vegan for the animals
- Go Vegan for the planet
- Go Vegan for your health
- Go Vegan to save humanity

Whilst Lucy was talking, Max had opened up a separate portal which was like a cinema screen with cartoons depicting everything she had been talking about, empty seas, farmed animals in factory farms all crammed in together, all the foods that she was describing and all the reasons to go vegan. It was incredibly powerful, Lucy words, the picture screen and the group chanting.

It was silence in the stadium, then lots of chatter. The stadium had recorded the speech and started to replay it on the large screens.

Max closed the portals. All of Lucy's friends cheered, clapped and congratulated her for the first speech.

"Thank you, Lucy, for going first and well done! Who is next?" said Max.

Pedro stepped forward. "I would like to focus on the rainforest Max."

"OK, great, ready, 3, 2, 1 you are live." Max opened up the portal again. The scene was another football match.

"People of Brazil, we come with an important message for you all. The rainforest is the lifeblood of the world, 20% of the Amazon rainforests have been destroyed, that is around 200 million acres since 1978, and each year, another 5 million acres are being lost. I live in the rainforest; it is our home, my family and friends, we all depend on the forest for our food, water and homes.

"Around 80–90% of the land that has been decimated is occupied by livestock or grain is grown to feed the livestock. The world's cattle eat enough grain to feed 9 billion people yet there are almost 1 billion malnourished people in the world, just using a portion of the grain would feed every hungry human mouth on the planet. Around 50% of our oxygen comes from the seas that have also been decimated. The oceans are dying, if the oxygen from the forest and seas reduces to a critical level, we won't be able to breathe. What can you do about that I hear you asking yourselves?

"We have to stand up to the big corporations and say no more decimating the forest, it is home to thousands of species not just humans. Stop eating meat, fish, dairy and eggs; tell your friends and family, we all need to change our thinking which will change our actions and consumption. We need to replant the trees that have gone so that we have a two-pronged plan to ensure we are all able to breathe in the future.

"All human beings on earth need to take action and talk to everyone they know. Please do your bit, if everyone does this, we can change the course of our future. It's not just about the future oxygen, there is an animal holocaust going on as I speak. 1,800 animals every single second worldwide are being killed, just for our pleasure.

"They feel pain and fear just like we do. They feel compassion just like we do. They are babies and toddlers when they are killed and have a desire to live a full natural life, just like we do. Please take action, think about what difference we can all make to ensure human life continues on planet earth, talk about it together and take action together. Please spread this message far and wide."

The group chanted:

- Forest for wild species not land for imprisoned animals
- Forest for wild species not land for imprisoned animals
- Forest for wild species not land for imprisoned animals
- Forest for wild species not land for imprisoned animals
- Forest for wild species not land for imprisoned animals

Again, Max had cartoon pictures of the forest before and after they started decimating it, starving people, dying oceans, suffering animals and animal carcasses hanging upside down dead.

Max closed the portal. Everyone clapped "Thank you, Pedro, great work. One more for today, who would like to go next?"

Jack stepped forward. "I would like to communicate about bullfighting Max."

"OK, ready, 3 2 1 you are live." Before them was a full stadium with a bullfight in action.

"STOP, please STOP. People of Spain. What are we doing? The Bull doesn't want to fight. He is not a fighter, it is us the human being that is the fighter. We have been brainwashed by our parents, them from their parents that this is normal behaviour. This is barbaric and is no different than putting an unarmed human slave in the ring with a tiger or lion; we would not find this acceptable. Animals are the same as us.

"They feel pain just like us, they feel fear just like us. They cry just like us. They want to live just like us. Imagine if beings from another planet watched this, they would see us as savages. What right do we have to torture this magnificent beast purely for our entertainment? Imagine that in the ring it was your brother or your son, fighting for his life, how would that make you feel? Have you ever asked yourself if this is OK and is this morally acceptable?

"Please think about this, please stop coming to these events, if no one came, they would be a thing of the past. We can replace this insanity with a festival celebrating this beautiful animal, we can all come together and dance in this stadium. We are an evolving species; this is part of our evolution, to respect each and every species and allow them to live a full life. Please think about this; please stop attending these barbaric events."

The cartoons were of men in the ring with no weapons and a fully alert, non-tortured bull. He was peacefully standing doing nothing, showing clearly that the bull was not naturally violent. Very young children sat with comical contraptions on their heads being brainwashed, a man dressed in nothing but a thong fighting a lion, a spaceship with beings watching the savage behaviour, a bull in pain, fearful and crying then a festival in the ring with all the people dancing around a big statue of the iconic bull.

The group chanted:

- Now is the time for change—time to end animal violence
- Now is the time for change—time to end animal violence
- Now is the time for change—time to end animal violence
- Now is the time for change—time to end animal violence
- Now is the time for change—time to end animal violence

The portal closed. Everyone clapped Jack. "Another great message, great job Jack," said Max.

Chapter 11

The next day, they all arrived at the same place ready for some of the others to communicate to their countries, but Max had a surprise for them all. "OK, everyone, today I thought we could have a day off, you can all do anything you like as individuals or in groups, discuss amongst yourselves what you would like to do and I will take you there."

Billy's group discussed what they wanted to do and decided to visit Unity again. So, Max advised them to all stand huddled together with their arms around each other, he then took them on the journey back to Unity. This time the ride was even more enjoyable, as they all knew what to expect so could take it all in a little bit more than the first time. The colours were even brighter in the wormhole than before.

Billy remembered, the streams of colour were changing, sometimes more red, sometimes more green sometimes more purple and colours not seen on Earth. The feeling of weightlessness was the same but somehow felt different being huddled together with his friends. Everyone had huge grins on their faces and their eyes were wide.

Billy noticed that if he focused hard enough, he could see through the colours. They were passing through space; he could see millions of bright stars, planets, moons and suns. He could see space dust and weird shapes in the distance and things he couldn't even name or describe, as they were not like anything he had ever seen. It was strange, although they were travelling at unimaginable speeds, everything he could see past the colours of the wormhole was still, it was as if they were travelling in slow motion.

Arriving in Unity, everyone took a deep breath as they took in the colours and the beauty around them. They were on a small hilltop looking down on a town, the people were all laughing and relaxed going about their day.

"People here do whatever it is they want to do. They are educated in such a different way that everyone finds a path that they really love, whether that is teaching, building, cooking, art, music, drama and more. There are no exams here, people just do what they love doing and if you do what you love doing, generally you are very good at it.

"There is something for everyone here on Unity and if you change your mind and want to try something else you can, anything is possible. We know that for a peaceful life, we all have to share our time, share our knowledge and share the wealth of the planet with everyone. We are all part of this planet; without the planet we would not be here. We have an equal opportunity to be happy and to do as we please.

"The land does not belong to anyone; we look after the land to pass it on to the next generation. All the fruits and vegetables are grown naturally by nature, they spread their seeds and everyone is able to help themselves. Farming does not exist as it does on Earth, it is not necessary. There is enough for everyone, just as there is enough on planet earth for you all."

A man was teaching a girl. She seemed to be really focused on an empty space in front of her, her hands looked as if they were holding a ball, but there was nothing there, her eyes were closed.

"Max, what is going on down there?" Anahira pointed to the girl and man.

"Oh, he is teaching her about energy, she has probably made something invisible and is now trying to make it visible. On Unity, we do not have greed or the need for acquiring things, we can have whatever we like, as we do not have the very rich and the very poor because there is no 'owning' land or resources. There is enough of everything for everyone.

"We all know what each other is thinking and feeling, so if someone is feeling a little confused or down, plenty of people are around to help and talk about it. We think and act as if we are all one, actually we are all one and we are part of this planet. Our ways of doing things are first and foremost with the land and the people in mind; therefore, there is no need for politicians, no need for armies and no need for nations or religions.

"All of these things cost a lot of money on planet earth, without them, there would be even more for everyone; if only people on planet earth could all be transparent and true and think and act for the good for all. This is why the next step in your evolution is so important because if you are all to treat each other as equals, first you have to see that every living being is equal."

People were playing music as others sat on the gleaming grass listening and watching, smiling and enjoying the buzz of the people around them. A man was sat painting the scene of the musicians and the audience.

"This has a feeling of a really nice chilled out festival," said Zeynep.

"This is life on Unity," replied Max. The buildings were out of this world, they were crazy shapes and colours, clearly whoever designed them had a great imagination. The air was clean, the sky was bright, it really seemed like paradise thought Billy.

The next day, they all gathered, and they were all excited about doing more speeches around the world.

Rohan was first up. Max opened the portal.

"3 2 1 you are live." Before them was a large temple, thousands of people had come to celebrate an annual festival.

"People of India, please listen up, we have a message for you all. The Cow is sacred to us, we honour the cow and do not kill the cow, but we drink the milk of the cow because it is so revered. We now have industrial milking factories here in India. These modern facilities do not care about the cow, they do not honour the cow. Their female babies are taken away from them as soon as they are born and will become a milk machine, just like their mums.

"The boys are sent for slaughter, as they do not produce milk. Cows in the modern dairy industry are constantly made to get pregnant to ensure that she always has milk, often this is done by artificial insemination, which is effectively rape. She really suffers as she is milked every day until she can no longer give milk, this is not natural for her as in the wild she would not be producing milk every day of her life.

"Once she has had around 5 years of forced pregnancy and continuous milking, she will be unable to produce enough milk to be profitable or she will collapse with sheer exhaustion, then she will be sent on a very long journey, with no water or food to be slaughtered in a state where it is legal to slaughter cows. Her natural life is 20–25 years.

"We are a population of many vegetarians because that is how we were raised, we have no wish to eat animal flesh; however, the milk is also not ours to drink; the milk is for the baby cow. What can we as individuals do about this? We can stop buying milk products. We can make milk from almonds, cashews, soya, coconut and more.

"The buffalo is not sacred to us, but they also still suffer the same as the cow. The buffalo is no different to the cow; buffalo, cow, cat, dog, elephant and fish, they are all the same as us, they all feel pain, they all get hungry and thirsty, they all want to live a natural full life.

"Please people of India think about this and ask yourself, is it OK for animals to suffer for our pleasure? Is it OK that animals die before their natural time? Is it OK for man to profit from animals? If you feel from your hearts, you will know the answer."

Max's cartoons flashed up as Rohan spoke: Humans honouring the cow putting garlands around their necks, a factory dairy farm at milking time with cows connected to the big milk machines as they go around like robots, baby cows on their own without their mums, a man with his whole arm inside the cow, cows collapsing and being dragged onto a truck, barely able to stand, being driven on dusty roads with no water, dying on route and calves drinking the milk from their mums in a field next to factories making nut milk.

The group chanted:

- Cows are being exploited and endure immense suffering
- Cows are being exploited and endure immense suffering
- Cows are being exploited and endure immense suffering
- Cows are being exploited and endure immense suffering
- Cows are being exploited and endure immense suffering

The portal closed.

Alice was next; she elected to talk about fur. "3 2 1 you are live." The portal reopened; they were at a fashion show.

"People in the fashion world, we have a message for you all. The fur items that you are making, wearing and selling are death. You are wearing death on your shoulders. You may or may not know how cruel fur farming is. Animals are trapped, hunted or bred into filthy farms. They are locked up in small changes and the wild ones get cage madness where they go around and around in circles, literally going crazy, they frantically scratch the cage trying to escape.

"Their deaths are barbaric, anal electrocution, carbon monoxide poisoning, strychnine suffocation are some of the methods. Once the fur is removed from their body, some are minced up and fed to their fellow caged prisoners. In

Greenland and the Atlantic frozen waters, beautiful baby Harp seals are bludgeoned to death and skinned, their carcasses are left to rot on the ice.

"Are these the actions of a civilised society? Is it morally justifiable to take the life of animals just for fashion? Our ancestors were in survival mode when they used the skin of an animal to keep warm, we are not in survival mode, the ones doing the killing and manufacturing are in profit mode. The people wearing the dead animal skins are doing it to make themselves feel good and are wrapped up in self-indulgence not giving a single thought to how that fur came into being.

"Well, I ask you all, would it make you feel good to personally kill these animals before putting them on your shoulders? Could you even do it? I feel that most people could not bring themselves to kill another animal. Please ask yourself, is it really OK to pay someone else to cause these atrocities when you could not bring yourself to do it?

"The wild animals living and breathing on planet Earth used to make up 99% of all living beings, it is now 2%, humans have taken dominion of almost all animals, and your fur coats and boots are the last of the wild animals in existence today. These animals don't want to be caught; they just want to live a natural life, having fun with their siblings, sleeping in the sunshine, breathing the clear fresh air in the countryside, running for fun. Please stop making, selling and buying these garments, once the demand has gone, the fur catchers will stop killing the animals and treating them in such a horrendous way."

Max's movie portal was cartoons of dead animals caught in traps and dead animals draped over humans with blood dripping out of them and a fur farm with rows and rows of cages with caged madness animals displaying crazy behaviour. The death by anal electrocution of a cute rabbit and a seal being bludgeoned to death. A caveman on one side wrapped up in a whole skin, a man in a suit with a wodge full of dollars in the other. Lastly, a woman in a glamorous fur coat full of her own self-importance was offered a live animal to kill, she ran away screaming for help.

The group chanted:

- Cavemen wore fur, it is time we evolved
- Cavemen wore fur, it is time we evolved
- Cavemen wore fur, it is time we evolved
- Cavemen wore fur, it is time we evolved
- Cavemen wore fur, it is time we evolved

Lars was up next, at a live music concert. "3 2 1 you are live."

"People of Norway. Please listen to our important message. Whales are a very important part of the ecosystem of our oceans. Our oceans are dying for many reasons; one is that we have overfished for many years and this has a detrimental impact on every aquatic species. Around 90% of fish stocks have been killed. Phytoplankton relies on whales and other large species poop as food as it is rich in nutrients.

"The Phytoplankton is food for small fish; the small fish are food for the bigger fish, so you see it is all interconnected. The Phytoplankton, algae and seaweed give us 50% of the oxygen we breathe. If we continue to kill whales, it will have a devastating impact on the air that we breathe. Once oxygen levels get below 10% of the air, we will all die. Please ask yourself, do you want to be the reason that the human race is extinct?

"Or do you want to make a difference with every other human being on the planet to secure the future for our grandchildren's children and their grandchildren? It's not only whales but also all fish that we need to stop killing, and the oceans need to be left alone to regenerate. Land animals are also having a devastating impact on the gasses in our environment as well as pollution in our water tables, toxins from poop are left untreated and are killing life in rivers and seas.

"Around 57 billion land animals are bred and slaughtered each year, just for our taste buds and pleasure. For too long, we have seen animals as stock not beings, property not individuals, products not young feeling animals. The terror we inflict on them on a regular basis without the slightest concern of their viewpoint we wouldn't inflict that terror on rapists or murderers.

"We have dominion over animals but we haven't the awareness to see that with it comes the responsibility to protect the vulnerable and keep the planet in good shape for future generations to enjoy. Animals feel fear and pain just like we do. Ask yourself is it morally justifiable to curtail an animal life just for our own pleasure? Please think about this, research yourself, ask yourself, how can you make a change to the course of humanities path?"

The movie portal opened up with a pod of whales swimming through the sea, small fish were being eaten by bigger fish, and they by bigger fish, next was a whale being harpooned many times and brought to its death and finally the dead zones in the sea showing no life at all and factory farms with thousands and thousands of animals in sheds.

148

The group chanted:

- Love won't kill sentient beings
- Love won't kill sentient beings
- Love won't kill sentient beings
- Love won't kill sentient beings
- Love won't kill sentient beings

Billy arrived at school to do another speech. This time, it was not necessary to arrive in his school uniform or hide behind the curtain. The headmaster knew he was coming and had assembled all the teachers to listen to what Billy had to say.

"Hello again, I was very surprised on my last visit that my words flowed so easily, I have to tell you I was very nervous. I want to say thank you for listening and for your wonderful reaction. Today I would like to talk again about cats and dogs. In Asia, 10 million dogs and 4 million cats are killed and eaten every year."

The whole room gasped. "To us here in the UK, this is without a doubt not acceptable. We cherish cats and dogs, they become part of our family, they bring us joy and keep many people company that would otherwise be very lonely and isolated. How would you feel if all the cats and dogs in Asia were shipped to the UK and slaughtered in one of our slaughterhouses, where we murder cows, sheep, pigs and chickens? Please show your hands now if this would this be OK?"

No one put up their hand. "I would like you all to ask yourself today, what difference is there between cats and dogs or chickens, pigs, cows and sheep? The only difference is our perception. We are humans on planet earth, they are animals on planet earth. Just like us, they suffer, just like us they feel fear, just like us they feel pain and just like us they feel joy and love.

"If only we would give them their freedom so that they could experience joy and love as we do. The world and UK farming has become just about profit for large organisations. We do still have some small farms; however, the majority of the meat on your plate has come from a factory farm, where the surroundings are really bad, they are in confined conditions, suffer mutilations without pain relief, are taken to slaughter at a young age, it is the equivalent age to us when we were toddlers.

"Meat is packed with labels to ease our conscience, free-range, red tractor approved or RSPA approved, it means nothing. The labels are nothing more than marketing slogans, we have all been fooled by this industry to believe that the animals don't suffer and we even pay more for the labels that sound like the animals are somehow protected and have nice lives, do not believe this marketing.

"Marketing was created to sell products, they are clever at using words to make the consumer want to buy the product. The industry also want you all to feel like the animals are happy and free, and they know that the majority of people believe the label; people literally take it as absolute truth. Please ask yourselves, is it morally justifiable to take the life of another animal way before its natural life just for the pleasure of our taste buds? Could you kill your dog or cat and eat it?

"If not, please ask yourself what is the difference? Cat pig dog cow chicken sheep are all sentient beings just like us. Industries that profit from the exploitation and abuse of animals hide behind a wall of secrecy and humans are lead to believe that the animals don't suffer, this is a lie. The only way for this exploitation to stop is for humans to stop being the demand. It is entirely up to you the consumers. It's in your hands, each and every one of you, it is everyone's responsibility, mine, my friends my family and yours." Once again everyone stood up and clapped.

Max gathered everyone together. "So, how are you all feeling and what feedback do you have from family and friends?" asked Max.

Alice was the first to reply. "It feels wonderful to be a part of this project Max, my friends and family are shocked that it is actually happening but are interested to know about everything you have shown us and told us. I have had calls from newspapers and TV companies Max, they want to do interviews with me, what do you suggest we do?"

Some others said together "Yea, I have had calls too."

"It's up to you Alice. Appearances on TV will certainly help spread the word, you just need to be aware that the interviewer will try to back you into a corner with questioning and make you look foolish and make everything you are talking about look like it is a crazy cult and a fad. So, as long as you feel you can handle the ridicule and the difficult questions, please go ahead and do whatever you are comfortable with.

"Some interviewers might be on board with compassion and love for all sentient beings, in which case it will be a breeze, but most people when they hear about veganism or equality for animals, ridicule it, this is because the conditioning/programming is so deep and so far-reaching that the minority look like the crazy ones.

"As you all know, once you wake up to the reality of what is going on, you then see that it is the majority that is acting crazy and that you once were the same and the only thing you wish for is that you had opened your eyes sooner and that everyone soon feels the same. So, to some up Alice, it is up to you what you do, just be aware that it may not be the outcome you would hope for."

Tala spoke next. "Max, it is surprising how much resistance there is from people. I do feel that we will get there and that people will start to be open to change, but a lot of people I have spoken to just don't understand, they just don't seem to make the connection with the fact that the animals feel the same as we do, and they are fearful of change, they don't like change, especially when it is something they have known to be 'normal' and done all their life, it is a bit like saying to yourself that your whole life you have been doing something that is wrong, this is tough for some people to admit."

"This is another human trait that is very common Tala. People will resist, they have only known what they have been shown by their family and society. Some will come to accept sooner than others, but once people around them are accepting and agreeing they will all soon follow. Wrong is wrong even if everyone is doing it. Right is right even if no one is doing it. It may take some time, but it will happen, it is already happening."

Tuan was up next, again at a football match. "3 2 1 you are live."

"People of Vietnam, we have an important message for you all. There are many among us that buy rhino horn and pangolins scales. Pangolins are now very rare in Asia, so they are being hunted and cruelly murdered in Africa along with rhinos. This is a barbaric trade that only exists because of our consumption. It is only people in Asia that have the crazy belief that the scales and horn have medicinal properties. It is mainly made up of keratin which is the same as our fingernails.

"This belief has been passed down from generation to generation, they are ancient beliefs which we have believed, please think for yourselves and consider it. Does it really make sense to you that they have medicinal properties? Or is it just that you have believed what your parents believed and them their parents.

We are following beliefs from thousands of years ago, we have evolved to change many things in our lives, yet this crazy belief still has a grip on many people in Asia.

"These beautiful animals are on the verge of being extinct, you will all have to stop taking it soon as there won't be any left to buy—so why not stop taking it now? Save the animals from being wiped off this planet and save your hard-earned money and use it on spending time with your family or time in nature, this will be better for your health and better for these animals that have done nothing wrong.

"They feel pain, just like us. They feel fear, just like us. They love their babies, just like us. They feel joy, just like us. Please, think about this, think about the direct impact you are having on these sentient beings and think about how crazy it really is that we are following like robots without giving it a thought of our own as to whether it is morally justifiable or whether it has medicinal value or is just an old wives tale."

The movie portal showed rhinos and pangolins in nature with their families then being killed and butchered for their horns and scales it repeated over and over while Tuan was talking.

The group chanted:

- Stop the violence before it's too late
- Stop the violence before it's too late
- Stop the violence before it's too late
- Stop the violence before it's too late
- Stop the violence before it's too late

Tala was next, the event was a rodeo. "3 2 1 you are live."

"People of The Philippines, we have an important message for you all.

"Bulls and Horses don't buck just because they are wild, but because they are in pain. You have all been led to believe that this is normal behaviour. It is not; it is monstrous and should be a thing of the past. A belt called a flank strap is secured around the body and the genitals. The animals are worked up by being slapped, teased and given electric shocks by rods and tormented to bolt out of the shoot in a frenzy.

"As the bull leaves the shoot a sharp tug on the rope that controls the flank strap is enough to cause the animal to start bucking in pain. The animals often suffer broken legs. Roping a baby cow whilst it is running away at full speed is totally abhorrent, but you have been brainwashed by your parents and them by their parents that this is OK.

"These animals, feel fear, they feel pain, they feel joy and love for their babies and fellow beings. This is not entertainment, but you are brainwashed to think that it is normal. In years to come, future generations will look back at this in shock that humans could be so cruel and find it entertaining to watch animals in pain and suffering and actually pay hard-earned money to watch such atrocities. This really is insane. Please stop coming to these events, once you all stop, the event will be a thing of the past."

The movie clip was running all the things that are done to them prior to being in the arena and the mother of a baby being roped is standing outside the arena watching with tears falling down her face calling out in emotional pain at what was happening to her baby.

The group chanted:

- Now is the time for change—time to end animal violence
- Now is the time for change—time to end animal violence
- Now is the time for change—time to end animal violence
- Now is the time for change—time to end animal violence
- Now is the time for change—time to end animal violence

Nicole Ricci was next.

"3 2 1 you are live." They were once again at a football match.

"People of Italy, we have an important message for you all. Have you ever wondered where exactly leather comes from? Of course, we all know it is dead animal skin, many assume the animal was already dead and think we may as well make use of the skin so what is the harm? A large percentage of leather comes from India where, in many states, it is illegal to kill cows.

"The cows are forced to walk in the burning heat for many days without food or water. They arrive at a transport point, to be crammed into the truck for many days travelling across India to another country or the Indian states where it is legal to kill cows. Many are dead on arrival due to the terrible conditions they have been forced to endure.

"The ones that are still breathing are forced to the ground, all four legs tied together to stop her moving, her throat is then cut, but because it is not a sharp knife, it is a long process of pain and suffering for the innocent animal. The carnage does not stop there. The men and women who work in the tanners, stand in baths of chemicals to tan the skin; they have no idea that they are probably going to get cancer or some nasty skin disease from standing barefoot in these chemicals.

"You as individuals are paying for this carnage every time you buy a purse, shoes, belts, wallets, jackets, sofas and anything leather. Please ask yourself, is it morally justifiable for you to sit on your comfy sofa or wear the soft leather jacket, knowing that a massive amount of suffering has been a part of the process for you to own your luxury items, the suffering to animals and other human beings? Faux leather is now almost as good as animal leather and it costs less with zero suffering. Please stop buying leather products."

The movie was showing exhausted cows being forced to walk in the heat of the Indian day, falling over and being forced back up, being forced into trucks and then finally their painful death. Then the Indian's working in the tanneries in bare feet standing in the chemical concoction.

The group chanted:

- Animal skins are not ours to wear
- Animal skins are not ours to wear
- Animal skins are not ours to wear
- Animal skins are not ours to wear
- Animal skins are not ours to wear

Max closed the portal and spoke. "OK, everyone, I just wanted to say what a great job you are all doing. Humans are inherently good, you have a lot to give and a lot of people in your world do give."

"So, why Max, have we got to this stage where we have got all these terrible acts of cruelty and immorality going on all over the world if we are inherently good?" asked Czar.

"This is evolution, Czar. Humans are inherently good, as well as the conditioning and things being normalised, humans needed to go through this hell to have a beatific cause—the first part of that cause is to free the animals. Humans essentially want to be happy and to be free. You cannot free yourselves from all the misery in the world until you have freed your cousins in the animal kingdom. Once that is done, you can take the next step to transform the world and start living to your full potential, which is a world of peace, togetherness and happiness for all."

"What if the world doesn't listen to us?" asked Tuan.

"Humans are on a path of self-destruction or self-understanding, self-destruction will occur if humanity does not look, listen and see what is really apparent and decide to be personally responsible for their own part in the future outcome. Feeling that the atrocities and the dominion of the animal kingdom are indeed immoral is the next step towards self-understanding.

"If everyone on the planet understood and felt that all beings are equal and deserve to live a natural life span, they would then begin to have more self-understanding. Humans have been on a technological path, a path of knowledge. It is time that you take the turning up ahead to one of a feeling path and togetherness path. Humans have emotional intelligence that is beyond that of the mind, the mind that has been driving your thirst for knowledge and technological advancement. We will talk about this in more detail later.

"The technology you have will help you achieve great things in the world. A small number of people are already doing great work on the path of oneness and sharing. Human's basic needs are water, shelter, food, safety and warmth. Not everyone has these basic needs; however, some are working towards a world where every human being has these needs met.

"By feeling that animals are worthy of natural life, humans will then start to feel that humans are all worthy of these basic needs which will be the next step after the animals are free. Beginnings hide themselves in endings."

"Max I have had a friend say to me that it is their personal choice to eat meat, how could I answer that question next time?" asked Ping.

"Of course, it is the personal choice, but that doesn't make it right—someone who personally chooses to murder another human, personally chooses to do so, but society deems this is morally wrong. The Chinese personally choose to rear, beat and eat dogs at the annual Yulin festival—in most countries you feel this is morally wrong, but it is the personal choice of the Chinese to do this.

"Rearing and eating chicken, sheep, pig and cow is morally unjustifiable—it is the same as eating a dog or murdering another human being. Humans are all in a self-made illusion, deluding themselves about what is really going on and don't want to think about it because you don't want to admit it or have to make sacrifices; generally, humans don't like change as it is perceived to be uncomfortable, but in truth, it is not, it is liberating."

"Max, I have just seen on my social media that some TV reporters are visiting farms without notice and are trying to get live film footage of what is going on," said Lars.

"This is no surprise as that is their job, a small number of journalists have been trying to expose what is going on; however, now that we are all sharing this information, all of the media will want to jump on the bandwagon, they will want to have full coverage to expose either the truth or to ridicule you all and show the 'nice' farms and what a lovely life the animals have in fields.

"This is all part of the plan, as I said before, had we taken over the TV broadcasting, it would not have been taken seriously; however, now, everyone wants to know what is going on and the TV companies are trying to get footage is just the start, next I predict they will be demanding investigations." Max smiled and ask who was up next.

Kemala raised her hand. "3 2 1 you are live." They were at a badminton match.

"People of Indonesia, please listen, we have an urgent message for you all. Here, in Indonesia, we hunt sharks for their fins mainly for export, without a single thought as to what impact it will have on our seas local to us. The ecosystem depends on a variety of species to be healthy, and apex predators like sharks are one of them. The more we fish these creatures the less healthy our seas will be.

"Phytoplankton feed off the poop of apex predators, small fish eat the phytoplankton, bigger fish eat the small fish, so you see, without the apex predators, the phytoplankton will reduce, which has a knock-on effect on the whole ecosystem meaning all other fish will be gone too. We are already overfishing all the other fish, so the impact is compounded. Phytoplankton, algae and seaweed give the planet 50% of the oxygen in our air, once all fish are gone so will our oxygen be gone, we will all die and take all other species with us.

"Fishing may be giving you money today, but money won't do us any good once we can't breathe. Every nation, every person needs to start looking at our future, it's not a great picture, there are many things we can all do to change the course that we are currently on, one is to stop fishing, times will be tough whilst we all find new ways to earn money to feed our families, but if we do not do this there will be no future for our children's children.

"We can't wait until the fish are gone, it will be too late so we have to act now. So please people of Indonesia, please go search yourself on the internet, talk to everyone you know, you will see that what we are sharing with you today is true."

The movie was playing a fishing boat catching sharks, slicing off their fins and throwing them back into the water, the shark slowly sank to the bottom of the sea and empty oceans of the future were also depicted.

The group chanted:

- No fish no humans
- No fish no humans
- No fish no humans
- No fish no humans
- No fish no humans

Keiki was up next at a sumo wrestling match. "3 2 1 you are live."

"Hello, people of Japan, we have a vital message for you all. Dolphins are social mammals; they feel joy and happiness just like we do. They feel sadness, pain and fear just like we do, so why do we drive these beautiful creatures into killing bays? It is mind-boggling what we are doing to all species in our seas. Around 90% of the tuna fish in the world's seas have been killed. One single company buys 40–60% of the Bluefin tuna; they have frozen many years of usage of this fish but continue to buy more tuna.

"They are only buying the fish because we humans continue to eat it. Once the tuna fish in the sea has gone, the company will make ludicrous profits because humans will pay the extra money not only to satisfy their taste buds but also to buy in top restaurants to satisfy their ego, showing off to their friends and family. Once it has all gone, the fashion will disappear, so please ask yourself, is it not better to create a new fashion of not eating it and then we will see our seas flourish.

"This would be a fashion to be proud of. Japan has many things to be proud of, let us add this to the list and lead the way in the world. Modern technology has enabled humans to almost wipe out most species in our seas, and once we do, this will have a dramatic impact on us, this will be karma. The oxygen in our air is created not only from trees and plants but also the algae, seaweed and phytoplankton in our seas, they need dolphins and all other fish to grow, they are all interdependent, once they are gone, our oxygen will be depleted so much that we won't be able to breathe.

"Another thing to ask ourselves is; what right do we have to take the life of another living breathing animal that wants to live and that feels pain and fear. We humans think we are superior, we are not acting superior, we are acting like barbarians. Please, people of Japan, ask yourself, is it morally justifiable to take the life of another being just for our taste buds?

"Please consider if each and every human being on this planet need to take responsibility for their own actions. If we all work together, we can change the future path. If we all do nothing, we have no one to blame but ourselves, we can't blame governments, we can't blame all the companies that are profiting from fishing, we can only blame ourselves because all anyone can control is their own actions; it's the only thing we can control. Please stop killing and eating sentient beings."

The movie was playing dolphins having fun together, doing somersaults and then being driving into bays and killed, then tuna fish being trapped in nets with all the other fish, gasping for air.

The group chanted:

- No fish no humans
- No fish no humans
- No fish no humans
- No fish no humans
- No fish no humans

Oskar Fischer was up next, the venue was a large circus. "3 2 1 you are live."

"Hello, Germany, we come here today to deliver you a message about animal ownership. Animals are not ours to own. Animals are certainly not ours to beat and torture to make them do tricks for the entertainment of us the audience and the profit of the circus owner. Elephants are incredibly gentle giants when they are in the wild. They are social animals and form deep lifelong bonds with their families.

"This is no life for such an intelligent and emotional being. These animals are slaves, they are chained and beaten. They are trained from a very early age, whipped and beaten; their spirits are broken to the point where he just does as he is told in fear of another beating. The only reason that this continues is because we pay money to come and watch. I beg you please stop paying for this cruelty.

"You are just as guilty for the beating that goes on behind the curtains as the person inflicting the pain. Humans violate the animal kingdom and we are betraying the animals. Not just in circus performances, animals in so many different entertainments and many other industries that exploit animals for our own gain. Animals are innocent beings caught up in man's greed and self-importance. Be the change that you want to see in the world, please stop coming to these events."

The movie was playing elephants in herds in the savanna, in nature the way they should be and being 'trained' from a very young age to do tricks. It really was a very sad thing to watch the spirit of the animal being diminished to a point where he just did as he was told for fear of being beaten.

The group chanted:

- Freedom not chains
- Freedom not chains
- Freedom not chains
- Freedom not chains
- Freedom not chains

Billy visited his school again.

"Today I would like to talk to you about exotic pets. Importers bring in exotic animals from all over the world. Sometimes they are illegally imported and are stuffed into very small spaces. The journey for these species begins in their natural habitat in places such as Australia, Africa, Brazil and the USA. They are caught by catchers and often change hands through many different people, finally arriving at the exporter.

"Birds often have their feet and beaks taped up and are shoved in tubes so that they are not detected at custom ports. Baby turtles are taped up; they are trapped inside their shells. Species such as snakes, terrapins, bearded dragons and tarantulas are shipped around the world. Some are transported by the hundreds in boxes with no water or food and as many as 80% are dead on arrival.

"These animals do not deserve to be stolen from their homes, shipped in horrendous conditions all over the world to end up next to their friends who are dead or dying or stuffed in a tube all alone and trapped all for the pleasure of a human to again be trapped in a tank or cage in our living rooms or bedroom.

What is it about us humans that we have the desire to own creatures and keep them in an environment that does not meet their needs?

"Tanks in living rooms are no different to prisons cells for humans except that the animals are 100% innocent. Many of these creatures live long lives up to 15 years, which is one long prison sentence. Actually, it is not just exotic creatures that suffer these long prison sentences, gerbils, hamsters, rabbits, guinea pigs, tortoises, lizards, fish, rats and more. The stress alone of being captured, then the travel is bad enough, but to then be trapped forever, this really is quite hellish for the animals and is wicked behaviour of us human beings.

"It is no different than us being captured by aliens, taken in a spaceship to a place far away, placed in a glass or wired cage in an environment that is totally weird and nothing like we have experienced before and kept there forever, often all alone with no humans to talk to with food that doesn't taste or look like food to us and then sometimes being picked up by the gigantic aliens and stroked.

"Please try and imagine this, how does it feel to you? This is a demand-driven industry, if we stop having the desire for these prisons, then the animals will be left to live their lives in the natural habitat they were born in."

Billy was surprised to hear from the head teacher that another local school had asked if he would do a speech, Billy, of course, was pleased to do so and said that he was happy to continue to speak at his school, as many of his peers had already decided not to eat meat, and he wanted to continue to speak and maybe even become the first vegan school to ever exist.

Chapter 12

Max gathered everyone together.

"As you all know, I have often said that I may teach you some of the things that I and my people can do, that most humans are not aware of; however, you all have these abilities but have forgotten. Meditation is the first tool that you need to learn before I can then teach you to communicate via telepathy, which is the first lesson of what you call ESP—extrasensory perception. There are many ways to meditate, on Earth some may say you have to do it a specific way, this is not true.

"To really follow this path, you need to go with your own instinct, do what feels right for you. You can start with meditation music to help you focus and quieten the mind but this is a stepping stone to help you meditate without music. Or put in earplugs with no music to help you go inward and block out some of the noise of the surrounding area like dogs barking or cars and planes. Find a comfortable seated position, close your eyes and focus on your breathing. Listen for the silence if you are not listening to music.

"The main objective is not to stop the thoughts but to quieten the mind and slow the thoughts. To become the observer of the thoughts just sit and focus. When you realise you are thinking, bring yourself back to your breath, the silence or the music. Do not get frustrated with yourself that you were thinking as thoughts will always come. Just keep bringing yourself back into focus.

"Acknowledge the thought and mentally note what it is; is it regret from the past or is it a worry or plan or fantasy of the future or is it simply something you need to do later that day? Whatever it is, let it go and re-focus. Meditate every day or perhaps twice a day, start with 10–15 minutes then build up from there to whatever feels right for you and practice, practice, practice. Another focus is the body sensations, feeling what is going on inside the body, on the surface of the skin and even just outside the body, what can you feel and then see what images or thoughts comes up.

"You will go on your own journey inward with a unique experience. Many people on earth do not like to discuss their experience; however, I would encourage you to share with each other, what sensations, visuals, words or pictures that come to you. Do not try to experience something specific that you have experienced before or heard about from a friend, just see what comes up and perhaps write down all your experiences, thoughts and feelings in a journal. We will then work on telepathy at some point in the future. OK, who is next?"

Ava stepped forward. "3 2 1 you are live." They were at a rugby match.

"People of France, we come here today to talk to you about the cruelty of an ancient tradition here in France. Gavage, the process of force-feeding geese and ducks to fatten them up to apparently improve the taste of the liver is a highly outdated tradition. The liver is enlarged by around 10 times its usual size, causing the bird to have difficulty in standing. They also suffer lots of other health problems such as damage to the oesophagus, impaired liver function, fractures of the sternum and many more.

"Some die of aspiration pneumonia which is caused when the grain is accidentally forced into the lungs or when birds choke on their own vomit. This tradition goes back to 2,500 BC—don't you think we should reconsider this tradition and ask ourselves if it is morally right to force-feed birds just for the pleasure of our taste buds?

"In 2,500 BC, they had many savage ways of doing things, many of which have now been outlawed as being totally unacceptable in the twenty-first century. Some countries have banned not only this process but also the sale and the import of any Foie Gras. Surely, we are more evolved and more aware than the people in 2,500 BC? We are conditioned from a very young age to believe that this is normal by our parents and them by their parents, it is not until you stop and really think about it that you realise how cruel it is.

"France is the biggest producer and consumer of this horrid food, people of France and the world please stop buying this product, it's the only way to stop the suffering of these birds. It's your choice, you can choose not to be the demand for such an old-worldly ghastly tradition or you can continue to pay for the suffering."

The cartoon screen was of humans force-feeding birds and their bodies changing shape as their liver got larger.

The group chanted:

- This is the evolution revolution; it is time for change
- This is the evolution revolution; it is time for change
- This is the evolution revolution; it is time for change
- This is the evolution revolution; it is time for change
- This is the evolution revolution; it is time for change

Jiemba was up next, it was at a cricket match. "3 2 1 you are live."

"People of Australia, please listen up, we have an important message for you all. The farming industry is out of control. Mass production has led it to change from farming to big businesses, this means that animal welfare has gone to the bottom of the priority and profit is the only driving force. Sheep in the wild do not need shearing, the only reason they now need it is that we have selectively bred the sheep to produce more and more wool for profit.

"The shearers are often paid not by the hour, but per sheep, so they work really hard and fast which means the sheep are handled in a totally disrespectful way; they get injuries and are very stressed throughout the whole process. We have many other materials we can use for our sofas, carpets, suits, jumpers and hats other than wool. Please buy none animal clothes and furniture."

The cartoon was showing the way that the sheep are manhandled during shearing.

The group chanted:

- Their wool, not ours
- Their wool, not ours
- Their wool, not ours
- Their wool, not ours
- Their wool, not ours

Ping was up next at a Thai boxing event. "3 2 1 you are live."

"People of Thailand, we have an important message to share with you. One hundred years ago, Thailand had 100,000 elephants, today we have only 2,000. These animals are very sociable and intelligent. They recognise each other, they mourn their dead, and they love and look after each other. They don't deserve to be chained as slaves and used for tourist selfies or to be ridden; they were born to be in the wild forests, with other elephants.

"They feel sad just like us, they feel pain just like us, and they feel lonely just like us. We do not have the right to own them, please let them go free; please ask your friends and family not to own elephants. More and more tourists are starting to find it distasteful, so this industry will end anyway. The tigers we drug are majestic animals; once again they are not ours to own, we chain, drug and lock them up in small cages, tigers that should be roaming the rainforests but are abused all for profit.

"This is brutal and vicious behaviour. Imagine if this was your mother being chained, while humans from other lands took selfies of her. Please, people of Thailand, look into your hearts, feel from your hearts, please see what we see; they are the same as us, we came from the animal kingdom, and they are feeling beings just like us."

The cartoon was showing elephants and tigers in their natural habitat and the poor animals looking very miserable, sad and lonely chained and drugged, as well as a Thai woman chained whilst having photos taken with tourists.

The group chanted:

- Freedom, not chains
- Freedom, not chains
- Freedom, not chains
- Freedom, not chains
- Freedom, not chains

Billy continued to get more and more invites to lots of different schools. His mum was so proud of him; her shy intelligent boy was now being asked to share his learning. When he first told her about Max, his new friends and Max's plan she thought that his imagination was running wild again, but he showed her some video clips on the internet of some of the groups' speeches. She was astounded and speechless. Proud wasn't the word for it, there wasn't a word she could think of that described how she felt.

"Thanks, mum, for trusting in me to leave school, it was really helpful for me to leave and then go back to speak to everyone."

They hugged each other, both with tears in their eyes at the amazing changes that were happening in Billy's life. Billy's mum even said she would think about going vegan with him which pleased him greatly. His new friends were also being asked to speak at lots of other schools; Billy was so excited that Max's plan was really starting to make a difference in the world.

As Max had predicted, the media were demanding enquiries into the inhumane slaughters and the terrible lives that farmed animals are forced to endure, the illegally farmed tigers, Illegal fox hunting, the fur, big game hunting and more. They were in a frenzy, they didn't know where or when the next holographic appearance would be, so they couldn't follow Max and the young groups, all they could do is follow up on all the details of the previous holograms and try to find out who all the young people were. Billy started getting calls from the TV channels and the newspapers; however, his mum had shielded him from the calls and suggested that he should focus on what he needed to do with Max and deal with the media later. Billy was pleased about this as he really didn't like the idea of being interviewed, he felt that speaking at schools and being in the holograms was enough for him at this time.

Vegan groups all around the world were stepping up the demonstrations, the smaller groups were coming together to create bigger groups, all meeting outside mega-farms, dog farms, slaughterhouses, media buildings, parliament and other government buildings. TV channels were becoming more interested in the vegan groups, what they were up to and what they thought of these young people in holographic projections. The sofas of the TV shows were full of vegans—Max's plan was happening; humans were talking about animal exploitation all over the world.

Billy was visited by the British secret service, as were some of the others from their respective countries' government departments. Billy didn't tell them anything other than the truth; holographic appearances were controlled by a being from another planet called Unity. They asked him many questions about the being, where was he hiding, where was his spaceship, how many 'aliens' were on Earth, where did they come from and what was their intention. Billy said that the 'being' just appeared and disappeared and that he had teleported them to places all over the world and the intention was to help change the direction of humanity to avoid a disastrous future. Billy wasn't sure if they believed him or not but they didn't arrest him as they had nothing to detain him for.

Eduardo was up next at a football match. "3 2 1 you are live."

"People of Peru, please listen, we have important news. Peru catches the second largest number of fish in the world. Fishing is not sustainable, we all rely on the seas to give us 50% of our oxygen, which comes from algae, phytoplankton, seaweed, and they cannot survive without fish in the seas creating the overall ecosystem.

"We have taken 90% of the fish in our seas, so pretty soon in the future, we won't be able to reverse the damage we have done so we all have to act now. No fish, no phytoplankton, no oxygen, no humans. Another massive impact is the animal agriculture industry; 57 billion land animals are being bred in the world for food which is polluting our water tables with toxic waste and our atmosphere with harmful methane.

"Our rainforests are being illegally chopped down, causing indigenous people to be forced from their homes, decimating the thousands of forest animal species and adding to the potential lack of oxygen in future years. Please ask yourselves, what can you do as an individual to make changes to our future. If we all believe that our individual changes won't make an impact, we will become extinct.

"If we all spread these messages, if we all take responsibility, we will make a difference. Please stop fishing, we know this will be hard to begin with, but there are many new industries that will replace the fishing industry. People worry about lost livelihoods, but they will be lost anyway, along with species and mankind unless we all make changes.

"Please stop eating fish, meat and dairy products, the only way to stop this is if our demand for the product disappears. We can't rely on big organisations or the government to do something. We have the power, 7 billion people, please think about it, talk about it and take action. Let's take back our power. Please stop eating beings with heartbeats."

The cartoons were showing the seas full of fish before our industrial fishing days and the present low fish stocks in the seas and the forests being cut down.

The group chanted:

- Friends not food
- Friends not food
- Friends not food
- Friends not food
- Friends not food

Dimitrij was up next at a football match. "3 2 1 you are live."

"People of Slovenia please listen we have an important message for you all. Slaughterhouses around the world are deemed 'humane'; this is not true. They hide behind closed doors and high walls so that we cannot see what is going on in these murder houses. Animals are lined up on death row in one-way paths where they cannot turn around with walls that they try to escape over, but are too high.

"They can smell the blood; they know what is coming. Often, they see their brothers and sisters being murdered, they can hear them call out in pain and fear. They are full of fear and do not want to die as they wait on death row for their turn. Unable to do anything, they can't save themselves; they cannot save their families and friends. Humans have complete dominion over them.

"Cows are stunned with bolt guns to the head, which often does not cause them to be unconscious, so they have to be stunned two or three times. Often, they wake up as they are hanging upside down by one leg and are fully conscious as they have their throats slit. Pigs are gassed in chambers where they scream and struggle as their lungs burn before dying. Some pigs and sheep are stunned with electrical prongs; some go through the same process as the cows, waking up before being killed.

"Chickens, turkeys, geese, ducks are hung upside down by both legs, they are dipped in an electric water bath which stuns them, many birds see the water bath and hold their heads up to prevent going head first into the water; they remain fully awake. Many other birds get shocked but wake up before they have their throats slit. The next stage is a scalding tank, which loosens the feathers, many birds are still conscious at this stage so are boiled alive. All animals feel pain, fear, joy and love.

"Please ask yourself is it OK that we do this? What right do we have to take the life of another being? We humans have thought of ourselves as superior to the animal kingdom for a long time, we have evolved to use tools, we have evolved to have a moral compass, it is now time that we evolve to see all beings as the same as us. Please ask yourself, could you take a knife and kill another animal?

"If the answer is no, then you are just paying for someone else to do something you inherently know is morally wrong. We have been conditioned to eat meat since the day we could chew. If you felt it was morally justifiable you would be able to slice the throat of any animal.

"They are terrified beyond belief, and they are utterly saddened, shocked and disappointed in the humans that have failed to protect them for doing absolutely nothing wrong. Humane slaughter is an oxymoron, humane means compassion and benevolence, slaughter means to kill. The two words just do not go together and it is not possible to humanely kill an animal that does not want to die. Please stop eating dead animals."

The cartoon movie showed the cows having the gun bolt to their head, being lifted up to hang upside down, waking up, struggling and having their throats slit. Pigs were being gassed and stunned along with the lambs and birds going through their process of death.

The group chanted:

- Don't buy the humane lie; animals do not want to die
- Don't buy the humane lie; animals do not want to die
- Don't buy the humane lie; animals do not want to die
- Don't buy the humane lie; animals do not want to die
- Don't buy the humane lie; animals do not want to die

Zeynep was up next. "3 2 1 you are live."

"Hello, Turkey, welcome to this, a message from us all. Ten thousand years ago, wild animals made up 99% of the total biomass of planet earth, human beings made up 1%. Today, human beings and the animals that we 'own' as property makes up 98% of the total biomass; wild animals make up 2%.

"Humans have stolen the free-living animals from the earth. Hunting is unnecessary and cruel. Animals feel fear, they feel pain, and they feel joy. They are the same as us; they love and protect their children. Why is it that we feel that we are superior and can take their life? Imagine, aliens landing, chasing us through woods and killing us off one by one, this is exactly what we are doing, hunting for the fun of it, please find another way to have fun.

"Hunting for food is just not necessary nowadays. We can sustain our bodies without meat. Meat is actually very harmful to our bodies; it causes cancer and heart disease. We can still eat all the same dishes, just omit the meat and add more pulses and vegetables. Please people of Turkey think about this, imagine you were the wild animal, would you want to live or die?"

The movie was playing humans chasing animals, then killing them with knives or shooting them. Aliens doing the same to men, women and children.

The group chanted:

- If it has a heartbeat, don't kill it
- If it has a heartbeat, don't kill it
- If it has a heartbeat, don't kill it
- If it has a heartbeat, don't kill it
- If it has a heartbeat, don't kill it

Billy was covering all the various subjects of the various exploitations from across the world. At one school speech, he covered them all.

"Friends, we have an animal holocaust going on as I speak. Animal habitats are being destroyed in the Amazon forest, their homes are being ripped apart, and they are dying. Not their choice, not good for them, not what they want and definitely not humane.

"Rhinos, pangolins and elephants are being hunted and killed for their horns, scales and tusks. Not their choice, not good for them, not what they want and definitely not humane.

"Lions, tigers, bears and more are being hunted and murdered just for fun. Not their choice, not good for them, not what they want and definitely not humane.

"Furry animals are being hunted and farmed for their fur; they live a miserable existence before their painful death. Not their choice, not good for them, not what they want and definitely not humane.

"Whales, dolphins and sharks are being hunted and killed for their meat and fins or for captivity into prisons, for our entertainment. Not their choice, not good for them, not what they want and definitely not humane.

"Bulls and horses are being tortured for human entertainment in rodeos, bullrings and on the streets; they suffer a long, frightening and painful death. Not their choice, not good for them, not what they want and definitely not humane.

"Cows are tortured and endure long journeys to their death for their skins, all to become leather for man. Not their choice, not good for them, not what they want and definitely not humane.

"Farmed animals are artificially inseminated, their babies taken away and tortured, kept in hellish filthy conditions and then sent to slaughter when they are babies and toddlers. They endure long journeys to the slaughterhouse and some even thousands of miles across the oceans to other countries to meet the final day before they are killed in an inhumane way. Not their choice, not good for them, not what they want and definitely not humane.

"Dairy cows are being abused for their milk and sucked dry until they are exhausted or their bodies unable to give enough milk to be profitable; at this point, they join the other farm animals in the journey of death. Not their choice, not good for them, not what they want and definitely not humane.

"Horses, dogs and other animals are being trained and forced to race for profit. Not their choice, not good for them, not what they want and definitely not humane.

"Fish are being pulled out of the seas at such a rate that they will become extinct in the coming years. Not their choice, not good for them, not what they want and definitely not humane.

"Birds, exotic fish and other animals are imprisoned in tanks and cages as pets. Not their choice, not good for them, not what they want and definitely not humane.

"Ducks and geese are tortured again and again for their feathers, all to keep humans warm, live-plucking is far more profitable than dead plucking; profit is repeatable again and again. Not their choice, not good for them, not what they want and definitely not humane.

"Animals are held prisoners and tortured with chemicals, forced to inhale substances and their bodies burned, all in the name of human safety. Not their choice, not good for them, not what they want and definitely not humane.

"Queen bees have their wings removed, their honey stolen and often the whole hive is killed once they have done all the hard work of making honey which they are making for themselves and their family. Not their choice, not good for them, not what they want and definitely not humane.

"Animals across the whole animal kingdom are captured, contained and stared at, all in the name of profit and so-called education and fun for children in circuses, zoos, aquariums, safari parks and sea-life parks; they live miserable existences. Not their choice, not good for them, not what they want and definitely not humane.

"Fish are caught for entertainment and thrown back into the rivers and lakes to be caught, again and again, suffering the hook, humans handling their delicate scales and removing the hook causing pain and sometimes death. Not their choice, not good for them, not what they want and definitely not humane.

"Crocodiles are bred and kept in enclosures all lying on top of each other waiting for their death to become shoes and handbags. Not their choice, not good for them, not what they want and definitely not humane.

"Geese and ducks are being force-fed that enlarges their liver 10 times the normal size, all for man's taste buds. Not their choice, not good for them, not what they want and definitely not humane.

"Sheep are being bred to grow more and more wool and are brutally sheared for the profit of man. Not their choice, not good for them, not what they want and definitely not humane.

"Elephants and tigers are being chained and drugged for tourists to have selfies, all for our entertainment. Not their choice, not good for them, not what they want and definitely not humane.

"Cats and dogs are being tortured and eaten in Asia, while their European cousins are being treated like family. Not their choice, not good for them, not what they want and definitely not humane.

"There is no excuse for animal abuse, but it is going on everywhere in all nations. We need to change our thinking which will, in turn, change our behaviour.

"Be kind, think about the consequences of your actions, think about the animals suffering for your pleasure, your taste buds, your entertainment and ask yourself, is this really necessary for me and is this morally OK? We can choose if we want to increase the amount of mercy in the world or the amount of misery in the world; Each and every one of us can make a difference simply by feeling compassion for our cousins in the animal world and choosing not to be a part of the abuse anymore."

TV Sofas were also full of anti-vegan campaigners. Saying that it was wrong that shops were now selling all these different new vegan foods, that it was just a hippy fad. It really was quite comical to hear the presenter asking questions, such as 'Do you think vegan food should be banned?'

'Yes' replied the campaigner.

'Even though the people who want to be vegan are doing it because they have compassion for the animals, they want to choose food for better health and it is better for the environment?'

The campaigner started to get angry he said 'the livelihoods of the farmers should be protected, the animals are there for humans to use and fish don't really matter as they don't really feel pain' He really was looking rather foolish he finished, 'all the vegans are insulting me and the rest of the population by accusing us all of being wrong to eat meat and accusing us of being no different to the Nazis and it is outrageous that they can get away with saying such things'

The presenter replied. 'Sir, if you are offended by people choosing not to eat innocent animals, then that really is your problem, they are not taking action against you. Their behaviour is none action, they are choosing not to be a part of violence, captivity and the slaughter of innocent beings'

'That is ridiculous, I am offended by what they are saying and doing'

'Sir, perhaps your offence is because deep down you know that they are right, and you just don't want to face it' That really was the last straw for the man, he got up and stormed off. Everyone in the studio was laughing; the TV company quickly took an advert break. Next up on the TV was an easy 15-minute vegan cooking show. Veganism really was the talk of everyone, even the ones who were vehemently against veganism were spending their time talking about it and sharing opinions.

Min-Seo was up next. "3 2 1 you are live."

"Hello, South Korea, we have an important message for you today. Most of the world do not eat dogs and cats. In Europe, America and Australia dog meat was eaten many years ago, now dogs and cats are part of the family in many homes. In more recent times, Hong Kong, Taiwan and the Philippines have banned the sale of dog and cat meat. Dog and cat flesh can be found on the menus in North Korea, South Korea, Vietnam, China and some African countries.

"We need to follow the world, let us not be the last country in the world to ban the sale of this meat. Also, farmed animals like pigs, chickens and cows are being farmed at an industrial rate. 57 billion animals worldwide are being murdered every year. Their poop is seeping into our water tables causing environmental damage to the rivers and seas, causing new diseases in the sea life.

"The methane from these animals is a big cause of the bad gasses in our atmosphere. Animals feel fear just like we do; they feel pain just like we do. Part of the evolution of mankind is to wake up and see that we do not have the right to kill any living creature. We are animals too, we just have more thinking ability and we have a moral compass. Please, feel from your hearts and ask yourself the question; is it OK to kill another being?"

The cartoon was playing the suffering of the cats and dogs, then the lucky ones that are part of the family and the farmed animals in their prisons.

The group chanted:

- Love animals don't eat them
- Love animals don't eat them
- Love animals don't eat them
- Love animals don't eat them
- Love animals don't eat them

Sven was up next. "3 2 1 you are live."

"Hello, people from the Netherlands. We have come here today to share an important message. Animals in zoos, safari parks, aquariums and sea mammal entertainment parks are very sad and lonely. Their natural needs are not being met, elephants in the wild walk for around 12 miles per day, in a zoo, they have little room to walk around.

"Animals are very sociable; they need their natural environment and their families to feel alive. Animals feel just like we do, they get lonely and depressed just like we do. People think they just need food, this is not true, and they need much more than food. Zoo's, safari parks, sea mammal entertainment parks and aquariums are not about conservancy, they are about profit. They may have conservancy programs in place, but mostly this is a marketing tool, to ease our conscience.

"We need rehabilitation centres and sanctuaries until the animals can go back into the wild, but we need to do this in the country that they came from, where the weather and habitat are appropriate and meet the needs of the animal. This industry is demand-driven, if we stop visiting these places, they will become a thing of the past.

"Aquariums and sea mammal entertainment parks house very large mammals in tanks, these tanks may seem big, but compared with what they have in nature, they are no different to small prison cells. In nature, they have thousands of miles of ocean all around the world and many of these mammals are migratory beings, they travel hundreds of miles a day, in tanks they just get to swim around and around purely for entertainment and profit.

"You may say that children and people would never get the chance to see these creatures if it wasn't for these places, that thought is coming from a place of what does it do for us humans, not from a place of what are the creatures needs. Imagine that it was your brother or sister in the cage being stared at by alien beings, every single day. He/she would have no room to exercise or display natural behaviour. Make no mistake, these businesses make a lot of money because we humans pay them, we are paying them to house the animals, we are paying them to capture the animals, we are the demand, we are the reason they still exist. Please consider this and stop visiting these animal prisons."

The cartoon was showing some animals in their natural environment and the cages/pens/tanks that they exist in. The animals in the wild looked alive, happy and at peace. The ones in captivity looked sad, miserable and lonely.

The group chanted:

- Natural wild lives not captive in prisons
- Natural wild lives not captive in prisons
- Natural wild lives not captive in prisons
- Natural wild lives not captive in prisons
- Natural wild lives not captive in prisons

Freja was up next. "3 2 1 you are live." They were at a racecourse.

"Hello, Denmark, we are here today to talk to you about racing. Horses and dogs do not want to race. We are led to believe that they enjoy the race and that they love to be trained. This is not true. Animals love to run, but for fun; you would never see them running for competition in the wild. The training of dogs is often done on a treadmill; please ask yourself, do you think this is 'caring' for the dog? Or is it a form of abuse?

"Horses are often trained to the point they get over training syndrome, which is manifested with different physiological and or psychological issues. Animals that are injured or are too old to race are dis-guarded, like slaves that can no longer work. Again, please ask yourself, is this caring for the animals? The animal has given the 'owner' everything, but he just throws them away to be slaughtered, or the lucky ones get new homes in animal sanctuaries.

"In some cases, they get so badly injured, that they are shot as the medical bills would be too expensive. Imagine the top athlete at the Olympics, falling, having severe injuries, he/she wouldn't be euthanised, money would be spent on operations and rehabilitation. The only reason this business exists is because humans are addicted to gambling and want to win money and the 'owners' want to make money. Please ask yourself, is this morally justifiable?

"If this was a family member of yours being forced to train, was locked up and then forced to race, would you consider this acceptable or barbaric? We are no different to animals, they have needs just like we do, and racing does not meet any of their needs. Please stop attending these events; they will become a thing of the past. We can have parties to celebrate the liberation of the animals instead of watching them being forced to race and get injured."

Cartoons were of dogs and horses in the wild displaying natural behaviours and the disasters that happen in racing; horses falling at the jumps, dogs on treadmills.

The group chanted:

- What do we need? Animal liberation
- When do we need it? Now
- What do we need? Animal liberation
- When do we need it? Now
- What do we need? Animal liberation
- When do we need it? Now
- What do we need? Animal liberation
- When do we need it? Now
- What do we need? Animal liberation
- When do we need it? Now

The next day, they all appeared, as usual, Billy was with his group.

Max started "OK, everyone, there is another place I would like to show you all, please hold hands."

All 28 of Billy's group held hands and were immediately teleported to a hot country.

"We are in South Africa."

Before them, they could see many lion cubs in a cage, they were really cute, about the size of a full-grown domesticated cat.

"These cubs are being bred just like calves, piglets and lambs, their mothers are artificially inseminated and just like dairy cows they are kept permanently pregnant."

"What for, Max?" asked Kemala.

"For various reasons, but as you all know, it's all about money. Many tourists and volunteers often pay thousands of dollars to help hand raise the cubs, thinking they are participating in conservation projects. The cubs are also used for tourist selfies, the tourist holds the cubs, which is a wonderful experience; however, if they knew the truth, they wouldn't want to be a part of it.

"When they are big enough, they are used for trophy hunting. Hunting for fun as you all know is something some people seem to get enjoyment from, killing a big cat feeds their ego. Once these wondrous animals are dead, their bodies and bones are then sold to the Asian 'medicinal' market. Lion's bones, teeth and claws look almost the same as tigers, so they are sometimes sold as tiger body parts.

"This export from South Africa is done under an official quota that is approved by The South African government. Unfortunately, this 'approval' further fuels the black market and encourages poachers to kill wild lions. So, the cute cubs are a 'triple earner' making it very irresistible to those who do not see them as sentient beings.

"This is very sad, as it will take three different types of demand to disappear before this horrid industry is a thing of the past. There are an estimated 8,000 lions held in captivity in South Africa, while there are only an estimated 1,300–1,700 wild lions.

"I felt the need to share this with you, there are so many more examples that I could show you, but this being a big cat, I felt it was important to share. Please tell the world not to have selfies with animals and that hunting for fun is not entertainment. Oh, and remember, all ask yourself to follow the money when you are attending anything to do with animals."

"What about animal sanctuaries, Max?" asked Khayone.

"There are some legitimate sanctuaries; you will get a feel for it whenever you visit a sanctuary if it is all about money or all about the animals. Often the sanctuaries are charities, not businesses and do not charge money to have selfies, they do not drug the animals and do not have a large entrance fee and may even have a donation box rather than an entrance fee.

"They may do some fundraising events; however, this is to pay for the food for the animals and the upkeep of the sanctuary. Even 'petting' farms at first may seem all about the animals but are about money, it isn't hard to work out, just see how much it costs you to enter and if once inside you have to pay for extras!"

Czar was up next. "3 2 1 you are live."

"Hello, Russia. Humans often say they want to be as free as a bird, so why do we cage them? Do we do it to care for the bird or to hear their song inside our houses? Or perhaps it is to show off our aviary to our friends and neighbours. Or is it simply a tradition that has been passed down from generation to generation?

"The earliest known record of humans caging bird's dates back to the ancient Sumerians, they caged them to teach them to speak a human language.

"In the middle of the sixteenth century, the term 'jailbird' was a slang word in England for a person in prison and the saying 'the bird has flown' was in relation to a person who had escaped prison.

"In the 1700s, miners would take caged canaries down a mine shaft with them, the bird would be singing the whole day. If it stopped singing, the miners knew to get out as the birds died quicker than humans when odourless toxic gasses were present in the shaft.

"When Leonardo da Vinci was walking by a place selling caged birds, he would buy the birds and set them free, giving them back their freedom.

"I guess the question we should be asking is not why we cage birds, but is it morally OK to do so? Birds were born to fly with the wind beneath their wings supporting them, swooping up and down. Bird song is such a wonderful sound no human could deny, but it is the right of the human to capture and cage a being that was destined to fly?

"We urge you to set free your caged birds and instead watch and listen for wild birds, this freedom you give them will make their song even sweeter to hear. Nature loved the birds and created trees for them, we created cages for them; that's not love that's ownership, imprisonment and torture."

Max's cartoon was of birds in flight and birds in cages. The caged birds were shouting: please set me free.

The group chanted:

- The songbird in its cage sings not for joy but for freedom
- The songbird in its cage sings not for joy but for freedom
- The songbird in its cage sings not for joy but for freedom
- The songbird in its cage sings not for joy but for freedom
- The songbird in its cage sings not for joy but for freedom

Khayone was up next. "3 2 1 you are live."

"People of South Africa, we are following in the footsteps of the western world. Our farming has become more industrialised and we are eating more and more meat. Raising animals for food is far more water-intensive than growing crops, about 10 times more water is required, Africa cannot afford to wastewater as we have thirsty people.

"Poop and wee from animals enter into the water tables and into the rivers and seas, this has a catastrophic impact on the wildlife within the oceans and rivers. Around 70% of the crops we grow are used to feed the animals; this is crazy as we could use this to feed the hungry people in Africa. On top of that we also export animals live to other countries, so we are using water to grow crops to feed and water the animals that are not even to feed people in Africa.

"We also feed the animals on fishmeal; this is having a detrimental impact on the fish stocks in our seas. It is also impacting on the South African penguin, as their food is being stolen by us. Imagine an Africa where everyone had water and food, how amazing would that be? This is easily possible if we all stop eating animals and give them back to mother earth.

"The impact of humans eating animals and fish is far-reaching. It even will impact the air that we breathe, as 50% of our oxygen comes from the seas, once we have taken all the fish from the seas, the phytoplankton, algae and seaweed will die, our oxygen will be depleted, we will become extinct. So please people of South Africa, please stop eating sentient beings."

The movie was showing industrial farming, thirsty and starving people of Africa, the suffering animals, the penguins struggling to find food.

The group chanted:

- Feed and water humans not farmed animals
- Feed and water humans not farmed animals
- Feed and water humans not farmed animals
- Feed and water humans not farmed animals
- Feed and water humans not farmed animals

Anahira was up next. "3 2 1 you are live."

"Hello, New Zealand, we have important news for you. Have you ever wondered about how honey in a jar is made? Bees in the world today are suffering because we have stolen their honey. Bees started making honey 200 million years ago, well before man showed up and humans have been taking the farming of honey to new extremes. There are between 80 and 100 million hives being farmed in the world. What is wrong with that I hear you ask?

"Well, big honey companies remove the queens' wings to ensure she does not fly away and take her worker bees with her and if that isn't cruel enough, they artificially inseminate her by putting her in a tube then poking and prodding her to impregnate her. They then wait for all the bees to travel millions of miles to produce the profit-making honey and then steal it. A single bee visits around 10,000 flowers per day.

"Bees can only survive the winter by storing and saving some of the honey, but humans take and give them a substitute called sugar water which isn't as nutritional as honey for the bees, so they now get diseases that they did not get when they were wild. Or, the farmer decides to kill the bees as it is less costly to just buy new bees in the spring. If he does this, his new bees may be posted in a box to him, a very traumatic time for the bees, a journey which they may not survive.

"All in all, they are exploited for profit and for human taste buds. Some organisations are mixing honey with other sugars, so you are not actually buying honey, it is fake. There are many alternatives like: rice syrup, molasses, maple syrup, cane sugar or dried fruit, so you see there really is no need to buy honey. Please don't support this violent industry, buy alternatives to honey."

The cartoon was of wild bees having a good time and farmed bees being inseminated and killed after the honey was stolen and of bees zooming around the earth finding flowers.

The group chanted:

- Honey is made for bees, not humans
- Honey is made for bees, not humans
- Honey is made for bees, not humans
- Honey is made for bees, not humans
- Honey is made for bees, not humans

Max teleported Billy and his friends to a demonstration. There were thousands of people walking in the city street. People had banners with many messages about animal exploitation, it was a peaceful demonstration with people chanting just like Billy and his friends did at the speeches. Some people were dressed up in pig and cow outfits, others had megaphones to chant with. The media were there taking pictures, filming and interviewing both onlookers about what they thought of all the holographic projections and the vegans who were marching asking them why they were vegan, what did they eat and how easy was it to be a vegan. There were famous people from actors, musicians, sportsmen, fashion models, TV presenters, chefs and more. Billy and his friends joined in the walk and as people recognised them, they ushered them to go to the front of the procession. A gangway opened up through the middle, the people were cheering them as they walked through the middle of the marching crowd. Eventually, they were at the front where many people held a very long banner, the people invited Billy and his friends to take over from holding the banner, the slogan read;

'It is time for change—freedom for the animals'

People standing on the streets joined the march, they continued to walk for some time until they reached a big urban park. At the park were many stalls selling vegan food and a band was playing music. Once everyone had arrived, the park was so full that there were people standing outside the fence watching to see what would happen next. The band stopped playing music and invited Billy and his friends up on stage. They each introduced themselves and said a few inspiring words about the global animal exploitation, the crowds were cheering and whistling. Billy at last felt like he belonged, he was accepted for who he was, he felt like he was part of a very caring and compassionate community and felt the happiest he ever had been his whole life.

Billy visited another school.

"We human beings have become like a cancer to the planet; it is not us that are cancerous, it is everything we do. Animal agriculture, air pollution, burning fossil fuels, deforestation, concrete cities, plastic pollution. The planet is suffering as it is being attacked by humans. Knowledge is power, what knowledge gives us is the opportunity to change the way we do things and the way we behave.

"It is new thinking that changes old ways and it is time for humans to change the way we do things around here, one by one, each of us, we all need to make changes to the way we are behaving. The easiest and quickest thing you can do as an individual is to stop eating meat, fish, dairy, eggs and honey. Why is this? Because the suffering is like nothing you can imagine. The impact on the planet is more than any other industry.

"Our rivers and seas are being polluted with poop. Our seas are dying as they are being overfished. Our atmosphere is being polluted with methane from animal burps. Our water is being consumed by animals when we have thirsty humans in the world. Our crops are being fed to animals when we have around 1 billion hungry humans. Our health is suffering, the more animals a nation eats, the sicker the nation gets.

"Farms are the same as death row, except the animals are 100% innocent and we are no longer blind to the injustices that are going on; the animals are no longer voiceless as we are their voice. Humans need to give the animals back their freedom, give the animals back to the earth and the earth back to the animals. We can coexist with animals and the earth in harmony.

"Choosing to eat one animal over another because one is smarter is like saying smart people matter more than not so smart people and people who think veganism is hard are thinking about themselves, people who think veganism is easy are thinking of the animals, the planet and the future generations.

"Vegetables are nature's little miracles they are there for the animals and for us and are packed full of all the nutrients we need. Silence and no action are complicity, it is time we all spoke up and shared this information with everyone we know, please spread this message with your family and friends, if we don't all stand together and work together, we will become extinct. This is evolution; Evolution of life. The evolution revolution."

Dinis was up next. "3 2 1 you are live."

"Hello, people of Portugal, we come here today to talk to you about animal rides.

"All over the world camels, elephants, donkeys and horses are used for tourist attractions. Animals are working to make money for humans, they were not created to work and to be held captive like prisoners, they were created to be free. Most of these animals are not treated with respect when they are not working, they have little space to run free, they are working and are treated as slaves.

"The animals are not doing it willingly; they are forced to work in really bad conditions, often standing all day in extreme heat, with little water and no relaxation. Please, people of the earth, do not participate in these rides, the animals get nothing for it and have a miserable existence."

The cartoon was showing the animals working and animals free in the wild.

The group chanted:

- Wild and free not slaves for humans
- Wild and free not slaves for humans
- Wild and free not slaves for humans
- Wild and free not slaves for humans
- Wild and free not slaves for humans

Ting was up next. "3 2 1 you are live."

"People of China, please listen, we have important messages for you. Elephants are being killed for their ivory and the biggest demand is here in China. As you may know, very recently the China government has banned all ivory carving. Ivory is a status symbol, please ask yourself; is it really worth having an ornament or piece of jewellery in exchange for the life of an elephant?

"Thousands of elephants die every year, just for the Ivory for us to display in our houses and on our bodies. It may be banned, but an illegal trade will persist if we continue to be the demand. Please do not buy ivory, it is death on your hands if you do. Even if someone tells you the ivory is old, please do not buy it as this will still fuel the future demand.

"Feathers are another commodity that causes tremendous suffering and death and 80% of the world's feathers come from China. We pluck the geese and ducks live which causes pain and suffering for the birds. You might wonder why on earth we do this; it is because the feathers grow back again and again.

"The bird will have to suffer this torture over and over until their bodies stop growing feathers; around 6 times and they are then killed as they are no longer a profitable commodity. Please, people of China, do not buy feather jackets, pillows and bedding."

The movie was playing elephants being brutally killed and birds being plucked live.

The group chanted:

- Animals feel pain just like us
- Animals feel fear just like us
- Animals feel joy just like us
- Animals love their babies just like us
- Liberate the animals; let them feel joy and love, just like us

Billy was up next. "3 2 1 you live."

"People of the UK, please listen to our important message. We in the UK pride ourselves on being animal lovers but we conduct painful tests and imprison animals. The UK has the highest number in Europe of animals in captivity having painful experiments carried out on them their whole life.

"Worldwide, it is estimated that 100 million animals are killed each year for these crazy experiments. Vivisection is performed in laboratories to have horrendous product testing conducted on them apparently for human's safety. Products are rubbed on the skin, in the eyes, ears and mouths of rabbits, mice, monkeys, dogs, cats, rats and more or they are forced to inhale or eat substances, and they are injected with chemicals.

"They are often then killed to examine the results. There are many extensive reports to show that they really are irrelevant experiments when it comes to product safety because products still need to be tested on humans and considerable proof exists that there is no correlation between what a product does to an animal versus the outcome on a human being.

"Products such as cleaning products, paints, dyes, inks, petrol products, solvents, tars, pharmaceuticals, toiletries and cosmetics. Please people of the UK, please sign the petitions that are on the internet to request that the UK government ban all testing on animals and to ban all imports of products that have been tested on animals. Please also buy products that have not been tested on animals.

"Look on the label of the products for the leaping bunny symbols or it may be in words 'not tested on animals'. If enough people stop buying the products that are tested on animals, the companies will have to change their methods.

"Let us show the world that we are animal lovers and we find these experiments totally unacceptable and barbaric. Evil prevails only when people stand by and do nothing."

The cartoons were playing the poor animals being tested.

The group chanted:

- Their bodies, not ours
- Their bodies, not ours
- Their bodies, not ours
- Their bodies, not ours
- Their bodies, not ours

Rina from was up next. "3 2 1 you are live."

"Hello, Israel, we come with an important message. Live imports into Israel of sheep and cows from Australia and Europe are suffering immense fear and pain and the journeys are extremely long. They are herded onto purpose-built ships, standing and laying in their own poop and are forced to travel thousands of miles, some die on route, if not, it is a journey to their final destination of death.

"Arriving at a slaughterhouse, where animals are treated with no respect, they are kicked and tortured before having a horrendous ending. The torture and death are no different than the Nazis concentration camps, in fact worldwide 57 billion animals every single year are savagely slaughtered, so it is actually more wide-reaching and more gigantic than the terrible atrocities that happened in world war two.

"People of Israel, we already have a high number of non-meat-eaters here in Israel, please talk to your family and friends, get this subject on the lips of everyone you know. Ask yourself the question, if this was your family being treated like this, would it be acceptable?

"If you were the cow or the sheep, how would you feel being owned, contained, abused, exploited and murdered? Watching your children taken away to be murdered and then your final fate; death. Please people of Israel, really feel from your hearts and ask yourself, is this morally justified. Do we have the right to do this?"

The cartoons were of the ships, with dirty, tired, thirsty and exhausted animals, being forced into the kill zone for the violent and brutal death in the slaughterhouses and the human concentration camps and the animal concentration camps.

The group chanted:

- All we need to ask of the animals is their forgiveness
- All we need to ask of the animals is their forgiveness
- All we need to ask of the animals is their forgiveness
- All we need to ask of the animals is their forgiveness
- All we need to ask of the animals is their forgiveness

The next day Max gathered them all together. "Max, we have written a song and wondered if we could all sing together?" said Jack.

"What a great idea, if you share it with the other groups, we can sing at the holographic events. Continue to share with people in your local areas and practice the song for a few days. We will then practice the song together until you are ready to go live."

Max took everyone back to their homes. A few days later they rehearsed together for many days. Two other groups had also written a song, so they all had three to learn, they then took the songs around the world.

Little Dude

Millions of animals born to die
Have you ever wondered why?
Follow the money and you will find
It's all for the profit of humankind
Did we ask them for their skins?
For their bodies to be put in the bin
What about their feathers and fur?
To be removed by an amateur

Hey there little dude
You are not our food
Hey there little dude
It is not right that you live in solitude
Hey there little dude
You won't be our barbecue
Hey there little dude
We now see the magnitude

Some die at a day old
Their cousins will be controlled
Whilst in the zoos they make old bones
This has been going on since the Flintstones
So what can you do to make a change?
Stop and think about their pain
Is your gain worth their suffering?
To them, this is all very puzzling

Hey there little dude
You are not our food
Hey there little dude
It is not right that you live in solitude
Hey there little dude
You won't be our barbecue
Hey there little dude
We now see the magnitude

It's all for the profit of humankind
Open your eyes as we have been blind
Innocent beings with feelings
Abused for human dealings
All they want is their freedom
All we do is mislead them
Rather than tanks, chains and cages
Let's free them and changes the ages
Choose to become more evolved
Then the earth's problems will be solved

Outrageous

Born in cages
All for man wages
Pets and crazy experiments
Are we still in the dark ages?
Horns, scales and ivory
Millions of hives and mass slavery
Chicks born to die and birds in an aviary
All they need is their liberty

This is all so outrageous
Man needs to become courageous
Speak out to your family and friends
As we all need to make amends

Birds that cannot fly
Might prefer to die
Sharks going around and around
Might prefer to drown
Dolphins taught to act
They didn't sign a contract
Horses and dogs made to race
They just want our embrace

This is all so outrageous
Man needs to become courageous
Speak out to your family and friends
As we all need to make amends

Animals that are forced into pregnancy
Just want to live in ecstasy
Pigs that suffer gore
Want again to be wild boar
Sheep are bred for meat and wool
They have had enough of this bull
Hens enslaved for their eggs
Just want to hide in a hedge

This is all so outrageous
Man needs to become courageous
Speak out to your family and friends
As we all need to make amends

Fish taken from the seas
Just want to be carefree
Animals abused for our entertainment
Want us to end this enslavement
We have used them for our progress and now we know their ecology
We have come very far and now we have our technology
When will it be time for us to give them a rest?
It's now time for us all to put ourselves to the test

Freedom Dream

If they were free
How would it be?
Songbirds would sing goodbye
To fly high in the sky
Tigers and lions would run upfront
To catch the days hunt
Dairy calves would love the taste
Their mummy's milk as her udder is embraced

Freedom to run, fly, swim and sing
What a wonderful world it would be to live in
Freedom to eat whatever they want
From Mother Nature's restaurant
Freedom to live their full lives
To be in nature and survive

Chicks would meet their mummy
Nestling just under her tummy
Rhinos would run as fast as they can
For fun, not from man
Hamsters would live in burrows made of dirt
Living in peace and totally unhurt
Sharks would swim for miles a day
Hunting for a tasty stingray
Cows would procreate the natural way
And enjoy all their calves' birthdays

Freedom to run, fly, swim and sing
What a wonderful world it would be to live in
Freedom to eat whatever they want
From Mother Nature's restaurant
Freedom to live their full lives
To be in nature and survive

Barn hens would smell the fresh air
And enjoy the nature of childcare
Bees would enjoy their homemade honey
Nature's perfection is not too thick nor runny
Sheep would take cover
In the extreme weather
Sows would feel the grass under their trotters
And spend their life dancing with sons and daughters

Freedom to run, fly, swim and sing
What a wonderful world it would be to live in
Freedom to eat whatever they want
From Mother Nature's restaurant
Freedom to live their full lives
To be in nature and survive

Ducks would swim and paddle
And roost to safety with a waddle
Geese would fly together
And preen all their feathers
Elephants would walk for miles and miles
Together with their family all with big smiles
Dolphins and whales would be at peace
Thankful for their prison release
Fish would still be the prey
But at least it would be the natural way

The groups continued on a daily basis to deliver speeches at schools and events across the world as well as singing the three songs. TV companies flew the groups around the world to sing the songs on live shows.

They all delivered many different speeches covering all the different subjects. The people of the earth continued talking amongst themselves about the young brave teenagers and of the impact that they were all personally having on the animals, the planet and the future.

Over the weeks and months that followed, meat, fish, dairy, egg and honey consumption decreased at an unprecedented level, farmers and fishermen turned their efforts into farming vegetables, solar power, plant-based milk and many more new ideas that had come into being. The farmers all shared 'best practices' with each other for the transition and new ways of working.

Governments set up 'transition' funds for people and businesses to apply for a grant for conversion to a new product. The rainforests were left alone as the need for more land faded. The fields that used to grow crops to feed the animals were now growing other plants or being planted with trees to enable forests to regenerate.

Animal ownership also started to reduce as people delivered their pets or slaves to animal sanctuaries or even back to the wild. New sanctuaries were opened, as more and more people did not want to continue to be a part of the exploitation. New businesses were formed from the workers that lost their jobs, or they found jobs in the new industry of plant-based living.

A vegan coffee shop opened in the UK, they offered all the various plant-based milk, cakes and savouries, the owner paid the workers more than the usual pay rate and sent all the profits to various animal projects, to the UK transition fund and to other local community projects. A very wealthy man liked the idea so much that he invested in many 'not-for-profit' vegan coffee shops all over the world and called the chain 'Unity Coffee'.

As with the first coffee shop, the profits went to help the transitions across the world and helped to start new Earthling Wild Zones that needed to be created for the new way of being; animals were on the path of getting back to being wild and free. Experts in land management came together to advise on how to 're-wild' the land to enable the animals to survive. Many rich people and big companies followed the lead of the Unity Coffee owner and donated money towards the EWZ's and the transition funds.

It really was amazing how humans all pulled together to help with the many changes that were needed for both the animals and humans. Max knew that in time the oceans would heal themselves and once again thrive. There was still a lot of work to be done on planet Earth, but this, the first challenge had really started to take the path of humanity onto another track.

Max gathered Billy's group together. "Wow, what an amazing transition that is taking place but we have one last job to do together. Many animals have been liberated; however, some businesses are not easily able to liberate large animals. We can't help all animals, but for some species, we can teleport them back to their real homes and I assumed you would all want to be part of that." The excitement in the air was electric.

Max continued, "Zoo's, safari parks, aquariums and sea life centres have a very big challenge; transporting the big mammals is very stressful for the animals and it is a difficult task, especially for the sea life. I need your help; the plan is for me to split up with you all and target these businesses in each of your countries. We need the permission of the owners to go ahead and free the animals, we can't go ahead without permission; however, with everything that is going on right now, I don't expect anyone to say no to a little help."

Max wasted no time, Billy found himself in a sea life centre that housed sharks, whales and dolphins in tanks. Billy explained to the manager that the being from planet Unity wanted to teleport the large mammals back to the wild, with his permission it could be done immediately. The Manager was delighted, as he had been worried about how they would deal with liberating their large animal stock now that no one was visiting the centre.

Max spent the day working with all of his friends across the globe teleporting elephants, giraffes, hypo's, tigers, lions, whales, sharks, dolphins, sea lions and more back to their natural habitat.

Back in Billy's room, Billy spoke. "That was for sure one of the best experiences Max, thank you. Watching the dolphins, whales and sharks swim off into the abyss and the land animals run around in excitement gave me goosebumps all over my body, it was one of the happiest days of my life Max, I am so grateful to have been part of such an amazing project. Thank you again, Max, for choosing me."

"Billy, you have yourself to thank because if you didn't possess the qualities, I would not have chosen you, so thank you too, Billy."

"Max, having liberated these animals, I am now thinking about the café with the birds, whether the café owner has brought more birds since we liberated them?"

Before Billy could blink, they were at the café, to Billy's delight the cages had gone, he laughed out loud and cried tears of happiness, knowing that he and his friends with Max's help were having such an impact on the world and the animals.

The next day Max teleported everyone together.

"What a stupendous job you have all done. Humanity has you all to thank, they should also thank each other for believing in you, believing in themselves and feeling that things had to change. There is much more that needs to happen on Earth; however, for now, things need to settle for a while before we work together again on the next step in this evolution revolution.

"I will be back in the near future, till then my friends, keep talking to the people, the wave of this change is now big enough that soon the animal kingdom will be back in balance once again. I will be watching how it all unfolds and when the time is right, I will come back. In the meantime, if you ever really feel the need to talk to me, just call me, in your thoughts, I will hear you, bye for now everyone."

Max was gone. There was a deadly silence as everyone felt his presence leave. He reappeared, laughing, laughing so much he was doubled over.

"I hadn't thought that one through, how were you all going to get home?"

Everyone laughed with him. "When you are ready, just call me and I will take you individually home."

He disappeared again. Everyone started chatting and exchanging phone numbers and social media details before calling Max to go home.

"Our grandchildren will ask us one day: 'Where were you during the Holocaust of the animals? What did you do against these horrifying crimes?' We won't be able to offer the same excuse for the second time: that we didn't know."

—Dr Helmut Kaplan (b. 1952)

Ingram Content Group UK Ltd.
Milton Keynes UK
UKHW022032120323
418425UK00007B/124